Defining Courage

Jill Daugherty

Copyright © 2014 by Jill Daugherty

All rights reserved. This book or any portion thereof may not be reproduced or used in any manner whatsoever without the express written permission of the publisher except for the use of brief quotations in a book review.

This book is a work of fiction. Names, characters, places and incidents either are products of the author's imagination or are used fictitiously. Any resemblance to actual events, locations or persons, living or dead, is entirely coincidental.

First Printing, 2014

ISBN 978-0-9887284-4-8 (Paperback)

ISBN 978-0-9887284-5-5 (ebook)

Open Mike Publishing, Denver, Colorado, USA

Cover design by Damonza

Visit www.jilldaugherty.com for more information about this book and the author.

1 2 3 4 5 6 7 8 9

"Knavery's plain face is never seen till used." –William Shakespeare (Othello)

Chapter One

I woke up and for one fraction of a moment so small that it didn't completely fill a split second, I forgot who I had become. For that too-brief flicker of time, I was back in Denver, in my old bed, in my old house. My mom was downstairs making breakfast. My dad and Brandon were stealing bacon faster than she could cook it. Maybe snow was falling. Maybe it was a warm summer day. I felt safe and loved and full of promise and potential. My whole life was ahead of me and I could make it anything I wanted it to be. And Simon was there in my short moment of confusion—alive and well and waiting to see me. It was the thought of Simon that brought down the illusion I was building in my mind. I wasn't in Denver. I wasn't safe. I wouldn't see Simon anytime soon.

I reluctantly opened my eyes to the reality that was waiting for me. A stream of sunshine was shooting through the crack in the curtains that hung at the window in my room. The sun didn't make as many appearances in Ireland as it did in Denver and I decided to hold onto that ray of sunshine as a good omen—as a sign that something good was going to happen. I did that a lot. I took normal, insignificant, happens-every-day kinds of things, and turned them into good omens. They always turned out to be nothing and I was always surprised and disappointed, but I needed hope. I needed something to hold onto that told me the battle I was fighting was worth all of the sacrifices I was making.

Ian and two of my guards, Nessa and Michael, were in the kitchen. I sat down at the worn wooden table and Ian put a plate of eggs and toast in front of me before turning back to the counter and getting a mug of coffee. We'd come to an unspoken agreement in the time we'd all lived together at Slan Lathair: Everyone gave me time to eat and have a cup of strong coffee in the morning before they spoke to me. That brief time of gentle confusion between dreaming and being fully awake was the only time I could delude myself into believing that everything was going to be okay, and I didn't want anyone to end that time prematurely by speaking to me and forcing me to face reality.

"What time are we leaving?" I asked Ian after I'd finished drinking the coffee he'd put before me.

"As soon as you're ready."

"'Ready' has so many levels," I said with a hint of grumpiness still lingering in my voice.

He smiled warmly and ruffled the hair on the top of my head before leaving the room to get everything ready for the trip to Ballecath. It would be our first trip back to Simon's home since we had returned to Slan Lathair after Thanksgiving. I was safer at the faery boarding school than at any other place on earth, but my parents and

Brandon would be at Ballecath for Christmas, and my absence might have caused a surge of undesirable emotions from my parents—confusion, worry, anger, suspicion. It was "suspicion" that concerned me the most. We couldn't afford to have my parents suspicious about anything I was doing in Ireland. It was best for everyone if they remained clueless about the new life their daughter was living.

I'd been nervous about my trip to Ballecath. Not only would I be more vulnerable on the road between my two homes in Ireland, but I would also have to drive past the spot where the Fomorians had attacked us on the same trip a couple of months before. I would have to see the field where I lost Simon. It was also my memories of Simon that made me not want to go to Ballecath. There wasn't a single place I could go on his estate that didn't send of flood of memories rushing through my brain and my body, and it was painful. I missed him so much. So very much.

"You doing okay?" Ian asked as we sat next to each other in the front of one of the SUVs in the caravan taking me back to Ballecath. I nodded, hoping he wouldn't see how panicked I really was. He took my hand in his and squeezed it—trying, I'm sure, to offer reassurance. The warmth of his hand around mine pushed some of my anxiety away. I liked that Ian could make me feel better, but I also felt guilty about the betrayal to Simon.

I hadn't been happy when Ian had taken over Simon's responsibility as my primary Guardian. Ian's presence had always been a constant reminder of Simon's absence. Our relationship had been strained, and at times combative, but since Ian had admitted to me that he believed, as I did, that Simon was alive, we'd developed a strong bond that was forged out of a common purpose—

finding Simon.

But it was more than that, and it was the "more" that tied my stomach in knots of guilt. Ian and I had kissed, and worse than that, we had confessed our feelings to each other. Ian could never replace what I felt for Simon and we both knew that, but there was a connection between us that had formed in Simon's absence. Sometimes I wondered if my feelings for Ian were real, or if I was just drawn to the closest thing to Simon that I could find. Ian and Simon had known each other since birth—over two hundred years. They'd spent a lot of time together when they were growing up and had shared a room for nearly a hundred and fifty years when they were at school. Like I had with my best friend, Lexie, Simon and Ian had developed similar personality traits over the years. Ian wasn't Simon, but he was so close, and I knew those similarities were clouding my judgment.

Other than the one time when Ian told me he believed Simon was alive, we hadn't kissed. If we'd believed that Simon was dead, we might have behaved differently, but if we believed Simon was alive, kissing someone else would have been a betrayal, and neither Ian nor I wanted to be responsible for doing something that would hurt Simon. So we didn't kiss. Not in a romantic way. He'd sometimes kiss my forehead or my cheek and we both knew that it was the only way we could feed our appetite for each other—or for whatever we were trying to pull from each other. Tiny nibbles of sustenance for the starving.

We couldn't stop the emotional bond that was developing between us, however. We were bound together by our love of Simon, by the overwhelming sense of loss we felt in his absence, by our desire to find him, and by our decision to keep the belief that he was alive between the two of us. The Guardians acknowledged that there was a traitor among us who was feeding information to Balor and the Fomorians. It was hard to sort out whom we could and could not trust, and for that reason, we knew it would be best to keep our beliefs a secret that only we shared. Isn't it funny how a secret can bind two people together so tightly?

As we drove down the long driveway to Simon's home, a flood of memories—thousands of memories—crashed through me. It hurt in a physical way to have such harsh reminders of what I'd lost, and I found it hard to breath. I pulled my hand from Ian's, not wanting to add guilt to the pile of emotions assaulting me. He didn't protest or exhibit signs that his feelings were hurt.

I stayed in the car for a few moments after Ian stopped in the driveway. I needed the time to compose myself before I got out of the car and had to talk with people as if I was still a whole person. It was getting harder and harder to hide the months of fractures that were breaking me apart, and sometimes I needed a moment to pull all the broken pieces together so I could present the illusion that I was going to be okay.

Ian got out of the car and walked around to my side and opened the door. He didn't say anything, or pressure me to get out. He just stood, quiet and supportive, waiting for me to ready myself for what came next. It seemed like even the simplest tasks required a tremendous amount of mental preparation, and Ian was always there, waiting for me.

When I eventually stepped out of the car, I caught a glimpse of my reflection in the side mirror; strands of red hair fell into my blue eyes—the same blue as Simon's eyes. I missed his eyes and the world that had been expressed in them.

"We should probably meet with the Guardians tonight," I told Ian as we walked into the house. "My family'll be here tomorrow, and it'll be harder to meet once they're here."

Ian nodded. "I'll let Sloane know."

"Thanks." We were silent for a few beats. "I'm going to go lie down," I finally told him. We both knew what that meant—I was going to Simon's room. We didn't acknowledge that, though. It was part of that unspoken rule between us.

Ian nodded again, but remained silent.

"I need some time alone," I told him.

Another nod. I knew he would do as I asked and make sure that my guards would leave me alone. I also knew that Ian would sit outside the door to Simon's room, waiting for me to come out, or waiting for me to need him. My heart twisted with the pain and pleasure of my love for Simon and of Ian's love for me. That love was getting all tangled together and I wondered how long it would be before I wouldn't be able to separate one love from the other.

I walked to Simon's room and closed the door behind me. I was focused on one goal. I kept my eyes lowered and tried not to see his room and everything in it as I walked to the closet and reached up to pull out a small wooden box that sat on a shelf. I opened the lid greedily, needing my fix as soon as I could get it. I pulled out the plastic bag that held the shirt I had hidden inside the last time I was at Ballecath. Simon's shirt. I had found it, unwashed, on a chair in his room. I held it in my hands for a moment, wanting desperately to hold it to my nose and breath in Simon, but I was terrified that his smell wouldn't be there anymore. But it was there—his smell—earthy and fresh and so completely Simon. Tears sprung to my eyes and I didn't try to stop them. I wrapped his shirt around me and let the grief wash over me.

Chapter Two

Mom sent a text saying they had picked up their rental car and were on their way to Ballecath. I decided I would use the time to do something I'd been putting off for quite a while. Something I knew was going to be difficult and unpleasant and possibly even dangerous, but I really couldn't put it off any longer. I needed to wrap my Christmas presents.

I went to my room—the room I had commandeered from Simon—and pulled all of the gifts I'd bought into the middle of the floor. Erin had given me several rolls of wrapping paper and an armload of ribbons, bows and tags. I threw them into the middle of the floor next to the gifts and sat in the middle of the festive mess, ready to do battle and determined to turn it all into something that embodied Christmas cheer.

I folded a cut piece of paper around the first gift and realized I hadn't remembered to get any tape. I stood and tiptoed through the piles I'd created to get to the door, but stopped when I saw Simon's desk. Surely he'd have tape in there somewhere. Everyone kept tape in their desk. I sat in his chair and started pulling open drawers, lifting folders and envelopes and small boxes, looking for just one roll of tape that would save me the long walk downstairs in search of Erin or Finn or someone who would know where to find some tape. I was about to give up when a large brown accordion folder caught my eye. It had been tucked below a stack of envelopes that I'd lifted in my pursuit of tape, and it had a large sticker with my name, birthdate, and address in Denver.

I pulled it from the desk and hesitated only a fraction of a second before making the decision to open it. It was old and worn, the edges bent and creased, the elastic clasp long gone and replaced with a string wrapped several times around the outside. I unwound the string and set it aside before opening the file and looking inside.

The first section was bulging, wider by far than the other sections of the file. I reached in and pulled out a large set of pictures with an old and faded ribbon wrapped around them. I pulled off the ribbon and looked through them, one by one. There was a copy of my school pictures from kindergarten through eleventh grade, but there were also a lot of candid photos. One of me and my parents on the front steps of our house. I was a baby, maybe a few days old, and my mom held me while my dad looked down at me with so much love and devotion. There was one of me at about four years old, crying while my mom bent down on one knee and scolded me in the park. There was another of me with Lexie, maybe thirteen years old, walking together in the mall. One of Brandon and me playing on our backyard swing, his black hair flying up as he hit the apex of the swing. One of Lexie and me on our bikes, riding down one of the streets that separated our two houses. Another of me sitting alone on the playground at my elementary school, looking on as my fellow classmates played around me. Me at our fourth grade play. Me at a friend's birthday party. Me skiing. Me swimming. Picture after picture after picture. At least a hundred. All of me.

I shook my head slowly, not able to come to terms with the contents of this folder. They'd known about me—been close to me—since I was born. My life had never been my own.

I rummaged through the rest of the folder and found copies of my report cards, dental records, medical records, and reports from people who had evidently been close to me. Mr. Warner, my social studies teacher from sixth through eleventh grade, wrote several reports about my progress in school, meetings with my parents, my interactions with fellow students and my extracurricular activities.

"Maggie is quiet and shy and seems to prefer letting her best friend take the lead in all aspects of her life. Attempts to get Maggie out of her shell only result in her retreating further into it."

"Maggie exhibits absolutely no faery ability and seems an unlikely choice to take on the task that may lie ahead of her."

Brandon stormed into my room and belly flopped onto my bed, pulling my focus from the pictures and the folder.

"Nice of you to meet us at the airport," he said in lieu of a hello. "We fly all the way from Denver to see you, but you can't even bother to come to the airport?"

I blinked for a moment, taken aback by the amount of time that must have passed while I sat at Simon's desk looking through the folder. I stood from the chair I'd been sitting in and went to sit beside my little brother on the bed.

"Good to see you," I said as I lay beside him and kissed his cheek. "How was your flight?"

He made a show of wiping the kiss away. "Long."

My parents came into the room, evidently unable to keep pace with Brandon on his way to see me. I stood and pushed the pile of unwrapped presents under the bed and hugged each of them, feeling so much of the tension I'd kept cinched inside of me loosen just a little.

I reluctantly wrenched myself from my family's arms, worried that if I lingered too long they might suspect that something was wrong.

"I'm guessing you want naps before dinner," I said.

"We slept most of the way on the plane to London, but showers would be good," my mom said.

I showed them all to their rooms before going downstairs to help Finn and Erin with dinner. Since my cooking skills were definitely lacking, my help generally involved chopping the vegetables they put in front of me, but I put everything I had into making sure those carrots were diced to perfection.

All of the faeries at the house joined us for dinner that night, nearly twenty of us surrounding the massive oak table. Those dinners, with everyone sitting around and laughing and telling stories, were difficult because they always reminded me of the one person who wasn't there.

"I'm sorry we're missing Simon again," my mom said when we were all seated and filling our plates. "Is he back with his mother?"

"Yes," I lied. The faeries couldn't lie, so it was it up to me to account for Simon's absence. When I had thought Simon was dead, I hadn't wanted to tell my family about his death because of the number of questions we couldn't answer. Once I decided he was still alive, I chose to continue to keep the truth from them. The faeries all supported me with the lies I chose to tell my family. "She's sick again, so Simon went to be with her."

"Will you not be going to see your mother for Christmas, Finn?" my dad asked. He put down his fork and leaned back in his chair, staring at Finn while he waited for his response.

"Not this year, no. Some work is keeping me at Ballecath."

It was vague enough that it answered my dad's question without being a lie.

My dad kept staring at Finn as if he was searching for something, but he didn't say anything.

"I'm holding you to your promise to go horseback riding, Brandon," Keelin said. Ian's twin sister evidently didn't feel the same animosity toward my brother that she felt toward me.

"Definitely," Brandon said. "I want the biggest, meanest horse you've got."

I rolled my eyes. "You are *such* a fourteen-year-old boy."

"Thank you very much. I take that as nothing but a sincere compliment."

"Then you obviously missed my sarcasm."

Some things never change.

ഗ◌ര

"*Nollaig Shona Duit*, Maggie," Finn said when I walked into the drawing room well before dawn on Christmas morning. I'd been restless since our return to Ballecath and sleep was a luxury that only other people got to enjoy. Even most of the faeries in the house were still asleep, and they didn't need nearly as much sleep as non-faeries did.

"*Nollaig Shona Duit,*" I said. Ian had worked with me on the correct pronunciation of "Merry Christmas" in Gaelic before we left Slan Lathair.

"You're up early. You know Santa can't come if you're awake." His eyes were twinkling with amusement, but I was too grumpy to be amused.

"I had a tough time sleeping," I admitted. "I miss him, even more now that I'm here."

Finn nodded knowingly. "I was just heading to the kitchen to make some tea. Care to join me?"

We went to the kitchen and Finn filled a kettle with water while I got out the cups and the tea bags.

"My dad seemed kind of weird at dinner last night," I said.

"Yeah. I noticed that too."

"Do you think he's suspicious?"

"I'd be surprised if he wasn't, all things considered."

"I really should have been more careful to surround myself with stupid people," I joked. "It would make deception a lot easier."

Finn smiled and changed the subject. "I want to give you one of your Christmas presents before everyone else wakes up. I'll just go and get it."

He left and came back a few minutes later with a small wrapped package. He set it on the table and I carried over our two mugs of tea.

"It's from Simon," he said as he pushed the package toward me. I looked at it, and looked at Finn, confused. "He ordered it before your birthday. It arrived after—"

My hand flew to my mouth and I pushed down the tears at my eyes. Simon had gotten me a Christmas present and it didn't matter what was inside. All that mattered was that it was from him and it was special for that fact alone. It was the closest I would get to having him with me on Christmas day.

I ripped the paper and when I saw what was inside, I sobbed, somewhere between a cry and a laugh. I wiped the tears that were running down my cheeks and laughed again while I opened the plastic holding the industrial-strength cell phone case inside.

"He meant it to be funny," Finn said. "He wanted you to throw as many phones as you needed to throw, but he also wanted to be sure he could always stay in contact with you."

I nodded, unable to speak through the tears that were streaming. It was the appearance of those tears that made me understand why Simon's gift was something Finn would want to give me when we were alone.

"Thank you," I whispered to Finn. *Thank you*, I said silently to Simon, hoping he would hear me, but knowing there was a good chance that he wouldn't.

We finished our tea in silence and I headed to my room to take a shower before everyone woke up. I had just finished getting dressed when Brandon came bounding into my room without knocking. I looked out the window and saw that it wasn't quite light outside, but it was very near dawn.

"*Nollaig Shona Duit*, Maggie," he said as he jumped on my bed. "Keelin taught me that at dinner last night. It's how they say Merry Christmas here in Ireland."

I jumped on the bed with him. "I know. What'd you get me?"

"Patience, woman. Come on. Let's wake up mom and dad and open presents."

"And who needs patience?"

He pulled my arm, dragging me off the bed, and we

went to the room down the hall where my parents were staying. Brandon jumped into bed with them and I followed, my breath catching in my throat when I thought about how normal this was. It was so hard for me to find pieces of normal in my new life and I wanted to soak up every second. The four of us scrunched together on the bed, our family doing what so many families do on Christmas morning.

"Let's go open presents," Brandon insisted.

My dad pulled Brandon into a headlock. "You're making a pretty big assumption there, Brandon. How do you know you even have presents?"

Brandon looked up through the crook of my dad's elbow. "I've been good. It's a lot easier when Maggie's gone. I don't have anyone to torment."

I turned my head from my mom's shoulder and looked at my little brother. "I miss being tormented by you."

"Well I'll do my best to get in some quality tormenting while I'm here. But let's go open some presents. *Now.*"

He pulled at my arm, but my mom pulled me closer to her and wrapped her arms around me. "Let's wait five minutes," she said. "Five minutes cuddling with my family is the best Christmas present any of you could give me."

"Good thing 'cause I didn't get you a real present," Brandon teased.

It was a gift I was happy to give, and while Brandon complained about valuable Christmas minutes ticking away, I think he was just as happy.

Chapter Three

Ballecath was completely decked out for the holiday. Simon's home had always reminded me of the estate homes used in period pieces for Masterpiece Theater. It was absolutely massive and filled with large paintings and tapestries and statues. It wasn't a complete throwback from another era, however, and a sixty-inch television with a complicated sound system was mounted on a wall across the room from an ornately carved, antique grand piano. Like the furnishings at Ballecath, the Christmas decorations were a mix of old and new. Every room had been decorated with lights and garlands and wreaths. There were at least five different Christmas trees in different rooms, and stockings were hung above most of the fireplaces. Strings of twinkle lights were draped around festive candles. Homemade gingerbread men hung on the trees beside the shiny and new ornaments. The mixture of decorations was so appropriate for this faery home where people who were hundreds of years old were able to use and embrace the latest technology as if they were born with a laptop in their hands and their

Instagram account already created.

I tried to be as cheerful as I could manage for my family while we went through the Christmas routine, but the feelings of dread that were always with me allowed only the thinnest of veils to hide my true feelings.

My dad didn't seem to be doing much better. He teased Brandon and expressed the appropriate amount of gratitude when he opened his gifts, but he seemed a little off. He kept looking back and forth between me and the faeries, and sometimes he would stare off into a distant place that only he could see.

"I really wish you'd come home with us," he said as he sat down next to me. I'd been sitting on the periphery of the group in a window seat, watching as everyone pretended to enjoy the holiday. The other faeries were just as worried and depressed as I was, but they too tucked those emotions away for the sake of my family.

I didn't respond to my dad's statement. Instead, I just leaned into his shoulder, hoping to feel the safety and security I'd always felt in my dad's arms. It wasn't there. I didn't hold out hope that it would ever be there again.

"You're obviously unhappy here," my dad continued as he tightened his arm around my shoulders. "And Simon's not even here any more. There doesn't seem to be much point in staying."

As we had at Thanksgiving, we told my family that Simon's mother was ill and that he had needed to leave his home to be with her. They seemed to have bought that explanation for his absence. Lexie hadn't. It was harder to deceive her.

"I can't come home," I told him. I hoped he couldn't hear the dejection in my tone. I wanted to go home so desperately and it took everything in me to keep from dragging him to the airport that second and catching the first plane to Denver.

He looked at me as if he were trying to assess my expression. "You know, Maggie, you can talk to me. About anything."

"Everything's fine, Dad," I lied.

"Everything's not fine, Maggie," he said with tenderness. "I can see how unhappy you are."

"It's just going to take a while for me to adjust to the changes," I reasoned.

He was quiet for a few minutes and we sat and watched while Brandon and Ian played one of the new video games Brandon had unwrapped earlier in the day. It used to be Simon who filled that role—playing video games with Brandon for hours on end. Ian had slipped in so seamlessly that I almost didn't notice the change.

"Let's take a walk," my dad suggested. I nodded, eager to leave that room. Eager to leave the memory of Simon. Eager to leave the realization that I almost hadn't noticed when Ian had filled Simon's role in my family—in my life.

We pulled on our heavy coats and walked toward the beach. Simon's beach. My dad seemed nervous and that worried me.

Jake, Simon's faithful yellow lab, ran toward us and nudged my dad's open palm with his muzzle. My dad responded by pulling both of his hands away from Jake and folding his arms across his chest before turning his back on the dog.

"Maggie, is there something about Simon and his family that you should tell me?" he asked when we were a good distance from the house.

"Like what?" I hoped my dad didn't notice that my heart was beating in triple time at the suggestion that there might be a secret to tell about Simon's family.

He hesitated. "Is there something unusual about them? Something you may not want to share with other people?"

He couldn't possibly know. It had been incredible enough when Lexie had figured things out, but we had been so careful with my family. Finn was repeatedly convincing them with his special faery ability that things were normal and that their daughter was safe. Had we missed something? Had we slipped up?

"Why would you think that?" I asked, deflecting the question.

"I've just noticed—things," he admitted evasively.

"What sort of things?"

He looked puzzled as his eyes moved down to where Jake sat at his feet.

"Things that feel—unreal."

"Unreal?" I asked, playing dumb.

He was silent again, staring absently at the horizon, his gaze fixed at the point where the ocean met the sky. After a virtual lifetime of skipped heart beats and hundreds of worse case scenarios running through my head, my dad started to talk again.

"I don't want to see it. I don't want to believe it. I keep telling myself that it couldn't possibly be true." His tone was flat and dreamy, his expression heartbreaking. "Not you," he continued. "It can't be you."

I saw tears in his eyes and knew he understood too much.

Finn, I called out telepathically, hoping he was close enough to hear me. *I need your help.*

I was relieved to see him walking toward us a few moments later.

He knows something, Finn, I warned silently. *I'm not sure what, but he knows something.*

Finn nodded and walked to my dad, putting his hand on his shoulder. My dad sighed heavily as if he was giving in to the inevitable. Tears fell silently from my eyes as I watched Finn once again alter my dad's memories. I walked away before he could finish. I didn't want to have to explain the tears. I went to Ian's apartment behind the main house and waited for him to join me. He wasn't far behind and when he got to the apartment door, he opened it and waited for me to walk inside before he followed, wrapping me in his arms once he'd closed the door.

"Someday this won't be so hard," he whispered gently.

"I need 'someday' to get here soon," I said, pulling away from the security of his embrace. "I need to do something. Now."

"What?" Ian asked, his tone logical. "We don't have any leads—on anything. We don't know where Balor is. We don't know where Simon is. We don't know where Lexie is."

"Why can't you use your faery ability to get someone to tell you where they are?" I asked, my tone accusatory. Ian was able to get people to tell him things they didn't want to tell anyone.

"I would have to know the right person to ask. It wouldn't do me any good to just ask every faery I meet to tell me where to find Simon or Balor or Lexie. If they don't know, I can't force them to tell me, and if I start going around asking everyone, it's going to raise suspicions."

"I need to do *something*—even if it's the wrong thing. I can't just sit around and wait for bad things to keep happening to the people I love while we figure out a plan of action."

He looked at me, his expression grim, but said nothing.

"If you were forced to make a decision today—if you had no choice but to act—what would you do?"

He sat down on the sofa in his living room and rested his elbows on his knees, his fingers tangled together in front of him. He remained still, quietly thinking, then looked at me with a reluctant expression—evidently a little wary to tell me his idea.

"Some people think Newgrange is the entrance to the Underworld," he said so quietly that I wasn't sure I'd heard him correctly.

"Newgrange?"

He nodded.

"What's that?"

"It's a Megalithic burial site near Dublin."

"In English?"

"Megalithic. It's a term for a big stone structure. Newgrange is this massive stone burial mound. It's older than Stonehenge or the pyramids in Egypt and there are some people who think it's actually a hidden entrance to the Underworld. But it's probably nothing more than a tourist attraction. They have this big visitor's center and a restaurant and they do tours and stuff."

"Wait. The entrance to the Underworld is a secret?"

"*Entrances*, actually. There are several. And not really a secret—just not widely advertised. Unless you have reason to be there, you aren't told how to get there."

"So why would we want to go to the Underworld?"

"I think we might find Balor there. Or Simon."

"But Danu's in the Underworld, isn't she? Why can't we just get ahold of her and tell her we want to go look for Balor? Wouldn't she take us to the entrance? She's Simon's mom, so I know she'd want to help."

"It's more complicated than that," he said as he stood and started to pace. "All of the different entrances to the Underworld lead to different places. Danu may not even know where to find the entrance that would lead to Balor's section of the Underworld. And I don't know how to contact her anyway."

"Let's ask Finn. Surely he would know how to get to his own mother's house."

He stopped pacing and leaned against the arm of the sofa. "But if we tell Finn that we want to talk to Danu, he'll want to know why. Besides, I imagine it's something they've already talked about, and if Danu knew how to get to Balor, I have no doubt that she would have by now."

"So let's go to Newgrange and see for ourselves. What do we have to lose?"

"Our lives."

"Small price to pay." I said with a slightly less than teasing smile.

He looked at me pointedly. "Your life, in particular, is a large price to pay."

I knew he was referring to the prophecy and the fact that I'd have to kill Balor if humanity had any chance of survival. Yup. That's right. The survival of the human race depended on me.

"We have to do *something*," I reiterated. "Let's organize everything we know and try to figure out our next step—even if it's a small one."

It's something we'd done before—poured over all of the information the Guardians had gathered. We spent hours with maps and charts, books and notes. Each time, we came to the same conclusion. We had nothing.

"Let's wait until your family leaves," he suggested. "They fly home the day after tomorrow. I think you need to spend as much time with them as possible. Then we'll focus on this. I promise."

I agreed reluctantly. I needed time with my family. It was the only time I came remotely close to feeling normal.

Chapter Four

A knock on the door to Simon's room woke me up early the next morning.

I have coffee, Ian told me silently from the other side of the door. Telepathic communication was absolutely my favorite of all the faery abilities. It was a pretty handy skill and I often wondered how I had managed to survive my entire life without it.

I grabbed one of Simon's sweaters and pulled it over my pajama top before crossing the room to open the door for Ian. He smiled apologetically and handed me one of the two mugs in his hands. I slogged over to the window seat and slid down the wall until I was in a sitting position. I turned my head to look out the window and saw that the sky was the mottled purple of a bruise. The sun was pushing at the horizon, ready to start a new day.

"Was there a purpose to your visit, or did you just want me to watch the sunrise with you?"

"There's been a mud slide," he explained.

"Balor?"

"Maybe."

"But I thought he was taking a break from natural disasters to focus on killing me." It was absolutely unbelievable that I could say those words without flinching.

"I guess he's decided he can multitask," Ian said with a shrug.

I leaned back and looked through Simon's window toward the ocean in the distance.

"Do you have any specifics?

"It happened in Chile and there are four thousand dead at this point. That's about all I know."

I took a big gulp of the lukewarm coffee. "We have to do something, Ian. We can't just sit around waiting for the ideal situation while thousands of people die."

"We need to wait until we have a viable plan."

"And what would you consider a viable plan? Are we going to wait until my safety is guaranteed? Because we're never going to get that guarantee, Ian."

"There are a lot of people dying now, but if we act impulsively and Balor offs you, *everyone* will die. We need to wait for a plan that's going to keep more people alive. Until then, we just sit tight."

"I think we need to focus on getting Simon back," I said. It was where every plan started for me. If we could get Simon back, he could help us with the rest.

"I want him back as much as you do, Maggie."

"I know you do."

"It's just that I've been thinking."

Uh-oh.

"What?"

"I honestly believe Simon was alive when he left the field that day. I believe he was alive when he talked to you, but it's been a really long time since you've heard from him."

"And?"

"And," he began, dragging the word out slowly. "I think we need to accept the fact that while Simon was not dead when he was first taken, he might be dead now."

"No we don't," I said matter-of-factly. "We don't have to accept that. He's not dead." It was actually something I'd thought about too, but I wasn't going to admit that to Ian. Thinking about it and acknowledging it were two entirely different things, and I was absolutely not ready to acknowledge that fact. Ian knew not to push the issue. He just nodded silently.

"I think we're back to Newgrange," I told him, wanting both of us to stop thinking about the idea that Simon might actually be dead.

Ian sighed again. "Even if we go to Newgrange, we don't know how to find the entrance. Plus, it's full of tourists during the day, and I'm sure it's heavily guarded."

"So, it sounds like our next step is to work on my ability to make myself invisible so we can get past all of the people."

"Nice idea, but I don't know how to teach you to be invisible. It's just something that will happen. We also need to recognize that not one of the Guardians in the house is going to allow you to do something so dangerous. If we go to Newgrange, it will be just the two of us—which will be more dangerous—and we'll have to figure out a way to ditch the Dream Team and the rest of the faeries."

"So let's figure it out," I told him, not wanting him to continue building obstacles around the closest thing we had to a plan.

"Let me give it some thought," he finally agreed. "Give me time to think it through."

I nodded, mollified by the idea that he was at least willing to consider it.

"I need you to promise me something in the meantime," he said in a somber tone when he stood to leave. "I need you to promise that you won't go off on your own—that you'll wait for me before you act."

I shook my head. "I won't. I promise."

Leaving Ian and the others was something I'd considered many times, but it was an unrealistic idea. I'd managed to get away from Ian and the Dream Team once before, but I knew that even if I got away from them, I didn't know enough about the faery world to make it very far. I needed Ian with me.

His expression relaxed with my promise and he leaned in to kiss me on the cheek, his hand resting softly on my shoulder. When he pulled away, I wanted more. I wanted him to kiss me again, to run his lips against mine, to hold me against him and make me feel safe and loved, but I fought the urge to pull him back to me. I cared too much about Ian to encourage a relationship where he would always be second best.

Ian smiled knowingly, sadly, and walked out of Simon's room.

&)CR

"I've been thinking," I told my family as we sat in the kitchen for breakfast later that morning. "Instead of flying from Londonderry to Dublin to catch your flight home, why don't we drive down to Dublin tomorrow so we can do some sightseeing down there. We could hang out for a couple of days, and you could catch your flight directly from Dublin."

Ian spit out the coffee he'd been drinking and started

on a coughing fit.

"Drink some water, Ian," I said impatiently, not willing to let him derail my plan to get to Newgrange.

Maggie, he said, a silent warning pushing through from his brain to mine. *You know you can't go to Dublin. It's too dangerous.*

I ignored him. I was willing to keep my promise not to run away from him, but I was too impatient to wait for him to develop some unrealistically ironclad plan.

"So, what do you think?" I asked my parents brightly, hoping my enthusiasm might sell them on the idea.

"I think it sounds fun," my mom said, matching my enthusiasm.

Maggie, Ian warned again.

"Great," I said. "I'm sure Ian would be happy to make the arrangements." I looked at him pointedly and saw that he had turned a bright shade of red. I wasn't sure if his color change was due to a lack of oxygen from the coughing fit or if it was a result of anger. Probably both.

"Why don't you come help me make those plans, Maggie," Ian suggested as he looked at me pointedly.

"Can't," I informed him. "I promised Brandon we'd play some tennis." I grabbed Brandon's arm and pulled him toward the back door, a piece of bacon suspended midflight on its way to his mouth.

"Hey!" Brandon protested as he tried to get the piece of bacon to make contact with his mouth. Jake was waiting outside the back door and he made a valiant effort to get the bacon before it made its way to Brandon's mouth, but Brandon was quicker. He let Jake lick his greasy fingers as a consolation prize.

"What's the rush?" Brandon asked as I hurried through the courtyard and out of Ian's immediate reach.

"I want to hurry and play before it rains," I defended absently.

"It's an indoor court," Brandon responded in a tone that indicated he thought I'd lost my mind.

"Yeah," I covered, "I just want to finish so we can get back to the house before it rains."

He gave me a "whatever" look, but didn't push the issue.

As I predicted, Ian came down to the tennis court after a while and sat on a bench beside the court to watch us play. He didn't look happy.

"Brandon, why don't you head back to the house," Ian suggested when Brandon and I had taken a break to get some water. "I want to play your sister for a bit." He raised his eyebrows and I was pretty certain he'd intended his words to have a double meaning.

"I'm actually worn out," I told him, not wanting to spend time alone with Ian until he had an opportunity to let his anger cool.

"Just a few minutes," Ian countered. "You know how bad I am at this game. I need all the practice time I can get."

"Later," I suggested.

"Now," he said firmly, staring me down.

Brandon seemed to sense the tension and scurried out of the building.

"Why the sudden interest in Dublin?" he asked when we were alone, unable to hide his irritation with me.

I shrugged.

"We can't go," he said firmly.

"Yes," I said slowly. "We can."

He shook his head. "No."

"Yes."

We stared each other down for a full minute before

Ian shook his head and looked away from me.

"We risked a lot just to bring you to Ballecath," he said. "Going to Dublin would be insane."

"I'm going, with or without your approval."

"You promised you wouldn't run away."

"I'm not running away. I'm telling you exactly where I'm going. I'll even leave a detailed itinerary if you're not going to come with me."

I could see his frustration growing.

"Why?" he asked. "Why Dublin?"

"I've never been—except the airport. The only places I've been for the past five months are Ballecath and Slan Lathair."

He looked at me suspiciously, but I could tell he was giving in. "You okay with an entourage?" I nodded, willing to make the concession in order to keep Ian from fighting me any more on the idea. "Fine," he said with a heaviness in his voice. "I'll make the arrangements."

"Thank you," I told him. I felt guilty about deceiving Ian, but knew it was a necessary deception.

Chapter Five

Sloane and Finn weren't happy about my "vacation" plans, but they didn't fight me on it. I think they knew it wouldn't do any good, and I also think they were determined, as
 Simon had been, to make sure I remained as normal as possible under the ridiculous circumstances that made up my life. In the end, it was decided that Finn, Erin, Alana, Sloane, and Aidan, would all make the trip with us. With Ian, that would give us the protection of six faeries, but they were all faeries my parents knew and it made sense for them to come with us. In addition to the faeries Ian told me about, I was certain other faeries would make the trip as well. I couldn't brush my teeth with fewer than ten Guardians watching over me, ready to stomp out any evil that might be lurking in my tube of toothpaste.

We took two cars for the four-hour trip from Simon's home to Dublin. Ian and I rode in a car with my family and the other faeries rode in a second car. Ian didn't like that he was the only faery in the car with me, but Brandon had wanted to ride with Ian, and my mom wanted Brandon in the same car with her so he wouldn't get too obnoxious (like her proximity ever helped), and my dad wanted to ride in the same car with me, and it just worked out that there wasn't any room for the other faeries.

Ian was pretty silent for most of the trip, a grim expression pulling at his forehead and eyes. It bothered me that I was making him worry, but I had to act. I couldn't wait around for "the right time" or "the perfect plan." I'd be waiting forever if that were the case. If Simon was alive, I had to find him. If he wasn't alive, I needed to know so I could move forward without him. Newgrange was the only lead I had and I needed to follow it until I met a dead end. *No pun intended.*

As we got closer to Dublin, I pulled out the guidebook I had slipped into my bag at Ballecath.

"Oh, hey," I said nonchalantly, as if I hadn't carefully planned every detail of this trip. "Newgrange is on the way to Dublin. We should stop. I mean, we'll be so close that it'd be silly not to."

Ian jerked his head in my direction and looked at me with fury. *NO!* He yelled silently. I flinched. Even silent yells threw me off balance.

"What's Newgrange?" Brandon asked.

I decided to play up his love of anything gross and macabre. "It's an ancient burial site," I told him. "It's like five thousand years old and there are all these old bones and people's ashes inside and stuff."

"Cool!" Brandon enthused. I could play my little brother like a fiddle.

NO! Ian reiterated in my head.

"I've heard of that," my mom said. "We should definitely stop if it's on the way."

"So, it's settled then," I said triumphantly.

"We really should get to our hotel," Ian said out loud in a much calmer tone than the one he'd used in my head. "We don't want them to give away our rooms or anything."

"They're not going to give away our rooms," I told him. "Check in isn't even until 3:00, so this'll give us something to do until then."

Maggie! We're not doing this.

"I'll just call Finn and tell him we're going to make the stop," I said, ignoring Ian's silent comment.

Our two SUVs parked next to each other in the parking lot. The faeries in the other car were all giving me wary expressions when they saw me, suspicious, I'm sure, as to my intentions.

"What are you playing at?" Ian asked fiercely as we walked along the path from the parking lot to the visitor's center. He'd taken my arm and pulled me back so that we were several paces behind the rest of the group.

"I think this is something my family will enjoy."

"That's not the reason for this little side trip, and we both know it."

"I just want to look, Ian. I'm not going to act."

"This is a really bad idea."

"I appreciate your concern, but we're still doing this."

We bought our tickets at the visitor's center and went to look at the exhibit while we waited for our appointed time to ride the shuttle to the burial mound. The exhibit gave a history of the burial site and the excavation, and the people who had lived nearby at the time of its construction. I tried to look for clues, but it was all pretty meaningless to me. While it was fairly interesting, I didn't see anything that might help me to find Simon or Balor.

Before we walked to the shuttle, I stopped at the gift shop and bought a couple of books about Newgrange, hoping they would give me some clues later if I couldn't find any during our visit.

The faeries all looked particularly nervous as we sat on the shuttle with the other tourists for the ride to the burial site. I really did feel awful for inflicting this trip on them, but I kept reminding myself that it was necessary. I had to do something. I had to act.

At the end of the shuttle ride, I looked up at the circular mound that was about the same size as a large circus tent. Clean, white stones formed the base of the massive structure, and a grassy roof topped it. We walked around the field that contained the burial mound, looking at the stones that were scattered in different areas. Our guide pointed out the pattern of the stones and told us the history of the site. We passed the large, ornately carved stone at the entrance and walked into the dark tomb. The opening was small and the guide warned us that if we were claustrophobic, we might want to consider waiting outside. No one stayed behind.

We stood inside, squashed together in the small opening in the middle of the rocks, and the guide gave us more information about the site, but I still hadn't heard or seen anything that I thought would be helpful. While she was talking about the winter solstice and the beam of light that would flood into the tomb, I started to lose focus. At first, I thought the warm flush that I was feeling was a result of too many bodies in a very small area, but as the warm flush turned into a painful burn, I panicked with the knowledge of what was happening. I had experienced the same burning throughout my body on two other occasions. The first time had been at the battle at Red Rocks when Balor had used a spell on me that sent me crashing to the ground in pain. Simon had been there to cast a spell of his own against Balor and I had been able to get away before any serious damage could be done.

The second time had been when I'd first moved to Slan Lathair. We'd never figured out who had done it that time, and I ended up losing consciousness because Simon wasn't able to do a counter spell against the person causing the pain.

As I stood in the tomb at Newgrange, I knew I was headed in the same direction as the time at Slan Lathair. Simon wasn't there to do a counter spell and I wasn't sure the other faeries would know how to do it. Even if they could, they probably wouldn't be able to figure out who was casting the spell that was causing the pain burning through me. Was Balor nearby or was it someone else?

I tried to steady my breathing, not wanting my family or the faeries to notice what was happening, but the pain was intensifying and I had to fight the urge to cry out.

What's wrong? Ian asked with panic in his silent voice.

I couldn't answer. The pain was unbelievable—beyond the pain I'd experienced on the two occasions when this had happened before.

I was aware of a shift in the room. Ian had me in his arms and was carrying me through the small opening in the tomb. I heard protests and panicked questions, but Ian didn't stop.

When we were outside of the tomb, I heard Finn talking to Ian, a strong sense of urgency in his voice. "Get her to the hotel. I'll clean up here, then we'll take care of her family."

As Ian rose from the ground with me in his arms, I saw Brandon standing beside Finn on the ground below, horror in his eyes. Then I lost consciousness.

Chapter Six

Simon's arms were wrapped around me and I felt safe and everything was right and real and good. I ran my fingers along his forearm, brushing the fine hairs lightly. He kissed the top of my head, pulling me closer to him as he did. I knew there was nothing that would feel as perfect as his arms felt at that moment. His right hand reached up to stroke my hair, and as it passed in front of my face, I noticed that the ring he normally wore on his right index finger wasn't there. Why wasn't it there? Ian. It was Ian's arms wrapped around me and I was simultaneously crestfallen that he wasn't Simon and horrified that I had been able to feel so good in Ian's arms.

I bolted to a sitting position, wanting to distance myself from the feelings of guilt and betrayal and disappointment that were running through me, working together to create a tidal wave of agony.

"Stop the car," I insisted. Sloane turned from where she sat in the driver's seat to look at me. My expression must have told her I meant business because she pulled over at the first opportunity, stopping in front of a dilapidated wooden building at the side of the road. I crawled over Ian and jumped out of the SUV. My breathing was rapid and shallow and I worked to calm myself down as the realization of what had happened at Newgrange started to sink in and mix with all of the other emotions I was trying to bury deep inside. I registered the fact that Ian had followed me out of the car before I turned away to throw up, the churning of emotion getting the better of me. When I finished, I stood and took the bottle of water Ian was offering.

"Don't tell me, 'I told you so,'" I said after taking a swig of the water. "It was the right thing to do. I didn't have any other options."

He didn't try to argue with me.

"Where's my family?" I asked.

"They're with Finn and Alana. Finn had to alter the memories of the people at Newgrange. Then he altered your family's memories. They're on their way to the hotel in Dublin."

I leaned against the stone building and let myself slide to the ground. I wasn't ready to go back to the tight confines of the car. Ian walked over and sat down beside me.

"Was it the same as that time at Slan Lathair?" he asked.

I nodded. "Do you think it was Balor?"

"I don't know," he admitted. "*Someone* knew you were there."

"And didn't want me there," I speculated. "I think there's something about Newgrange that someone doesn't want me to find out about."

"Or they just followed us from Ballecath and waited for a good time to attack you."

"We stopped for lunch before we got to Newgrange. They could have attacked me then."

He was silent, looking nervously between the old building and the car.

"Let's get to the hotel before my family starts asking questions about where I am."

We stood and walked back to the car. I knew this wasn't over. Ian was angry and would stay angry for a long time before he'd be able to forgive me.

∞☙

"Do they have a DAM museum here?" Brandon asked as we walked along Grafton Street with every other tourist in Dublin. The pedestrian mall was packed with people and all six faeries in our group kept looking around anxiously, watching for any trouble that might come our way.

I sidestepped to avoid three women loaded down with shopping bags. "We're in Dublin, Brandon, not Denver. Why would they have a Denver Art Museum in Dublin?"

"Uh. Hello. They might have a *Dublin* Art Museum. It would still be the DAM museum."

"Actually, it would be just be the DAM. If you say 'the DAM museum,' you're pretty much saying 'Denver Art Museum museum.' That doesn't make sense."

"It might not make sense, but it's more fun the way I say it."

A flash of memory from my first date with Simon darted into my brain. We'd gone to the Denver Art Museum and he'd had a conversation with Brandon that included a lot of DAM puns. Before I could lose myself in the memory and the sadness it brought, Ian pulled on my arm to get me out of the path of a group of rowdy teenagers coming our way.

"We don't have a DAM, as such, in Dublin. We do have several art museums, however," Erin offered.

"He doesn't care about art," I clarified. "He just likes saying DAM."

Brandon shrugged, clearly not embarrassed that I'd just outed him as a goofball. "So the DAM art is out. I can't leave Ireland until I've had a Guinness."

"Not gonna happen," my dad said.

"Why not? They put Guinness in baby bottles here because there's no drinking age."

"Afraid you've been mislead, my young friend," Ian said. "The drinking age in Ireland is eighteen. You're still a few years shy of your first pint."

Brandon seemed offended. "One of my friends told me you could drink at any age here."

"You have friends?" I teased. Brandon elbowed me mildly in the arm.

"Your friend was wrong," my mom said. "And even if he wasn't—even if you could legally drink in Ireland at fourteen—your parents would still say no."

"You're no fun," he said, but there was no bite behind his words. He knew he couldn't drink, but he was having fun messing with everyone. "No Guinness. No DAM art. What are we going to do then?"

"Let's start by getting off Grafton Street," my dad said. "I think every single tourist in Ireland is packed on this street today."

"We could head to St. Patrick's Cathedral. They have a nice tour," Finn offered. "Or Trinity College. We can take a look at the Book of Kells in the library."

I braced myself for a snide comment from Brandon about his two choices being a church or a library, but it didn't come. It seemed like he was finally figuring out when teasing crossed the line and travelled into disrespectful territory.

We ended up heading to the Dublin Zoo. When Brandon first made the suggestion, I pointed out that we have a much larger zoo in Denver and that we should do something unique to Dublin. He insisted on the zoo, however, saying he wanted to check it out to see if the animals had Irish accents too. I'm pretty sure he was kidding.

"Look, your cousins," he said as we walked toward the chimpanzees.

"My cousins are your cousins, little brother."

He smiled but didn't come back with a witty retort.

"Do you remember the first time you guys took me to the Denver Zoo?" he asked as he leaned against the railing.

I leaned with him. "It was hilarious," I said. "You ran around from exhibit to exhibit screaming 'awesome' every time you saw something new. You'd see one animal and run to it, then see another animal out of the corner of your eye and run to that one. It was in the middle of the winter and it was absolutely deserted, and you just ran around like a mad man."

"I was so exhausted I fell asleep in dad's arms before we made it to the car."

"Do you remember that day? You were so young."

"I remember a little, but I mostly remember you guys telling the story."

"Yeah. I know what you mean. Sometimes I'm not sure if I'm actually remembering something that happened or remembering the story Mom and Dad told me about what happened."

"Yeah."

He looked to where our group was standing apart from us a few yards away, then looked to the ground.

"I really wish you'd come home, Maggie," he said. "Mom says I shouldn't say anything to you because you're old enough to make your own decisions, but I miss you and Ireland's kind of a creepy place."

"Creepy how?"

He looked at me for a moment, but moved his eyes back to the ground.

"I don't know. It just feels creepy."

Even with his eyes lowered, I could see that they were glistening.

"Are you crying?"

"No," he insisted as he turned away from me.

"Brandon, it's okay to cry. It's not something to be ashamed about."

"I'm not crying. My eyeballs are just hot."

"What?" I asked, certain I'd heard him wrong.

"They're hot and that's making them sweat."

I burst out laughing and patted his shoulder.

"You are such a freak."

"No, *you're* the freak," he said quietly.

"It must run in the family."

He turned around and hugged me and broke apart that little piece of my heart that belonged only to him.

"I miss you, Maggie."

"I miss you, too, Brandon."

ಞಲ

"Did you have a good Christmas, Maggie?" Albert asked when everyone was back on campus after the end of the holiday. I'd become friends with Albert, Gertie and Jane in the fall after we bonded during a misguided trip to a party without the Dream Team.

I'd stopped taking classes with the other students

after the battle with the Fomorians because school was no longer a priority for me. My sole purpose for returning to Slan Lathair was to hide from Balor since, for whatever bizarre reason, he would die if he came on campus.

I stayed in a cluster of cottages on the other side of campus from the school with Ian and the Dream Team, so Albert, Gertie and Jane made it a point to come and see me two or three times a week. The cottages were small, and a bit rustic, but they were comfortable. The walls were all stone, inside and out, and the floors were wooden. Ian and I each had a bedroom, but we shared a small bathroom with very old fixtures. The living area was made up of a small living room that was dwarfed by the large stone fireplace, and a small kitchen with room for a wooden table and four chairs. Our cottage was basic and old fashioned, but it was cozy.

"It was great to see my family," I said. "What did you guys do over the break?"

They started telling me the details of their vacations and the holiday and all the stuff they'd gotten for Christmas. I loved that I could sit and chat with them about nothing significant.

"Emma asked about you," Jane said when the conversation died down.

I looked at her, confused. Emma was one of our fellow students who lived to torment me and had actually been the reason for my misguided trip to the party in the fall. If she was asking about me, it couldn't be for a good reason.

"Was she trying to find out how she can poison my food?" I asked.

Everyone laughed.

"She asked if you were back on campus yet," Jane

said.

Albert shook his head slowly. "That can't be good. I can't imagine she'd want to plan a 'welcome back' party for you or anything."

Before any of us could comment, Ian came into the room and told me it was time to make my way to the main campus for my daily magic lesson. Ian tutored me in all of my academic classes, but I went to the main campus for a magic lesson with one of the staff, Mr. James. Albert, Jane and Gertie walked with us to the main building on campus and we parted ways outside of Mr. James' classroom.

"Did you practice at all over the break?" he asked when we were alone in his room. One of my favorite things about Mr. James was that he insisted the Dream Team wait outside during our lessons.

"Not really," I admitted. "It's hard to practice with my family around.

"Understandable. Well, let's get to it then." He pulled two cushions out of a cabinet and threw them on the floor. My lessons with Mr. James often required us to sit on the cushions and meditate about whatever skill I was working on.

"Invisibility today, I think," he instructed.

I sat on one of the cushions and closed my eyes. I spent an hour trying to picture myself as invisible, but it didn't work. Mr. James had actually been shocked at the level of magic I'd been able to achieve in such a short time. I could communicate telepathically with any faery. I could make flame sprout from my fingers. I could throw my dagger, Bob, and summon him to me. And I could still lie. Mr. James said the fact that I had mastered any magic at all in only one month was downright awe inspiring—his words, not mine. That said, I still couldn't make myself invisible, nor could I fly—two skills faery children mastered soon after they learned to walk.

"I hear you made an unscheduled trip to Newgrange over the break," Mr. James said as he walked me to the door at the end of our hour together.

"Good news travels fast," I said wryly.

"Be careful, Maggie," he said with his hand on the doorknob. "Especially when your family is around. You wouldn't want anything bad to happen to them because of a poor decision you made."

I took a deep breath and nodded my head before walking through the door. Ian and the Dream Team stood in the hallway waiting for me.

"Jane said Emma was asking about me," I told Ian on our walk back to the cottage.

"Was she wanting to know your food allergies so she could poison you?"

I laughed. "That's what I thought, too. But I was thinking about her during my magic lesson."

"Weren't you meant to be meditating on your lack of ability to make yourself invisible?"

"I get distracted sometimes."

He nodded with a smirk.

"Anyway, I was thinking about the note Emma sent to me last fall."

Emma had slipped an anonymous note into one of my books that said she had information that could help Simon and me with our quest to defeat Balor. The note said to meet on the beach so I could get the information.

"What about it?"

"Well, the note said she knew what Simon was trying to do and that she could help him, but how did she know what Simon was trying to do?

"I think she was bluffing. Simon's work was something we kept quiet about."

"You don't think she's involved with the Fomorians?"

"I doubt it. Her parents are Guardians."

I shrugged. "But she could be going against their values. It wouldn't be the first time a teenager rebelled against her parents."

"I think she was just bluffing. Emma's vindictive and snide, but I don't think she's evil."

"Yeah, you're probably right."

At that moment, I looked up and saw Emma standing in the middle of the sidewalk, a malicious glare settling on me.

"Speak of the devil," I muttered.

"Maybe literally," Nessa, one of the guards flanking me, mumbled into my ear.

"What do you want, Emma?" Ian asked with impatience.

"Oh, nothing," she said in a way I'm sure she thought sounded totally innocent. It didn't. I thought Emma had made an attempt at kindness toward me soon after I'd returned to Slan Lathair after my birthday, but that peace had been short lived. She still seemed to take pleasure in making my life on campus miserable. "I was just wanting to talk to Maggie. Alone."

"Not going to happen," Ian said as he put his palm on the small of my back in a protective gesture.

"It will only take a moment," Emma said as she grabbed at my elbow.

Several things happened at once. Ian put his hand on my other elbow and jerked me away from Emma. The Dream Team positioned themselves around me, cutting off contact with Emma. And I did some magic. I didn't think about it. It just happened, but I knew it was me. I could feel it in my soul. I could feel myself controlling it.

I used my mind to break a branch off of a nearby tree and sent it hurtling toward Emma. It knocked her in the head, but it wasn't powerful enough to knock her off her feet.

"Ow!" she protested as she put her hand to the spot where the branch hit her. "Was that really necessary? I just wanted to talk. I'm not going to hurt her, you stupid bunch of goons!"

Ian and the Dream Team looked shocked, their mouths hanging open and their eyes wide.

"What?" Emma asked defensively.

"Who did that?" Michael, another member of the Dream team, asked.

"Yeah," Emma said. "I'd like to know the answer to that question, as well. It really wasn't very nice."

Not here, Ian said silently. *Let's get her back to the cottages before we talk about this.*

The Dream Team closed ranks around me and we walked toward the cottages.

"Oh, fine!" Emma yelled to our retreating backs. "Just leave me here on my own. I'm injured, you know. I could need medical assistance. Not that anyone cares or anything."

Nobody stopped walking or even turned around to look at her.

"Who threw that branch at Emma?" Ian asked when we were standing in the solitude of the cluster of cottages. He was obviously angry.

"I did," I admitted, ready to face Ian's wrath. "I honestly didn't intend to hurt her. I didn't even think about it while I was doing it. It just happened."

Everyone's mouths hung open again and their eyes were wide.

"*You* did that?" Ian asked with awe.

"Yes. I'm sorry."

"You can move objects with your mind?" Michael asked.

"I guess so. I mean, I never have before, but something in me just snapped when I saw Emma standing there looking so mean and determined to make my life hell. I should have just walked away, but it just happened before I could think about it."

"It's okay, Maggie," Ian said. "We're just surprised you can do magic that advanced. None of *us* can make anything fly like that."

"You make your daggers fly through the air," I pointed out. "Why wouldn't you be able to make a small branch fly?"

"It's different," Ian said. "Our daggers have magical properties of their own which help them come back to us after they're thrown. The only thing magical about that branch was you."

"Oh," I said, a little bewildered. I knew I was developing magic faster than most, but I hadn't realized that I was able to do magic that Ian and the others couldn't do. The thought should have made me feel more powerful, but instead it made me a little scared.

Chapter Seven

I tossed and turned for hours, trying, but failing, to rest my mind so I could sleep. Ian's words chased me around in circles and made my head spin. A month ago, I couldn't do any magic at all—except talk to Simon telepathically—and now I could do magic that my guards couldn't. They'd been practicing for hundreds of years. It didn't seem possible that I should be able to match them. I certainly shouldn't be able to surpass them.

I finally gave up on the fantasy of sleeping that night, and pushed the covers aside before getting out of bed. I wanted to test my magic. I hadn't thought before sending that branch toward Emma, and I wondered what else was inside of me that I hadn't thought about.

I started with the easy stuff. I used my mind to rip apart the papers in a notebook and pushed the pieces into a pile. I lit my fingertips on fire and shot flame toward the papers and ignited them, completely ignoring everything Smokey the Bear had taught me. I'd never extinguished flame with magic, but I'd once seen Simon create a small amount of rain. I focused on what I wanted to do and a little bit of drizzle spit out from under my hand. I used my mind to push the stream of water and was able to create enough to put out the small fire I'd created.

I was pretty impressed with myself, but I didn't stop. I tried to think of the most impressive piece of magic I'd seen and immediately saw the image of flying tree trunks spiking themselves into the ground before catching fire. It was that piece of magic that had allowed Balor to steal Simon away from me. I remembered the shock of seeing those tree trunks flying over our heads as if they were weightless pieces of grass. I remembered seeing them impale the ground around Simon, surrounding him and cutting him off from anyone wanting to help him. I remembered the tips of the trunks bursting into flame, creating a bonfire twenty feet above the ground.

I wasn't ready to try moving tree trunks, but I could start with sticks. If I was going to have any chance with Balor, I had to come as close as possible to matching his magical ability, and sticks seemed like a good enough place to start.

I moved to the window in my room and pushed it open. I looked around on the ground outside and picked out twenty or so twigs about a foot long. I focused my mind on picking them up and letting them float in the air. The twigs did as I asked and hovered above the spot on the ground where they had been resting before I disturbed them. I closed my eyes and focused on moving the twigs again, this time sending them flying around me. I looked up and saw the blur of them above my head. I closed my eyes again and sent them diving to the floor around me, and then I lit the tips of them on fire. *Sorry, Smokey.* I sat back against the heels of my feet and basked in the warmth of the fire for a moment before I created a small rainfall in my little circle that extinguished the flame.

I took a deep breath, trying to calm myself from the magnitude of what I'd just done. When I looked up, I saw Ian standing before me. He looked amazed and shocked, but he also looked concerned and I wondered why.

"Holy crap," he whispered disbelievingly, his eyes wide. He kept looking between me and the charred sticks fused into the small puddles around me. "Did Mr. James teach you to do that?"

I shook my head. Ian closed the door and walked over to kneel beside me.

"Does he know you can do that?"

I shook my head again.

He looked around at the mess, then stood and offered me his hand. "Let's clean this up."

He left and came back with some old towels and we worked to clean up the wet floor. We scrubbed away at the spots where the sticks had left charred marks.

"I think we might have to sand these out," Ian said when we couldn't get the spots out. I closed my eyes and focused on the spots disappearing, but when I opened my eyes, they were still there. I could evidently make a mess magically, but I was going to have to clean it up the old fashioned way.

I changed into some dry clothes before going to stand by the fireplace in the living room.

"Maggie, do you know how monumental it is that you're able to do magic at that level?" Ian asked. He still seemed concerned about what he'd seen me do.

"I think so."

"It's just so unreal. I mean you still can't make yourself invisible, but you can do *that*." He waved his hand around in the direction of my room. "How long have you been able to do stuff like that?"

"Just tonight," I admitted. "I wanted to see if I could, so I tried."

He shook his head, still having a tough time coming to terms with what he'd seen. "Even very skilled faeries like Simon and Balor spend years training to do magic at that level, and you just decided to give it a go? See what would happen?"

"I don't get it Ian," I said, starting to get a little angry. "You and the other faeries have been pushing me to learn magic, but when I learn too fast, you get mad at me."

"I'm not mad. Just worried."

"Why?"

"I'm not sure how Balor will respond if he finds out. He might decide to—" he let the thought hang in the air, but I was pretty certain I knew what he was going to say. If Balor knew I was starting to improve my magic, he'd work harder to come after me and kill me. As it was, he thought he was up against a helpless human girl, and that threat probably didn't seem worth a lot of effort. If he found out I was developing magic, he'd want me out of the picture before I became so skilled that I would be a match for him.

"I don't think we should tell anyone about this," he suggested. "Maybe Sloane and Finn, but that's it. And I think you should tone it down when you're with Mr. James. Make it look like you're not learning at fast as you are."

"I get not telling people, but why keep it from Mr. James. I trust him."

"I trust him, too. I just don't want to put him in a position where he might slip up and tell someone inadvertently."

"Okay," I agreed. He seemed relieved. "It really scared you to see me do that, didn't it?"

He nodded. "Now I know you can truly kick my ass. I don't stand a chance." He smiled and pulled me to cuddle into his arm.

☙❧

Despite my newfound magical abilities, my routine at Slan Lathair went on as usual. I woke up each morning and went for a run, came back to the cottage and showered and had breakfast before I sat down with Ian to do some lessons that I never, ever, gave my full attention. Ian would get frustrated and lecture me about the importance of finishing my education while my eyes glossed over. One of our stomachs would grumble mid-lecture and we'd make some lunch. Then we'd do some training outside with the Guardians until it was time to go to my magic lesson with Mr. James. That particular hour had become a big waste of my day. It was the one time when I was encouraged by Ian to lose focus and not perform to the best of my ability. After the magic lesson, we went back to the cottage to study Irish folklore and mythology, and the faery way of life. Then it was time for bed and we started all over again—day after day after day.

"I've been thinking a lot since our trip to Newgrange," I said one evening when we were sitting alone together in the living room of our cottage. "I don't want to stay at Slan Lathair anymore." He shot me an incredulous look. "Not all the time," I clarified. "I need to be out there—doing something."

"You experienced first hand what 'doing something' led to at Newgrange," he reminded me.

"So it didn't work out the way I planned. If you're not

failing on a regular basis, you know you're not taking enough risks in life."

He stood and walked a few paces away from me. "That's terribly profound, Maggie." His words were oozing sarcasm. "I'll be sure to have that etched on your tombstone after you've taken one risk too many."

"Has sitting here doing nothing brought us any closer to finding Simon? Has it brought us any closer to finding Balor?"

"And what if Simon isn't alive anymore? What if you risk your life to find him, but he's already dead?"

His words were like a slap in the face. I hadn't heard Simon talk to me telepathically for a very long time and I knew there was a possibility that he was already dead, but hearing the words out loud always stung.

"I've thought this through. It's not a decision I take lightly. I'm going to go and look for Simon, and you can come with me or not. That's up to you."

"Where are you going to look? You don't even have a clue where to start."

"I'm going back to Newgrange. I still think there's something there."

"There's nothing there, Maggie."

"You know that for sure or are you being intentionally oppositional?"

I could see the frustration building inside of him.

"It's dangerous," he finally said.

"I know."

"I can't lose both of you. If Simon is dead, and you die finding him—I couldn't make it without either of you in my life."

I could see tears glistening in his eyes and knew how much the thought of losing me scared him.

"Are you worried I'll get hurt or killed, or are you

worried I'll find Simon? That he might come home?" My voice was barely a whisper. I hated to ask him those questions, and I was pretty sure I knew the answer he'd give, but I had to be certain.

"I want Simon to come home." His tone was patient and soft. I was glad he wasn't angry. "I would rather have both you and Simon alive and safe. I will gladly let my heart break apart every moment I see you together, because that's a pain I can manage. But the pain I would feel if both of you died *isn't*. I'd have to die with you."

I stood and went to him, taking both of his hands in mine.

"Then help me do this," I told him with as much tenderness as I could manage. "I have a better chance of surviving if you help me."

He hesitated before nodding reluctantly. I could have cried with gratitude. While I was definitely doing a better job of getting in touch with my brave and fearless side, I still had a long way to go and having Ian by my side would make everything I had to do easier.

"But no more manipulation. You have to agree to tell me everything—all of your plans."

"Deal," I agreed. "But no more trying to shelter me."

"As long as we're both breathing, I'll want to protect you. That's not going to change."

"There's a difference between protecting and sheltering. I can live with protecting, but sheltering's gotta go."

"Semantics."

"An important distinction. Do we have a deal?"

"Yes," he said reluctantly, "we have a deal."

I wrapped my arms around his waist and hugged him to me.

"Well, now that we've got that sorted out, any idea what we do now?" I asked when we'd pulled away from each other.

"I guess we should start looking through those books you bought at Newgrange. We'll need to know the place inside and out before we go there."

I blushed. "I didn't know you saw me buying them. I was trying to be stealth."

"I see everything," he told me with a teasing smile.

I smiled back and I felt the warmth flow through me. I hated having Ian mad at me and seeing his smile did a lot toward making me happy.

"Let's keep this between the two of us, though," he suggested. "I think Sloane would have me pulled as your primary Guardian if she knew I was supporting you in this. We also don't know who the traitor is, so I think it would be best to just not tell anyone."

"Yay. More secrets," I said unenthusiastically.

Chapter Eight

I became obsessed with Newgrange. I studied books until every word and illustration was etched on my brain and became a part of me, and when there was nothing left in the books to memorize, I searched the web for articles and information. I studied excavation reports and looked at pictures of different symbols carved into the rocks. I read about the history and the folklore associated with Newgrange, as well as Knowth and Dowth, the two lesser-known burial mounds in the vicinity. I was convinced Newgrange was the key to finding Simon, but I wasn't sure if that conviction was a sign that I was on the right track, or a sign that I was truly desperate.

When I wasn't searching for clues about Newgrange, I was working with Ian on my faery skills. I was able to retrieve Bob with regularity and was working on improving my accuracy when throwing him. Yes, "him." I had started to feel an energy from Bob when I held him in my hands and when I threw him. He didn't talk to me—obviously, because that would be totally weird—but it felt like he could communicate with me, and I had started to regard him as a friend. Just one more thing to add to the checklist that the men in white coats would use to have me committed for the rest of my life.

I also worked on making myself invisible. I would equate that pursuit with trying to make a six-ton elephant fly through the air using a piece of thread. How do you even begin to teach yourself to accomplish that skill? Because I was desperate to try *something*, even if it was wrong, I imagined different states of mind that might encourage invisibility. I imagined my skin folding in on itself. I imagined myself being brushed away in little wisps of air. I tried to make my mind a complete blank.

"Can you see me now?" I asked Ian one evening when we sat in our cottage together. I had tried picturing myself floating away, my body weightless and free.

Ian sighed and looked up from the book on Newgrange he was reading. "Yes."

"Can you see me now?" I asked after I tried to imagine my skin camouflaging itself like a chameleon.

"Yes," he responded after looking up once again.

"Can you see me now?" I asked, imagining myself under a flow of water, my body becoming translucent as it was washed away.

Ian looked up once again, his expression filled with exasperation. "Maggie, even if you make yourself invisible to humans, I'll still be able to see you."

"I know, but it'll look different." I had noticed the shimmering that surrounded any faery making themselves invisible, like heat waves rolling off the pavement.

"I don't see the shimmer around you," he confirmed. "And you don't need to keep asking me. Just look at your arm. You'll see it yourself."

"Yes, but it's not nearly as fun as pestering you," I teased. Ian smiled and put down the book he'd been reading.

"Why don't we go into town for dinner," he suggested.

I was incredulous. I had fought with Ian so many times about the fact that I wanted to go into town, but he thought it was too dangerous.

"Who are you and what have you done with Ian?"

He smiled. "We've been cooped up here too long," he explained. "Besides, in light of what we're planning, a trip into town with the Dream Team seems about as dangerous as swimming in two inches of water while wearing a life preserver."

He made a good point. We'd spent way too much time in our cottage and the area immediately surrounding it. Our days were divided between honing my faery skills and studying Newgrange. We needed a break.

We only took Nessa and Michael with us in our SUV, but other members of the Dream Team followed in another car.

"They have cheeseburgers," I said dreamily as the four of us sat at a table together in one of the local pubs. "And fries! I can't remember the last time I had a cheeseburger and fries!"

Meals at the cottage were bland and unimaginative. We seemed to eat canned soup and grilled cheese several nights a week and it was a rare day when we had anything other than scrambled eggs for breakfast. I wanted grease and calories and fat and carbs.

"You may not like Irish cheeseburgers," Ian told me without taking his eyes from his own menu.

"Why?"

"They mix the hamburger with mashed potatoes before they fry them, then put a slice of baked potato on top."

"Why would they do that? That totally ruins the—" I

stopped when I saw a smile dawning on Ian's face. "You're messing with me."

He nodded, still smiling.

I shook my head, annoyed. "You should be careful who you mess with, Ian," I warned. "You never know when they might decide to get revenge."

"Is that a threat?" he asked, his eyes twinkling.

I returned his smile, but didn't answer.

Nessa started talking about a band that was supposed to be playing in a nearby town and we decided to drive the eight miles to go and watch them. I was still surprised by Ian's easiness in agreeing to let me go anywhere outside of the boundaries of Slan Lathair, but I didn't question it. I was grateful for some time away from the routines we'd established since Simon had gone.

The music the band played was unmistakably Irish folk music. I loved the upbeat jigs they played and the lyrics sometimes made me laugh. The slower songs were sometimes depressing and the lyrics that told of lost loves and broken hearts hit too close to home.

Albert, Gertie and Jane showed up with a group of Slan Lathair students about an hour after we did. We pulled a bunch of tables together so they could all join us.

"Emma was asking about you again," Gertie said when the band took a break.

"What is up with that girl?" I asked. "I guess I can see why she'd want to torment me when we come face to face with each other, but she's actually going out of her way to seek me out so she can be mean to me."

"She's an odd one," Jane said. "I wouldn't worry about it."

"Considering you're always surrounded by this lot, I don't think she's much of a threat," Albert said as he cocked his head in the direction of the Dream Team.

"Not a threat," I agreed, "but a definite annoyance."

The band started playing again, making it nearly impossible to be heard without yelling, so we ended our conversation and listened to the music.

"Dance with me," Ian requested as he held out his hand when a slower song was playing.

I hesitated for a fraction of a second, then put my hand in his and let him lead me to the area in the middle of the pub that had been cleared of tables and chairs. A couple of other people were already dancing, and Ian and I joined them. He held me close and swayed with me in his arms and it felt good.

After our good friend, Max, had died the previous spring, we'd had a counselor come in and give everyone a talk about stress management and dealing with grief. I thought most of what the counselor said over simplified the intensity of how we were really feeling, but as I let Ian hold me to him in the pub that night, I thought about an analogy the counselor had given us that day. She told us that when you're on an airplane, if there's a loss of pressure and the air masks drop from the overhead bins, they always tell you to put your own mask on first, then help others around you who may need help, because if we don't help ourselves first, we may pass out and be unable to help anyone. She went on to explain that this was how we should conduct all aspects of our life. If we didn't do a good job of taking care of ourselves first, we wouldn't have the mental or physical ability to take care of those around us. I told myself that the down-time in the pub that night was going a long way toward restoring my mental and physical strength and that I'd do a better job of finding Simon and bringing him home if I took care of myself first. It was hard not to think about Simon and where he might be and if he was still alive while I was dancing with Ian, but I worked to give my mind a vacation for a couple of hours, knowing I'd go back to giving my search for Simon everything I had when those couple of hours were over.

Ian and I sat in the backseat together on the way home and I reached over as we drove along the dark roads and took his hand in mine. He looked over as our skin touched and even in the darkness I could see his hurt and confusion, but I could also see how much he cared about me. Did he love me? I had no doubt that he did. Did I love him? Not the way he wanted me to. Not the way he deserved to be loved. And because of that, I wanted to pull my hand from his. I wanted so much more for him than I could ever give, but I couldn't bring myself to pull away—not in that moment or any other moment. I needed his closeness, but knew it was just a substitute for being with Simon. When Simon was back, I wouldn't need Ian anymore—not in the same way—and I felt heartless and evil.

I know, Maggie, Ian said silently, gently.

I looked up at him, wondering if he had guessed my thoughts.

I know you wish it were Simon's hand you were holding, he confirmed. *And I know that if we get him home, you won't want to hold my hand anymore. I'm okay with that.*

You deserve better than this.

He squeezed my hand and rubbed his thumb against the side of my index finger. *Someday, I will find someone who can love me as much as you love Simon, but right now, I'm happy to have this. I'm happy for the time we can spend together and the closeness we can share today and if it's gone tomorrow, I'm okay with that.*

Do you realize how horrible I feel?

You're not doing anything wrong, Maggie.
Then why does it feel like I am?

He reached over and pulled me to him, not caring, evidently, if Nessa and Michael witnessed the intimate embrace we shared.

ಬಂಡ

I turned around quickly, spotting the tree with the target almost instantly, and threw Bob, knowing he would hit the bulls-eye before he even left my fingers. It was a new game Ian had come up with to help with my target practice. He had me turn my back to a group of trees while he and the other Guardians tacked different targets on various trunks. Each target had a different color in the center and when Ian told me to turn around, I was to find the one with the red center and throw Bob toward it.

"Unbelievable," Ian said while shaking his head. "You've hit it the bulls-eye every time. And you do it in less than a second. I don't know if it's the ring, or Danu giving you more powers, or some latent ability inside of you, but you're absolutely amazing."

I closed my hand around Bob after calling him back to me. "Well thank you very much," I said with a sarcastic bow.

"I don't know how to challenge you any more. I don't know how to make it any harder."

"You and the Dream Team could be moving targets for me," I teased.

"As much as I'd like you to get some practice with the real thing before you have to go after Balor, I'm not real crazy about the idea of you coming after me with Bob. I don't think I can hold my own against you any more."

I blushed, knowing he was paying me a compliment, but also knowing it was true.

We gathered our things and walked toward the cottages. It was a cold night, but I felt more refreshed than uncomfortable. I could feel the frosty air moving toward my lungs and it energized me.

"I wish I never had to hit anything but trees," I confessed to Ian. "I know Balor is evil and all, and I know his death would mean that so many other people would get to live, but I hate that I have to be the one to kill him. I don't even like to kill spiders. I always find something to scoop them into and set them free outside."

"Spiders may be scary, but they're not evil. Balor is undeniably evil."

"But isn't there another option? Couldn't we throw him in a dungeon or something instead of killing him?"

"He'd get out. His magic is too strong. The only way to stop him is to kill him."

"But doesn't killing him make me just as bad as he is?"

"Balor kills for very selfish reasons. He thinks only of himself and what he wants. Your motivation comes from thinking of others."

"But is it any better?" I insisted. "I have to murder a man."

Ian stopped walking and took one of my hands in his. "You want to know the biggest difference between what Balor is doing and what you're planning to do? You question it. You ask yourself if it's morally correct. You have a powerful internal struggle that I'm sure keeps you up at night. Balor never asks those questions. Balor doesn't struggle with what he does."

Chapter Nine

Jane and I went into the town near Slan Lathair to do some shopping. A gaggle of guards stayed close behind as we walked from shop to shop. Ian had resisted when I told him I wanted to go, pointing out that I could buy whatever I needed online. I reminded him that I had returned from town several times, completely unscathed. I also told him I needed new bras and that it was something a girl really needed to try on. Being that he'd never needed to buy a bra for himself, there was no way for him to know if that was necessary or not. I also told him I'd prefer he not make the trip with me. I could see how hurt he was when I'd made that request, but we needed some time apart. He'd been by my side almost constantly since I'd moved to Ireland and I figured he needed a break as much as I did.

As it turned out, my shopping choices were ridiculously limited. There was one store that sold a lot of twill and wool, but I'd gotten my fill of wool when I'd had to wear my school uniform the previous semester; and while I knew they wouldn't actually make bras out of wool, just the thought made me shiver. Jane told me they sold clothes at the grocery store, but we both agreed that clothes sold in a grocery store were probably a little sketchy. That left a sporting goods store. It looked like I'd be getting a few sports bras.

We walked around the store after I'd tried on a few things to see if there was anything else I needed before we headed to the cash register. It was a small store, but the owners had taken advantage of every available space in order to squeeze in a surprising variety of merchandise. There was a small clothing section, a section devoted to team sports, and a hunting section. I noticed they had a lot of dagger accessories—sheathes, holsters and sharpening tools—but no daggers.

"Our daggers are usually passed between family members or handmade," Jane said when I pointed it out.

"But don't the people in town think it's a little odd that all the students want dagger accessories, but nobody wants an actual dagger?"

She shrugged one of her shoulders dismissively. "They know."

"What do you mean?"

"They know about the faeries. There are certain towns around Ireland that are close to a lot of faery activity and everyone in the town knows about the faeries—like this one and the town near Ballecath. It's really hard to hide who we are when there are so many faeries in one place."

"So the regular people know about the faeries?"

She nodded. "Some of them *know* know them. Faeries and regular people are always hooking up and stuff."

"Really?" I knew Ian's mom had been a regular human, and so was Quinn, Sloan's husband, but I didn't know it was commonplace.

"I dated a human from town a while back. He was a

really nice guy, but he said it weirded him out that I never got any older. He's married and has kids now. His son's about my age. He flirts with me when I see him, but I think it'd be strange to date a guy, then date his son later."

"Yeah. I can see how that would be uncomfortable."

After leaving the sporting goods store, we headed to the one and only coffee shop in town. It was a rainy and gloomy day and I felt like I couldn't get warm. The people in Ireland seemed to take the rain in stride, but I hadn't been able to get used to the feeling that I was always wet or damp. I'm pretty sure my socks hadn't stayed dry for a solid twenty-four hours since I left Denver.

I pulled a few napkins from the holder on the table and tried to blot some of the excess water from my face. Jane was wet, but she didn't appear to have a need to dry off.

"Hiya, Jane," our waiter said when he came to take our order. "I haven't seen you at the local lately. They keeping you busy up at that school?"

"Yeah. Lot's of homework and whatnot. You?" She was turning a dark shade of red.

"Same, yeah."

"That's him," she said in a conspiratorial tone when Colin left the table. "The son of my ex."

I turned and looked to where Colin was standing behind the counter.

"He's cute. You *should* date him."

"No. I could never kiss him after kissing his dad." She shivered with the thought. "You should date him though. You're the same age, and you've never kissed his dad, so you have that going for you."

I tried to blow her comment off, but I felt my face fall

and my stomach twisted in a knot.

"Oh my god, Maggie, I'm so sorry. Of course you're not ready to date anyone. It's too soon."

I took a few breaths and tried to distance my emotions from the tears that were threatening to fall. "It's okay," I told her when I felt like I could say it without choking up.

"I forget sometimes. I mean Simon hasn't been at school for almost two years—except to visit you. I forget that he's not just out working or something."

I nodded, not quite trusting the new flood of emotions that were washing over me to get along with the tears that were trying very hard to push past the rim of my eyes.

She took one of my hands in hers and leaned toward me across the table. "I know how much you loved Simon. It's probably going to be a long time before you feel like dating again."

The tears let loose. I couldn't stop them against the powerful force of my emotions. I hoped I never had to date anyone else. I hoped Simon was still alive. But what if he wasn't? What if I never saw him again and I *did* have to start dating someone else? I knew it would never be enough. I knew that not even Ian could take his place and make me feel whole again.

I wanted to confide in Jane. I needed someone to talk to about Simon and about Ian and about everything I'd been feeling, but I couldn't tell her about Simon. Ian and I had agreed. I could, however, tell her about Ian. I trusted her and I knew she wouldn't betray me and I really needed someone to talk to.

I pulled my hand from hers and used both of my palms to wipe away the tears from the face I'd just dried a few minutes before. I did a quick look around for the

Dream Team and made sure they were out of earshot before I said the three words that were causing me so much pain and confusion.

"I kissed Ian," I said, unable to look at Jane when I did.

"Ian who?"

I gave her a pointed look.

"*Your* Ian?"

"I feel horrible. It was so bad for so many reasons." I took a deep breath to steady myself before I went on. "And my best friend ran away and I don't have anyone to talk to about it and not talking about it makes everything feel so—heavy."

"Wait. What? Your best friend ran away?"

I nodded and rubbed my hands against my jeans, trying to stop the itchy burn that always settled in my palms when I was upset. I took several cleansing breaths, determined not to let any more tears fall. The Dream Team started to close ranks, but Jane shook her head in their direction and probably said something to them silently. I'm guessing she told them I was a real nutcase and about to blow a fuse. They went back to their seats on the other side of the coffee shop, but they kept shifting their gaze in my direction, worried, I'm sure, that I might really lose it.

"Okay," Jane said with extreme levels of calm. "You kissed Ian. Let's tackle that first."

I nodded, ready to lessen the weight on my shoulders.

"Was there anything that led up to it or was it totally out of the blue?"

"It surprised me when it first happened, but looking back I'm wondering if I should have known. Ian saved my life after Simon—after what happened to him. I wanted to slip away, but Ian wouldn't let me. I know it was hard for him too, but he didn't think of himself. He just thought about me and making sure I didn't lose myself."

"So, you're confusing gratitude with romantic love?"

"I don't know. Maybe. I guess so. I *was* really grateful. Not just because he saved my life, but for other stuff too." I didn't tell her that I was grateful because Ian believed Simon was alive.

"I think that's pretty normal, Maggie. He saved your life and you guys are hardly ever apart. It would be hard *not* to grow attached to him. He's here, and Simon's not, and I'm sure it's pretty confusing."

I nodded again and rubbed my palms. "I think the worst part is that I don't want to push Ian away. I like the way I feel when I'm with him, but I know it will never be the same as it was with Simon, and I know I should discourage him, but I *want* him near me. I want him to fill in the gap Simon left."

"Have you told him all of this?"

"I think so."

"Maybe you should tell him again, just to be sure, then let him decide how close he wants to get."

"You're right."

"Of course I am," she said with a teasing smile. "Now, moving on to the best friend."

I thought through what I could tell her without giving away too much.

"She ran away and I haven't heard from her since Thanksgiving. I don't know if she's safe and I don't know if she's coming back."

Jane looked at me with sympathy and pity. "You've got no one to talk to then."

I shook my head. "I lost both of my best friends within just a few weeks."

She reached over and took my hand in hers again.

"Gertie and Albert and I are here for you, Maggie. You have three people to talk to now, and you have a plan. You're going to talk to Ian and clear the air. Is there anything you can do right now to feel better about your best friend?"

"I keep e-mailing her, hoping she's checking it, but I don't know what else to do."

"Do her parents have any idea where she might be?"

"They don't even know she ran away." I filled her in on what I knew, telling her that Lexie had run away to find Max's killer and that we had told her parents she was going to finish her senior year in Ireland with me.

"Good lord, Maggie, how have you not exploded by now?"

I shrugged.

"Talk to Ian. Start there, then we'll move on to fixing the rest."

It felt so good to have an ally. I had someone to talk to and someone to help me figure out how to fix all of my problems, and I felt a lot better.

Collin came back to the table with our coffee. He appeared startled when he looked at my face and I was pretty sure I wouldn't have to worry about fending him off. There was no way anyone could be interested in a crazy American girl who looked like she'd just lost her best friend—two of them actually.

We finished our coffee and made our way outside and into the rain. I didn't try to hide from it as we walked back to our car. I lifted my head to the sky and let the rain wash over me and clean away the tension I'd been holding onto. I felt better and I understood why the people in Ireland didn't seem bothered by the rain.

Chapter Ten

Ian was sitting on the sofa in front of the fireplace, reading a book, when I came back from my trip into town. I placed my bags on the floor by the door and went to sit with him.

"How was shopping? Did you get everything you need?"

"More or less," I said.

His forehead furrowed as he looked at me closely. "You okay?"

"Yeah. I was just talking to Jane about some stuff that kind of upset me."

"Did you guys fight?"

"No, nothing like that. We just talked about some stuff."

"Like?"

"Like Simon and you and me and human/faery relationships."

"Ah."

"She suggested I talk with you about how I feel. She thinks if we clear the air, I won't feel so guilty."

"We don't have to clear the air, Maggie. I know how

you feel."

"Indulge me."

He stood and took a few steps away from me before turning back around. "You love Simon in a way that makes your heart ache. He makes your world have meaning and he gives you joy, even when there are so many reasons not to feel joyous. You would risk your own life to save his and life without him will always be sad and bereft."

He sat down on one of the overstuffed chairs near the fireplace before he continued. "You love me too, but not in the same way. I fill a little piece of the hole left in your heart when Simon left, but just a little piece. You like having me around, and I give you a feeling of comfort, but it will always be about Simon for you. Even if we find out that he's dead, your heart will belong to him. You'll be able to rent out a small section to me, but for the rest of your life, whether he is dead or alive, your heart will always belong to him."

He leaned forward and rested his elbows on his knees.

"Does that pretty much sum it up?"

"Uh, yeah. I think you have a better handle on it than I do, actually."

"I will be your friend forever, if you'll have me. And if, at some point, if you want to try for more, I'm willing to give it a go, but I will always know that you were wishing it was him."

"How can you sell yourself short like that, Ian? How can you settle for less than you deserve?"

"Because, actually, I think you're more than I deserve."

I walked to him and sat on the arm of the chair, leaning into his shoulder.

"*You* are more than *I* deserve."

He poked my ribs with his finger. "And don't you forget it."

☙❧

"Make sure to call your mom today," Ian said at breakfast a few days later. "It's her birthday."

"How do you know that? Are you my secretary now in addition to being my body guard?"

He looked at me and cocked his head. "You asked me two days ago to be sure to remind you."

"Oh, yeah. Sorry."

"Here—this might help your memory a bit." He placed a cup of coffee on the table in front of me.

"Thanks." I held the cup close to my nose and took a deep breath. I loved the smell of coffee even more than the taste and wanted to savor it for a moment before I took my first sip.

"Ian, when did your mom die?" I asked as gently as I could after I set the mug back on the table. The thought of calling my own mom had made me think about his and I wondered how long he'd been without her.

I saw his whole body tense up before he answered. "A long time ago."

"How old were you?"

"It happened my first year at school."

"Did she die of old age?" Ian's mother wasn't a faery, so she would have aged much faster than his father.

I could see the blood rush to his face and wondered what was causing his discomfort. Was he embarrassed? Angry?

"I'm sorry, Ian. I'm being really thoughtless. I shouldn't've asked you about your mom."

"Balor killed her," he said quietly.

"Oh." I shouldn't have been surprised, but I was.

"She was already really old when it happened," he assured me. "It just hurts that he was the one to do it."

"Oh course it does. We don't have to talk about, Ian. I'm really sorry I brought it up."

"There's more to this story, Maggie." His voice was low and he didn't look me in the eye when he spoke. "More that you really need to know."

"Okay." I wanted to be able to listen to whatever Ian needed to tell me about his mom, not only so I could understand what happened to her, but also because I wanted to be a good friend to Ian. He was always there when I needed his support and I wanted to offer that same support to him.

Ian twisted the end of his napkin in his fingers, back and forth, back and forth. "Maybe I should have told you sooner. I don't know. I guess I'd like to never tell you."

"It's okay, Ian. Whatever it is, it's okay to tell me."

His hands were shaking by this point and when he saw me looking at them, he tucked them between his knees, squeezing them tight.

"Simon was involved with my mother's death."

"What do you mean?"

"It happened when Simon was living with Balor—after Balor had kidnapped him. Simon's an incredibly gifted faery, which isn't surprising given who his parents are. Finn noticed early on that Simon had the gift of compulsion."

"What does that mean?"

"He could convince people to see things that weren't real, or to do things they didn't want to do. It's a skill he inherited from Balor."

"So he could make someone see a bowl of ice cream that wasn't really there? That sort of thing?"

"Exactly. One of our dogs passed away when we were little and Simon convinced Keelin that he wasn't really dead. She would play with the dog Simon created in her mind and she thought he was real."

"It's like Finn's faery ability. To make people believe things that aren't real. Or your ability to make people think they want to tell you something that they don't."

"It's similar, but more powerful. Finn can make someone believe that there was a bowl of ice cream on the table yesterday when there wasn't. I can make them believe that they really want to tell me they ate the ice cream. Simon and Balor can make someone see it now. They can make them taste it and feel it and experience it, even though it's not real. Finn changes memories and feelings. I can make someone want to tell me things. Compulsion is different. It's a lot more powerful and Finn didn't want Simon to use it—even if using it meant making someone feel better. It's a dangerous skill to have and he worked really hard before we went to school to help Simon control that particular gift. There's a very fine line between talking someone into something and using compulsion to control them. Finn didn't want Simon to cross that line. But Balor kidnapped Simon our first year at school and he encouraged Simon to use compulsion to get what he wanted. He even went so far as to make Simon feel weak if he *didn't* use it."

"So sort of like Finn's ability and your ability on crack."

He shrugged. "Sort of."

He went back to twisting the ends of his napkin before he continued with whatever it was that he needed me to know.

"Balor decided to kill my mother—probably for no other reason than as a training exercise for Simon. He told Simon to use his compulsion to get my mother to come with him to a place in the woods where Balor was waiting. When she got there, Balor slit her throat while Simon watched."

I felt my stomach lurch and hoped I didn't throw up. He was just a little boy. How could his father do that to him? How could he make his own son watch something so unbelievably horrible?

"Finn was able to get Simon back soon after that. Simon really fought Finn and wanted to go back to Balor, but the effects of Balor's compulsion on Simon started to wear off and Simon started to understand what he'd done while he was with his father. He vowed never to use compulsion again—even if it was for a good reason—and as far as I know, he never has."

"Wow. I totally get why your dad doesn't trust him."

"My dad is thinking with his heart. He was hoping to have a few more years with my mother and he lost those. Nothing we say can convince him that Simon isn't the evil bastard his father is."

"He thinks Simon faked his own death so he could go back to Balor."

"He told you that?"

"No. He told Sloane and I overheard him. It means that he thinks Simon's alive, though."

Ian nodded and looked deep in thought. "He thinks he's switched sides."

"Do you think he has?" I knew in my heart it wasn't possible, but a little confirmation couldn't hurt.

Ian stood and walked to the sink, rinsing out his coffee mug under the tap. He didn't turn around to face me when he finally answered.

"I think Balor is really good at compulsion. It's possible that he could convince Simon to join him. But I also know that Simon was developing his powers more and more, and if Balor has him, I'd like to think that Simon is able to fight him."

Yeah. Not so reassuring.

ಐಲ

"Maggie, come to me." I was dreaming and Grandma Margaret was calling to me, but I couldn't see her. I couldn't get to her.

"Come to me, Maggie Girl," she persisted. "Push through and come to me."

I didn't know how to get to her. I could hear her, but I didn't know where she was.

"Maggie, he's here. He's here. Push through and come to me."

I woke up, breathing rapidly, sweat running down my back and temples. Normally my dreams with Grandma Margaret were very real and vivid. This one had been like a regular dream—confused and surreal. I'd had a dream like that once before. It was the dream when Grandma Margaret told me Simon had to go to "him." It was that dream that had caused Simon to leave on his quest to find Balor. The dream that landed me at faery boarding school. The dream that may have ultimately been responsible for Simon being taken away from me.

She'd said, "He's here," but who was "he" and where, exactly were they? Near me? With Grandma Margaret? Then a hard lump formed in my throat when I thought of another possibility. What if she wasn't talking about Balor? What if she was talking about Simon and she was telling me that Simon was with her? If they were together, that could only mean one thing. He was dead.

I put my hand over my mouth to stifle a sob. I believed with complete certainty that Simon was alive when he'd been taken from that field when the Fomorians ambushed us. I believed he was alive when I'd heard him speak to me telepathically, but it had been so long since I'd heard him. I talked to him all the time, but he never responded and the idea that he might have died since the last time I heard him was something I thought about often. Having Grandma Margaret confirm it was more than I could bear.

But she hadn't said Simon specifically. It could mean any number of things. It could just be a dream—a regular dream that meant nothing. It was only a remote possibility that it meant something, but that small possibility would keep me awake with worry for the rest of the night.

Chapter Eleven

I ran into Jane, Gertie and Albert one evening after my magic lesson and they invited me to hang out with them in Jane and Gertie's dorm room. I pounced on the opportunity to do something so normal. A few members of the Dream Team waited outside in the hallway, and when I looked out the small window in the room, I saw that several more were stationed on the ground below, but none of them came into the room with us. They were doing a better job of giving me some space and I knew that was Ian's doing.

"You should join us for the students versus staff football game this weekend," Gertie said while we sat on the beds and ate from bags of junk food the girls had stored in their closet.

"You totally should," Jane agreed. "It would be fun to have you play with us."

"I'm not really a student here anymore," I said. "I only live on campus because Balor can't get to me here."

Albert reached into a bag of chips that had been lying on the bed. "You take magic lessons with Mr. James. That makes you a student." He made a face after putting a chip in his mouth. "What flavor are these crisps? They're disgusting." He looked at the front of the bad. "Haggis and black pepper? Why on earth would you buy these?"

"They sounded interesting," Gertie said with a shrug.

"Well they may be interesting, but they definitely aren't good."

"Stop with your whinging. No one's forcing you to eat them." Gertie grabbed the bag from Albert and pulled a few of the chips out for herself.

"So, back to the game," Jane said. "Will you play?"

"You'd be better off if I didn't. I've only played a couple of times in PE class. I'm not even sure I know the rules." Football in Ireland meant soccer, but I'd always passed on joining the soccer teams when I was growing up in favor of playing tennis. I knew you had to kick the ball and try to get it into the net, but that's where my soccer/football knowledge ended.

"It's just for fun," Albert assured me. "You should definitely play."

After a lot of begging and whining from all four of us, they succeeded in wearing me down and I agreed to play. We were required to wear the sportswear portion of our uniform so it was a good thing I hadn't torched it all while practicing magic. I'd certainly been tempted, but had resisted that particular urge. So the following Saturday I pulled on the black track pants with the two green stripes running down each leg and the green fleece pullover that was the required uniform when playing sports at Slan Lathair. I didn't have cleats or shin guards, so Gertie let me borrow her spares.

Ian and the Dream Team walked with us to the soccer field and sat in the stands with the younger students and the staff who had opted not to play. When I looked to where he was sitting before the game, I noticed Gracie, Alana's daughter, sitting near him and went up to say hello. She stood on the bench and reached up to wrap her little arms around my neck. Gracie was much older than me, but she looked like she was about six.

"How are you, Gracie?" I asked while she was still attached to my neck.

"Good. We're learning about butterflies in class, and I wanted to keep one but that's cruel because they need to be free."

"Well, that was kind of you to let it go."

"I wouldn't want to be kept in a cage. That wouldn't feel good."

"No, I don't suppose it would."

She started to wiggle in my arms and shimmied down to the ground.

"I have to go now," she said, and she went to sit with some friends her own age.

I took the field with the other students to do a few warm ups before the game.

"Maggie, I need to talk to you."

I turned around to see Emma standing behind me.

"Emma, I'm sure whatever you have to say isn't something I want to hear."

She rolled her eyes and started to walk away, but turned back around after she'd taken a few steps.

"I just want to warn you," she said impatiently. "I think you should be careful who you trust."

"You don't need to worry," I assured her. "I already don't trust you. There was no need to give me a warning."

"I wasn't talking about me, you idiot," she said before finally walking away.

I only had a minute to think about why this girl who

seemingly hated me felt a need to give me a warning before the ref called us together to start the game.

"We're playing a basic game here," our ref for the day reminded both teams. "No flying. No invisibility. No magic of any sort."

I groaned internally. I was pretty certain my only chance of not making a fool of myself on the soccer field was going to have to involve magic. Without it, I was doomed.

It was a cold and gray day, but it wasn't raining and I figured that would make my time on the field a little less miserable. Then I saw that Emma was on my team and the prospect of misery was suddenly very real. The girl definitely didn't like me, something I was pretty sure was a result of a kiss with Simon when they were both younger.

Jane, Gertie and Albert coached me along while we played. Their main piece of advice was to pass the ball to someone who knew what they were doing and I was definitely okay with that. Emma did her best to make sure I didn't ever get the ball. She shoved me and elbowed me and even tripped me on one occasion.

"You do realize we're on the same team," I finally yelled at her.

She shrugged dismissively and took off running toward the ball.

After a couple of hours on the field, the students squeaked by with a four-three win. I hobbled to the benches on the sideline with the rest of my team to change out of my cleats.

"I'm sure I have at least fifty bruises under my sweats," I complained. "All I want right now is a hot bath."

"No baths yet," Albert said. "We have the victory

bonfire. The staff has to build a fire for us and cook our dinner. It's tradition."

I took a deep breath and pushed aside my aches and pains to make the trek from the soccer field to the beach for the bonfire.

"Emma really crossed a line," Gertie said as we walked. "She just wouldn't lay off."

"I know. All of my bruises keep reminding me."

"We tried to keep her away from you, but she always managed to slip through."

"Don't worry about it. Maybe now that she's beaten me up, she's gotten all of her anger out of her system and she'll be nice."

"Not likely," Albert said.

I cursed Emma silently while I moved slowly down a steep hill, every bruise and sore muscle screaming in pain. The path was slick with the ever-present mud that covered Ireland and it was hard to keep myself upright as I made my way down. Eventually, the inevitable happened. I tripped on a rock sticking out of the ground, lost my footing, and ended up on my butt in the mud.

"You okay?" Ian asked as he rushed to help me to my feet.

"Fine," I said tersely.

"Do you want to go change before the bonfire?" he asked, unable to contain his smile.

"No. I'm good. I was already covered in mud anyway."

"You need to be careful on this part of the trail. I'd prefer you not fall over edge." Ian gestured with a tilt of his head toward the sharp drop at the side of the path.

"I'm not going to fall, Ian. Stop being so overprotective."

At the same moment that I finished my sentence, I

heard a scream, then the scraping of gravel and a thump behind me. We all turned around and saw that Jane had fallen over the edge Ian had just warned me about. She landed on a large boulder, which prevented her from falling to the bottom of the steep hill, but she wasn't moving, and when I got closer I could see that her head was bleeding.

Ian flew to where Jane was lying. Gertie and Albert started to follow, but Ian stopped them. "Stay there. This ledge is too small for all of us."

They both looked worried, but they didn't move any closer to the ledge.

"Is she okay?" Albert asked.

"She must have hit her head on the boulder," Ian said as he leaned down to her. "Jane. Jane." He rubbed her face, trying to get her to wake up, but her eyes remained shut. Ian and I exchanged a look. We both knew this was very serious. "Gertie, go and get a healer."

"Albert, go with her please," I added, not wanting him there for what I had planned.

When the two of them were out of site, I carefully climbed down to Ian and Jane.

"I'm going to try to heal her."

"You're not a healer, Maggie."

"How do you know? I've been able to do a lot of stuff lately that's pretty unbelievable. It's worth a try."

"I don't want anyone to see you doing magic at that level."

We'd been the last to leave the field and the rest of the students were already on the beach. I could see them from where we were, but I knew they were all having too much fun to look in our direction for long. Even if they did, they wouldn't know what I was doing from that distance. "Nobody will see."

"It's too risky."

"Ian, she's hurt. Badly. Look at how much blood she's losing."

I didn't wait for him to make a decision. I took Jane's hand in mine. I wouldn't allow myself to wonder *if* it was possible and instead told myself that I *was* a healer. I *could* do this.

I watched the blood continue to flow from the gash on the side of her head.

"It's not working," I said.

"Try pushing up her sleeve so you can touch more of her skin."

I did as he said and held both of my hands to her arm, but nothing happened.

The healer from school flew toward us with Gertie and Albert a few minutes later and touched his hands to Jane's arm. Ian and I climbed back to the path so that he would have plenty of room next to Jane. The blood stopped flowing from her cut and the color started to return to her skin. Within less than a minute, her eyes were open and, with help from the healer, she was sitting up. The healer used a wet wipe to clean the blood from Jane's face, then helped her to stand and make her way back to the trail.

"Maybe we should skip the bonfire," I suggested after we'd all questioned Jane and made sure she was okay.

"No way," Jane said. "I feel good as new and I wouldn't miss this for anything."

"Do you think you can manage to stay on the trail this time?" Albert teased.

Jane pushed him and he lost his balance, coming very close to going over the same edge Jane had just gone over.

"Let's try to walk the remaining one hundred yards to

the beach injury free," Ian said while rolling his eyes.

I sat apart from the rest of the group and stared into the enormous fire the losing team had built. My inability to heal Jane had been a very humbling experience. I'd been getting overly confident about my ability to do magic and was starting to feel invincible. Failing at something—especially something as important as saving a friend—was like a slap of reality hitting me hard upside the head.

Ian came and sat in the sand beside me. "So you're not a healer. You're still pretty bad ass."

I didn't smile. I didn't comment. I wasn't in the mood to humor him.

"Seriously, Maggie, it's nothing to be upset about. Even among faeries, healers are rare. It's not a common ability."

"No. You're right. I shouldn't be upset. It's good that I couldn't heal Jane. I needed a reminder that I'm vulnerable. That I'm weak."

Ian laughed out loud. "Weak? Are you putting me on? You're the polar opposite of weak."

"Compared to Balor, I'm weak, and that's all that matters."

"Don't let this shake your confidence. You're letting it mess with your head and *that* will make you vulnerable. Focus on what you can do. Not on what you can't."

He was right. There was no sense in wallowing in self-pity. Whether I was a healer or not, whether I could do magic or not, whether I could match Balor's magic or not, I had no choice but to try to kill him because the alternative was unbearable.

"You're right. I should focus on my strengths. I can't do anything about the skills I don't have, but I can work with the skills I have."

"That's the attitude!" he said enthusiastically. "So, let's enjoy this little victory party tonight, and tomorrow, we'll get back to the work of saving the world."

We stayed with the group for a couple of hours before the sun set and the rain started. Despite my faery inclinations, I was cold and wanted to get a hot shower.

"Have you emailed Lexie lately?" Ian asked when I walked into the living room after cleaning up and changing into my pajamas.

"She never emails me back. And I think if she's found anything that could help, she wouldn't wait for us to email her. She'd want to tell us right away."

"I still think it would be good to email her. Let her know we're trying to keep her in the loop."

I nodded and stood to get my laptop. "Oh, I keep forgetting. I have a folder that I found in Simon's desk. I think it's just a bunch of pictures and school reports. I doubt there's anything that could help us, but it might be worth looking through it, just in case."

"What sort of folder?"

"A folder about me, with pictures of me and stuff."

"Yeah. The Guardians kept a folder like that on all the Margaret O'Neills they were looking at. I'll look through it while you send Lexie an email."

I went to my room and grabbed the folder and my laptop before going to the kitchen table to sit with Ian. While Ian looked through the folder, I started typing an email to Lexie, asking her if she had any information that might help us and telling her, once again, to come back to us.

"Maggie?" Ian interrupted my typing. "Did you see this?"

I looked up to see the small, black notebook Ian was holding in his hand. It was a little larger than a deck of

cards and about half an inch thick.
　"What is it?" I asked.
　"Simon's journal."

Chapter Twelve

I took a deep breath and held my hand out to Ian. He handed me the journal, a look of concern passing over his face.

"Should we look in it?" I asked. "I mean, it's his journal. It's private."

"If it can help us find him, we should look. Do you want me to read it so you don't have to?"

"I'm fine," I assured him, but the truth is that I wasn't sure if I could handle looking through Simon's journal.

I opened the first page and saw that it was dated about the time we first met. He talked about getting to know Max and his family and his dread about starting school in August.

I understand the necessity of getting close to this girl, but it seems like a bit of overkill. What makes her any different than a dozen other girls we've met over the years? Yes, she has the physical characteristics listed in the prophecy, but so did several others. Each one of them turned out to be a dead end, and this one probably will as well. I miss Keelin. I miss my home. I want to meet this latest Margaret O'Neill and get it over with so I can go back to my life.

It hurt to read his words. He didn't even want to meet

me. He was thinking of Keelin.

"I'm going to read this outside by myself," I said. Ian didn't try to stop me when I put on my coat and scarf.

"Here," he said before I walked out the door. "You'll probably need this." He handed me a flashlight and his fingers brushed against mine and it made me feel just a little bit sadder.

I walked to one of the benches that sat in the middle of the circle of cottages and settled in for a long and difficult read.

School starts tomorrow. I'm anxious to get this over with so I can get back home. I know everyone is hoping it's her. Balor is out of control and the sooner we find her, the sooner we can stop him. And I want that too. But I also just want to go home. It's hard to think about falling in love with someone else when I already love Keelin. But that's what the prophecy says. It says I will fall in love with the one who will ultimately kill Balor. I'm trying to keep an open mind, but I'm finding myself not even wanting to like her...

...Love is such a personal thing—for everyone but me. My love, and the object of my love, has been the topic of discussion for as long as I can remember. Sometimes I think that's why I hang on so tightly to the love I have for Keelin. I want to protect it and keep it just for the two of us because I know it is likely the last time I will be able to love privately. I think that is one of the reasons I'm dreading the first day of school. If this is her—if this is the Margaret we're looking for—I will have to let go of the quiet and personal love I feel for Keelin in favor of a more intense and public love with this faceless girl from the prophecy, and how can that possibly be better than what I have now? Finn and Erin have done such a wonderful job of protecting me from the prying eyes of the faery community, but that will all end when we find the girl. My life, as I know it, will never be the same...

...It's done. I've met her, and a lifetime of preparation was not enough to equip me for that first meeting. I have always believed in

the prophecy the way I believe in God. It's an abstract possibility, but there is little evidence to support the true existence. A part of me has wanted it to be real, if for no other reason than because it means we stand a chance of defeating Balor, but her existence, and the proof she brings that the prophecy is real, will also bring pain and hardship. Those are qualities in life that I have grown accustomed to as Balor's son, but they are not qualities I want this girl—this lovely girl—to ever experience...

...She's beautiful and kind and shy and sweet. How could I have ever doubted my willingness to be with her? Of course it is different. But in so many ways it's better. The presence of a boyfriend was not something I had ever considered. If he were good to her, it might be easier, but he's an idiot and he treats her so poorly. Finn says to give it time, to let love find its way, but how can she fall in love with me when she's with him? And yes, I do love her, so completely. What I feel for Keelin is a comfortable love. What I feel for Maggie consumes me...

...I love her too much to let her face Balor. I keep thinking that if I fight my feelings for her, she won't have to be the one. If I don't love her, she won't have to risk her life. Being away from her is torture, but being with her is just as difficult. I want to kiss her and run my fingers along her beautiful face and tell her how much I love her, but doing that would send both of us jumping into the abyss without a parachute. If I force myself to stop loving her, will she still be the one?...

...I kissed her, and I want to feel guilty about it, but I just feel elation. I had fantasized so many times about what kissing her would feel like, but my imaginings couldn't hold a candle to the real thing. But that kiss sealed her fate. I will never stop loving her now and because of that, she is doomed...

...I know the time is coming. I must tell her everything about me. About her. About us. She's starting to ask questions and there is no doubt that she is the one. I could never love anyone as much as I love Maggie, and for that reason alone, she must be the one. It's

also the thing that makes it so complicated. The one I love will have to face an impossible future, but the fact that I love her makes me want to protect her from ever finding out. From ever having to face Balor...

...Seeing Maggie kiss Luke ripped my heart to shreds. I never knew pain of that level even existed. It's the love I have for her that made it so hard to watch, but it's that same love that must let her go...

I was sobbing, and Ian was there, standing beside me.

"Can I sit down?"

I nodded, unable to talk. He sat beside me and wrapped his arms around me and let me cry for Simon.

ಬಂಣ

Seeing our love grow through Simon's eyes was so overwhelming and I decided I would need to read his journal in small doses. Ian offered again to read it for me, but having someone else read it felt like an invasion of privacy—for both Simon and for me.

Ian looked through the rest of the file I'd found in Simon's desk and said he didn't see anything significant. It was filled with different pieces of information that would help the Guardians determine whether or not I was the Margaret O'Neill mentioned in the prophecy. We already knew I was, so even more confirmation of that fact was just a waste of time.

I was still determined that Newgrange held the key to finding Simon, so we spent a lot of time reading the books I'd bought and doing Internet searches. There wasn't anything obvious in what we were reading, and I knew I would have to go there to find what I was looking for.

I suggested to Ian that we talk with Mr. James. We'd

started to create a bond in the hour we spent together each day and I knew he'd be a good source of information.

"Do you think we can trust him?" Ian asked.

"Yeah. He's a good guy. If we ask him not to tell anyone, I know he wouldn't."

He hesitated again before nodding slowly. "Okay, I trust your judgment. But let's plan out what we want to tell him and what we don't."

"Okay. What should we tell him then?"

After talking for a while, we decided to tell him that we thought Simon was alive. There was no other way to find out what we wanted to know without offering up that piece of information. We would not, however, tell him the reason for this suspicion. Ian said he didn't want anyone to know I'd heard Simon after he was taken from the field.

Ian came with me the following evening for my magic lesson with Mr. James.

"You know my rules," Mr. James said to Ian. "You'll have to wait outside."

"Actually, Mr. James, we wanted to talk with you," I said.

We told him about our suspicion that Simon might still be alive and our interest in Newgrange, and asked his opinion on how we should move forward.

"Well, you're right about Newgrange being the opening to the Underworld, but I'm not going to offer you step by step instructions on how to get there. It's too dangerous—especially for you, Maggie. Your magic isn't advanced enough to handle a trip like that. No, it's best to give this information to Sloane or Finn and let them deal with it."

It wasn't the answer I wanted to hear.

"Do you think it's possible that Simon's still alive?" Ian asked.

"It's always possible. Balor can do some amazing magic. But the question would be why? Why fake his own son's death?"

"We think he might want Simon to join his side," Ian said. "He tried it before. Our first year at school."

"Yes, I remember."

He stood and moved around his desk to stand in front of me. "You need to be careful, you know that lass?"

I nodded.

"There's a lot riding on your survival, but I've also come to like you a bit." His mouth twisted in a crooked smile. "I don't want to see you hurt—or worse. Stay away from Newgrange. Leave the hunting to Sloane and Finn. Give yourself time to work on your magic here at Slan Lathair. Will you give me your word that you won't try to get to the Underworld? That you'll stay away from Newgrange?"

I nodded, knowing I had absolutely no intention of keeping that promise. If Mr. James wanted me to stay away, I knew there must be something there worth investigating.

"Well that was a complete waste of time," I told Ian when we left Mr. James to head back to the cottages.

"True that," he said with a twisted smile.

A very involuntary snort-laugh forced itself out of me. "Oh my god! You just said 'true that.'"

He smiled in my direction. "I'm just cool like that."

"No," I said. "No, you're not. You most definitely are *not* 'cool like that'. And the fact that you just said you're 'cool like that' only proves that you're not 'cool like that.'"

"You're words hurt," he said, putting his hands to his chest in an overly dramatic way.

I butted his shoulder gently with mine. "No they don't."

"Okay, they don't."

We walked into the cottage and Ian put the kettle on for tea.

"I was thinking about something when we were talking with Mr. James," he said while getting mugs out of the cabinet.

I pulled tea bags out of the canister on the counter and dropped them into the mugs before turning around and leaning against the counter. "What's that?"

"Well, my first thought was to use my special skills to force Mr. James to tell us what he knows. The only problem with that, though, is that he would remember me doing it and it would cause some serious problems."

"Understandably."

"Yes. So, my next thought was that if you could use compulsion, you could get him to tell us what we need to know, then get him to forget that you made him."

"Yeah, but I wouldn't want to do that to him. We have some trust built up between us and I think messing with his mind like that might make him stop trusting me."

"Well, then I had another thought."

"Oh, yay! *Another* thought."

He rolled his eyes at my fake enthusiasm before he continued. "If you could use compulsion, we could skip using it on Mr. James and just use it when we go to Newgrange—like if we run into a guard or something."

"Yes, great plan, except for one little minor detail."

"You can't use compulsion."

"Bingo."

"But we don't know that, do we? You've never tried."

"You're right," I said, a little shocked that the idea hadn't occurred to us before.

"Well don't act so surprised. I've been right before, you know."

"Yeah, but not often."

"Nice. You're confidence in me is so overwhelming."

"You are such a drama queen," I told him while I poured water from the kettle into our mugs. "So, how can we test your theory?"

"Try asking me to tell you something I wouldn't want to tell you."

"Like what?" I asked. We sat down across from each other at the kitchen table, a steaming mug of tea in each of our hands.

"I don't know. I don't want to give you any ideas because then I'll be thinking of it and it'll be easier to get out of me."

I took a sip of my tea and tried to decide what to ask him. I thought of a question I could ask that he wouldn't want to answer, but it was a cruel question and I tried to think of another.

"Don't spare my feelings," he prodded. "This is too important."

I took another sip of my tea, trying to prolong the moment when I would have to ask the question. I started to open my mouth to speak, but he stopped me.

"While you're asking it, you need to focus on pushing through to my brain and forcing me to answer.

I nodded. "Okay." I stood and walked to the counter, leaning my back against it and focusing on the floor. "Do you love me?" I asked. I wasn't sure if it was a question he wouldn't want to answer, but it was definitely a question I didn't want to ask. As the words left my mouth, I gave myself the mental image of knocking down brick walls inside of Ian's head.

"Yes," he answered quietly. "But you already knew that."

"When did you know?" I was still looking at the floor, still making sure I sent a message to Ian with my words that he had no choice but to answer me.

"When you went missing. The night Emma sent you a note telling you to meet her on the beach."

I felt like I needed to make it harder for him. Maybe these questions were too easy if he was answering them so quickly.

"Did you ever blame Simon for his part in your mother's death?"

"Yes."

I continued to stare at my shoes while a silence fell over us. I knew that was definitely a question he didn't want to answer and the fact that he had was confirmation of my power, but I didn't feel good about any of the answers he'd given.

I heard his chair scrape against the floor and assumed he was going to walk away, too angry or ashamed to face me, but within moments, I saw his sock-covered toes standing in front of my own. He pulled me to him and I rested my head against his chest while he stroked my hair.

"When it first happened and I found out he had been there, I did blame him. I was just a kid and I believed what my father told me. But as I grew older, I started to understand the pull Balor had on Simon and I didn't blame him anymore. I don't blame him now."

I lifted my head to look at his face.

"This is too easy, Maggie. There is nothing I wouldn't willing tell you if you asked. I have no secrets from you."

"Then how can we test this?"

He pulled away from me and went to pick up his mug of tea. "If you can get me to say the word "tower" in the next minute, I will do your laundry and cook all of your meals for a month. I really hate laundry and cooking, so I'll definitely be motivated to not say it. If I don't say it, though, you do all the laundry and cooking for a month."

"Deal."

I focused on pushing through his brain, knocking down the walls, and taking it over as my own. I didn't use any words. I just thought about making him believe that saying "tower" was the only important thing in that moment. The only thing that mattered in the world.

"Tower," he almost shouted after a few seconds. His eyes were wide with shock. "You did it."

I nodded, feeling just as shocked as he looked.

"Okay, then. You can force me to tell you something I don't want to. That's good. That's helpful. Now try making me believe something that's not real."

I thought for a moment and decide to make him believe his tea was actually pickle juice. Within moments, he took a sip and spit it out in the sink. He looked at me, understanding what I had done.

"Pickle juice?" he asked.

"Mm-hmm."

"Well, that settles it. You can use compulsion. You can move objects with your mind. You can create rain with your mind. You've got Bob coming back to you every time you call. You can speak telepathically. Anything I'm leaving out?"

I shook my head. "I think that sums it up."

"But you can't fly, and you can't make yourself invisible."

"Thanks for the reminder."

"It's just really puzzling that you can do magic beyond anything most faeries can do, but you can't do the very basics."

"I'm an enigma," I said ruefully.

"'A riddle wrapped in a mystery inside an enigma.'"

I looked at him and laughed. "What in the heck are you going on about?"

He chuckled. "It's an old quote."

"Well, I guess it does sum up this particular problem rather nicely. I thought about talking to Mr. James about my inability to fly and make myself invisible even though I can do a lot more advanced magic, but then I'd have to admit that I can do more magic than I've been letting on."

"Yeah. Good point."

"Maybe you should try pushing me off a cliff. If I have a choice between flying and dying, maybe I'll choose flying."

"It's the maybe-you-won't part that keeps me from giving that a try." He was smiling again and I was glad our brief game of Truth or Dare hadn't forced a wedge between us. My questions had been so personal and I didn't want him to feel embarrassed that he'd answered me.

"Ian, if you want to force me to answer a question you ask me, it would be okay. I mean, it's only fair since I forced you."

He looked at me with a curious express. "I promised I'd never do that to you."

"I know, but I'm giving you permission."

He took my hands in his. "First of all, I promised, and if I break that promise, it will cause me physical pain. Second, even if that weren't the case, I don't feel a need to get even with you. I understand why you asked those questions. They were tough ones to answer. You did good."

I rubbed my thumb back and forth across his open palm, focusing my eyes on the lines and ridges of his hand. He reached his other hand to tuck under my chin and lifted my face to look at him.

"I hope you already knew the answer to the first question, though."

My heart skipped a few beats and I nodded my head, not trusting myself to talk in that moment.

Chapter Thirteen

I took a little piece of Simon to bed with me that night. I wanted to try to read a few passages of his journal before I fell asleep, but if I'm being totally honest, I was hoping that reading his words would induce a Simon-filled dream.

There were several more pages of Simon's love and concern for me. A few entries talked about how amazed he was to see me accept my role in his world with such bravery and dignity. I wished I could be that girl Simon saw. I wished I could live up to the picture he painted of me in his journal.

After I started attending school at Slan Lathair, his journal seemed to also serve as a place to write down pieces of his research. Between the entries about how he felt about me, he jotted little pieces of unconnected information.

...Where is Birog?...Tir na nOg? Is the Morrigan back?...Lugh's magic spear??...Donegal?...Tory Island?...Tara??? Ruled by UiNeills...Fir Bolg?...

There were so many words that were foreign to me, but I didn't even understand the words I knew. Judging by the number of question marks, Simon didn't fully understand either, but he must have had a reason for writing those particular words and phrases.

I got out of bed and took the journal to the living room with me, wanting to show Ian the second half of Simon's journal, hoping the words would have more meaning for him than they did for me. Ian was still awake and talking quietly with Michael and Nessa.

"Are we being too loud for you to sleep?" Ian asked when he saw me come into the room.

"No. I was up reading. I have a couple of questions. Do you have a minute?"

"Of course." He stood and walked back with me to my room, shutting the door behind him. I showed him the part of Simon's journal with the words I didn't understand.

"Well, Birog is the woman who made the prophecy about you," he said. "All of her other prophecies came true, so people pretty much just trust what she says, but she disappeared a couple hundred years ago. I can understand why Simon would want to get in contact with her to see if she knows anything that might help with what you have to do, but nobody's seen or heard from her. I'm not really sure about the rest of it. We can start researching it all in the morning, though. The school's library would be a good start. We might be able to dig up something in the really musty section."

We never got a chance to do our research. Ian came to me the following morning after I'd finished my coffee and asked if I felt up for a walk. The look on his face told me he wasn't interested in fresh air and exercise. He wanted to talk with me about something. I refilled my coffee mug and walked outside with him.

"There's been a development," he said after walking

beside me for several silent minutes.

"Of course there has," I said with a heavy sigh.

"I got word about an hour ago that Balor's planning to send some of his people here to Slan Lathair—for you."

I nodded and was hit by a sudden irrational desire to go back to the old days when information of that caliber would send me straight toward a panic attack. Not anymore. It seemed like barely a day went by when there wasn't a threat to my life or the life of someone I loved.

"I'm surprised he hasn't done it before now," I said. "He can't get to me while I'm at Slan Lathair, but he can send any of his followers here to kill me." I said all of this in the same tone I would use to discuss the benefits of fleece over wool.

"Sloane and Finn and the others are on there way here. Sloane's arranging to add a few members to the Dream Team."

I thought about the implications of what Ian was saying, and quickly came to one very clear conclusion.

"We need to leave here. Now."

Ian shook his head. "I still think Slan Lathair is the safest place for you."

"I don't want to leave to get away from the Fomorians—although that's a nice perk to leaving. I want to leave because if we don't leave now, I'll never get away. There'll be way too many people wanting to protect me now."

"No," he said firmly and without hesitation.

"Well, I'm going. You can stay if you want."

"Knock it off with the emotional blackmail, Maggie," Ian said as I started to turn away. "It's starting to get old."

I turned back around and decided to explain my

thinking. I owed him that much.

"Ian, I wouldn't be able to live with myself if I didn't think I'd done everything I could to find Simon and bring him home. I know you understand that because I know you feel the same way."

"Yes, I do, but I also know that I couldn't live with myself if you ended up dead. Not only would it be impossible for me to live without you or Simon in my life, but I also couldn't live with the knowledge that I was ultimately responsible for the deaths of every human on this planet because I let you die."

"Well, the way I see it, the human race has a better chance of survival if I find Simon. I can't do this without him. And I don't mean that in a 'he's my soul mate and I can't accomplish anything difficult without him by my side' sort of way. I mean that he has skills and knowledge that you and I don't have. We need him."

I could see him softening toward the idea, but I knew we didn't have time for him to think through all of the possibilities. Sloane and the others were on their way and we needed to leave before they got to Slan Lathair. Once they were on school grounds, it would be next to impossible for me to slip away unnoticed. Sloane had told me I was free to come and go as I pleased since I was eighteen, but I didn't want to have a discussion with the Guardians about the fact that I was leaving. Someone close to us had betrayed us on several occasions, and I knew it would be better to slip away quietly.

"Ian," I prodded, hoping he heard the urgency in my voice.

"Two minutes. Just give me two minutes," he implored. I nodded and Ian turned his back to me. He laced the fingers from both hands together and rested them on top of his head. It was a stance I'd seen Simon take when he was upset or worried and it reminded me of the urgency of leaving. I took a few deep breaths and waited while Ian thought through his decision.

"Sloane's going to kill me. Slowly and painfully," he said as he turned around. "I'm doing this against my better judgment."

"Your resistance is noted. Now let's go."

"We need to do this right if it's going to work," he said. "I have a plan."

"Oh, good. A plan," I said dubiously. "Well, let's hear it then."

He gave me an impatient look before he continued. "When we go back to the cottage, I want you to throw one of your fits where you say you're sick of being smothered by the Guardians around you, then stomp off to your room and tell everyone that you want to be alone. Use that really imperious tone you get sometimes."

"This plan isn't painting a pretty picture of me."

"Shh!"

I flourished my hand, palm up, encouraging him to continue. I might have made a sarcastic face while I was doing it, but he ignored me.

"Once you're in your room, you have five minutes to throw some things in a backpack. Make sure no one's outside, then go out your bedroom window and wait for me. I'm going to put some things in a backpack and put it outside my window. Then I'm going to tell the other Guardians that I'm going for a walk. They'll think you're still in your room sulking, and we'll meet outside your window and I'll fly with you to the nearest car rental agency."

"Why don't we just take one of the SUVs?"

"They all have tracking devices."

"So?"

"So, if we plan to ditch your guards, I don't want anyone to know where we are. If we tell the Dream Team or any of the Guardians, the traitor is likely to find out and you'll be completely exposed to an attack."

"Good plan."

"You ready?"

I nodded and we walked toward the cottage. I did exactly what Ian had told me to do, even using the imperious tone he had mentioned. Nessa and Michael didn't even bat an eye, and it hurt a little that they would take my fit in stride. I thought I'd been doing a better job of accepting my role and the need to be protected, but I had evidently developed a reputation with my guards that would be difficult to shake off.

I went to my room and threw some clothes, toiletries, my laptop, Simon's journal and two of the books on Newgrange into a backpack and climbed out of my bedroom window. Ian was waiting there for me and we ran toward the woods before he lifted me onto his back and flew with me piggyback style.

※

"Can you send a text to Sloane letting her know you weren't kidnapped by Balor while I get a car? Tell them I'm with you. Maybe they won't worry so much if they know you're not alone."

We were in a car rental agency in a town I didn't recognize. I sat on one of the hard plastic chairs in the waiting area and dug through my bag for my cell phone.

"Ian," I called after him as he started to walk away, "can you get something other than a black SUV?" It seemed like black SUVs were the car of choice for the

Guardians and after a year of little else, I thought a change would be good.

He smiled and nodded.

I sent a text to Sloane telling her that Ian and I were okay and that I'd decided to go look for Lexie. Ian came back a few minutes later and we walked to a silver sedan.

"If you lie in a text, does it still cause you pain?" I asked as I pulled my seatbelt around me.

"Yes."

"You've tried it before?"

"Yes." The look on his face told me he was reliving the painful result.

"Was the lie you told worth it?"

"Absolutely not."

I smiled, but didn't ask him for any more details.

"I'm going to drive about a hundred miles east," Ian told me as we pulled out of the lot. "Then we'll throw away our cell phones and head back in this direction before going south. That way, if they search for our cell phones, they'll think we were headed in the direction they found them. We'll also want to get as much money as we can out of our bank accounts so they can't trace our credit cards."

"Have you done this before?" I teased. "You've thought of all the details in a short amount of time."

He flashed me a mischievous smile. "I've been on the other end of this scenario. I know what they'll look for to find us."

"It seems so weird to be hiding from Sloane and Finn and the others."

"We're not hiding from *them*. We're hiding from the person who's taking information to Balor."

I knew he was right, but I really felt bad about deceiving the people who had put their lives on the line to protect me.

"Where are we headed after we set a false trail?"

"Newgrange," he said. "It's the only idea we've got, so we might as well check it out. Mr. James was pretty adamant that we stay away, which tells me there might actually be something there worth checking into. At the very least, we can check it off our list of possibilities if we don't find anything. We'll get a hotel room tonight and decide what we want to do tomorrow. I want to find Simon and get back to the others before Balor has a chance to get to you."

"Fine by me," I told him, relieved that we were finally going to do something instead of sitting around and waiting.

We ended up driving about an hour and a half past Newgrange before stopping at a hotel in a town south of Dublin. Ian wanted to continue to throw everyone off our true destination, and he thought driving past Newgrange would make them think we were headed somewhere else. We checked into the hotel and put our things in the room before heading to a pub for dinner. Ian looked nervously around the restaurant and I knew it made him uncomfortable to know that he was the only person guarding me.

"Let's get something and eat it back in our room," I suggested.

"I think that would be best," he said with relief. We ordered at the bar and walked the short distance to our hotel.

"So, what's the plan for tomorrow?" I asked as we walked along the main street of the quiet town.

"I was thinking we'd go to Newgrange and look around after it gets dark."

"Let's just go tonight. Why wait?"

"We need to rest. Both of us. If we do find an entrance to the Underworld, we're going to need to be in top form."

I nodded and was suddenly struck with a horrifying thought. "I left Bob at the cottage."

Ian smiled. "He's in my backpack. I found him on the counter after you went to your room. Were you using him to dice carrots again?"

I smiled sheepishly. Ian and the rest of the Dream Team thought it was disrespectful to use Bob for mundane household tasks, but Bob didn't seem to mind.

"I feel bad that we're making the others worry," I told Ian, the thought of Bob making me think of Michael's horrified expression as he'd watched me use my trusty dagger to make a salad. "I know without a doubt that we needed to leave, but I wish there was a way we could have done it without making them worry."

"We can always go back. Just say the word."

"No, I don't want to go back, but with any luck, we'll find Simon soon and bring him home and they won't have to worry anymore."

"Until you decide to go after Balor."

"Yeah. Until then."

He smiled indulgently and opened the main door of the hotel at the edge of town. It was an old two-story building made of whitewashed stone. The furniture, artwork and bedspreads were a bit shabby and out of style, but it was clean and comfortable and it didn't smell like cat pee, so I was happy.

We opened the bags of food at the tiny, round wooden table in the room and started to eat our burgers and fries.

"If we do find an entrance to the Underworld at Newgrange, how long will it take us to get there?"

"No idea," Ian mumbled through a mouthful of fries.

"I'm not looking for an exact time. Just a ballpark figure would be good."

"I really have no idea. It could take a few minutes or a few weeks for all I know. I've never been, remember?"

"Well I've never been to Russia, but I have a reasonable idea of how long it would take to walk from one end to the other."

"The Underworld is different. It's location and entrances are kept secret in order to protect the people living there. There are no maps and we can't just hop on a bus that will take us straight to Balor. Unless you have a specific reason to go, you're not told how to get there."

"Well, you're instilling a heap of confidence in this trip."

"We can always back out," he reminded me.

"No we can't. You know that."

"I know, but I thought it was worth mentioning. Just in case you've changed your mind."

"I haven't changed my mind. I just wish there were someone we could trust enough to tell us how to get there."

"Anyone we could ask wouldn't tell us because they wouldn't want you to go. They'd think it was too dangerous for you. And they're right. I'm planning to have a thorough psych evaluation done when we get back because I must be out of my mind to help you with this."

"You're not out of your mind. You know I'd go, with or without you, and I'm safer with you."

"Please tell that to the firing squad Sloane hires to murder me when we get back."

I chuckled, but wasn't one hundred percent convinced that he was exaggerating.

Chapter Fourteen

We decided to sleep in shifts so one of us could be awake and alert in case there was any sort of trouble. Even though I was developing my faery abilities at an astonishing rate, I still needed far more sleep than Ian did. We agreed that I should sleep through the night, and he would sleep for a while when I woke up. We couldn't go to Newgrange until after dark, so we'd still have plenty of time for Ian to sleep and for us to get our things together before making the drive back to Newgrange.

Ian told me he wanted to study the area around Newgrange on Google Earth and took out my laptop while I climbed into bed. For all of my whining and complaining about privacy, it felt good to have someone in the room with me again while I slept. Ian had told the Dream Team to back off soon after Simon had gone and it wasn't until that night in the hotel with Ian that I realized how much I missed it. I was soothed by the occasional rustling sound he made as he shifted his weight on the bed, and the blue glow from the computer that reminded me, even as I slept, that the world would keep on turning—at least for one more night.

I didn't wake up until after nine the next morning, but I knew we were still in good shape. We grabbed some breakfast at the pub before heading back to the room so Ian could get some sleep. I took out the books on Newgrange, and realized I had studied them so much that I already knew them by heart. I decided to do as Ian had done and look at Google Earth. It was hard to read the different landforms that showed up on the maps. I was able to make out Knowth and Dowth, two lesser-known tombs near Newgrange, but I wasn't sure what to make of the odd circular indentations in the earth and the deep tracks that zigzagged across the landscape. The "street view" option didn't provide a clear picture, so I was left with a lot of unanswered questions about the landforms that dotted the fields in the area.

I closed my laptop and tried to quietly process all of the information I knew about the ancient site, but it was hard to know which pieces were important and which weren't. I made lists in my head of the things I knew and tried to categorize everything into neat piles. The meanings of the rock carvings in the area. The locations of Knowth and Dowth in relation to Newgrange. Details that was pure fact vs. speculation or myth. I didn't discount any piece of information, no matter how farfetched it seemed.

By the time Ian woke up, I knew I was as ready as I would ever be. It felt like there wasn't a single fact about Newgrange I didn't already know.

We left the hotel after dark and headed north. We stopped and got something to eat on the way, and bought some energy bars, beef jerky, dried fruit and water for our backpacks. We were both at a complete loss for what to expect, but if we did manage to find the entrance, I thought the chances of us finding a McDonalds drive-through along the way were pretty slim.

Parking at the visitors' center seemed like an invitation to trouble, so Ian positioned the car behind a copse of trees at the side of a deserted road behind Newgrange. We got out of the car and grabbed our backpacks and I was suddenly struck with the enormity of what we were doing. We were looking for the entrance to the Underworld. We were looking for Simon and for Balor. If we succeeded in achieving any of those objectives, my life would never be the same again.

"No matter what," Ian told me as we stood together in the darkness, "we stay together."

I didn't want Ian far from me on this quest, so it was an easy commitment to make. "We stay together."

"No matter what," Ian reiterated.

"No matter what," I promised.

The walk from the car to Newgrange took about half an hour. We looked out for security guards and alarm systems as we moved closer, but didn't see any. We did our best to stay as concealed as possible. We knew there was a good chance that there was a security guard around somewhere, maybe checking on the other locations before looping back to Newgrange. We also knew that we would, in all likelihood, be joined by other faeries—theirs and ours.

A flutter of excitement jolted through me as we walked to the entrance of the massive burial site. "I have no idea what we're looking for," I admitted.

"I guess we should just poke around a bit," Ian suggested.

We walked around the various stones that made up the circle of Newgrange. I looked for signs in the many symbols that were carved into the rock, and would occasionally poke at one to see if it would give way to a hidden entrance. No such luck.

"Do you think the entrance is actually inside the tomb?" I asked Ian as we stood at the back end of the structure.

"It's possible," he agreed. "I have a feeling, though, that they seal that part up at night."

I shrugged. "We don't have anything else to try."

As we walked back toward the entrance, Ian stopped short and grabbed my hand.

Faeries, he told me silently.

Whose? I asked as an electrifying terror coursed through me.

Ian shrugged and started to run toward a small, stone outbuilding with a dome-shaped roof behind the main mound at Newgrange. There was a small circular entrance cut into the stone about a foot off the ground and Ian pushed me through before crawling into the opening himself. As we sat huddled together silently, I noticed a faint shimmer on one of the rocks that made up the inner wall of the outbuilding. The shimmer was in the shape of a symbol I'd seen on a website about Newgrange. It was made up of one larger circle, with a smaller circle inside of it. The top of each circle was cut out, leaving an opening in each. I didn't have to think long to remember that it was the "passageway" symbol, and my heart started to beat furiously.

Ian, I said as I pointed to the symbol. His eyes opened wide when he saw the shimmering shape and he moved over to take a closer look. I watched as he pressed against the symbol with his palm, and a section of earth in the middle of the building opened up. The opening was completely black, but I could see another shimmering symbol further inside the tunnel and I knew we'd found the entrance to the Underworld.

Ladies first? I asked. Fear and anticipation were rising inside of me and I worked hard to get control of it before it took control of me.

Together. Ian said as he took my hand, and we climbed together into the unknown.

Chapter Fifteen

We pulled the flashlights Ian had brought from Slan Lathair out of our backpacks once we were in the tunnel. It went in only one direction, so that made things a little easier—no decisions to make regarding which way to go. It was a low tunnel, only three or four feet tall in places. While there were some stretches tall enough to allow me to stand up straight, Ian had to walk stooped over the entire time.

After about a half an hour of meticulously slow progress, the tunnel ended abruptly. Several steps had been dug into the wall at the end of the tunnel that led to an opening above.

"I'll go first," Ian offered. I wanted to argue. I wanted to tell him that this whole trip was my idea and if there was a risk to be taken, I should be the one to take it. Unfortunately, my mouth had other ideas. I was unable to protest and Ian was climbing out of the tunnel before I could find my voice.

He walked out of view for a moment before coming back to the opening of the tunnel.

"Come on up," he told me.

I climbed the built-in steps and pulled myself up. As soon as my feet hit the ground above, the opening closed, completely concealing the tunnel below. I looked around and saw a circular tomb that was similar to Newgrange. It was about the same size, but there weren't as many rocks at the base and there were several smaller burial mounds surrounding it.

"Where are we?"

"Knowth."

"Knowth?" I asked Ian, completely incredulous. "But that's only like a mile from Newgrange.

He nodded.

"Why would there be a tunnel leading from Newgrange to Knowth?" I wondered aloud. "There's a road going between the two that would be a lot easier walk."

"That symbol back at Newgrange," Ian said. "The tunnel wouldn't have opened up for anyone—faery or not—unless they were a Guardian, but why would we need a tunnel from Newgrange to Knowth?"

We both sighed simultaneously, then sat down on the damp ground.

"Did we go through all of this for nothing?" I asked. He didn't answer, but I knew he was thinking the same thing.

"Hey! You two! Up the yard with ya! Get your hole on somewhere else!"

Ian and I both jumped up and saw the security guard walking toward us.

Ready to try some Jedi mind tricks? Ian asked silently.

I'm not sure I have a choice. This dude looks pretty angry!

"Did ya hear me? I said to get out of here!"

I focused on pushing through the poor man's brain and letting him know there was something that urgently needed his attention at the visitors' center. I knew using compulsion was a necessary evil on the path toward saving the world, but I still felt guilty. The guy was just doing his job. I pushed away the guilt as I continued to tear down the walls in his brain in order to convince him to leave and forget he'd ever seen us. He did as I urged him to and turned, a confused but docile expression on his face, and left us alone.

"You're getting scarier and scarier every day," Ian said when the man was out of earshot.

I started to reply, but something flashed on a large stone standing upright a few yards in front of me. I had a moment of irritation at being momentarily blinded before I realized that it was another passageway symbol.

"Ian," I said, pointing.

He walked to the stone and put his hand against the symbol. The earth between us shifted and another tunnel was revealed.

"Round two?" he asked.

"Why not."

We climbed down and used our flashlights to look around. Like the other tunnel, this one had a low ceiling and only led in one direction. There was nothing to do but walk, or go back. We walked.

And walked. And walked. And walked. And walked. *Would it have killed them to build a road down here?* When we could, Ian would fly with me on his back, but the tunnel was often so low that flying was difficult. I would have been excited about the forward progress, but the tunnel didn't seem to have a downward slope. I always assumed that "Underworld" implied a world under the one we lived in. Other than the three to four feet we had climbed down to get into the tunnel, we didn't seem to be going down any farther.

"Why don't we stop for a bit," Ian suggested after

we'd been walking for several hours. It was hard on me to have to stoop in the places of the tunnel with a low ceiling, so I knew it must be horrible for Ian since he had to walk stooped over the entire way.

We sat down on the dirt floor and got out the food and water in our bags. We both ate just enough to keep us going, not knowing how long the supplies would need to last. We didn't stop long before we were on our feet again. We were both anxious to get to the end of the tunnel.

After several more hours, and several more rest breaks, I noticed that the ceiling of the tunnel started to get higher. Ian noticed, too, and eventually he could stand up completely. My adrenaline was pumping with the knowledge that we were almost there—wherever "there" was.

When the tunnel opened up completely and revealed a sunny forest, I didn't know what to think. Was it a human forest or the Underworld? It looked completely normal. Huge trees towered above us, boulders were scattered among the trees, and I could hear birds singing. The sun was seeping through the trees and dappling the forest floor with light. But the light was wrong. Rather than having one source of light, as we do with the sun, the light seemed to be coming from multiple sources. And, it wasn't a burning light, but a soft glow.

"Is this the Underworld?" I asked Ian.

He nodded, took my hand in his, and started walking away from the tunnel.

"Do you need to sleep?" he asked as we continued our walk.

I was exhausted. I was pretty sure we'd been walking for a good eight hours, but I also knew that I was too full of adrenaline to sleep. I shook my head. Might as well keep walking.

"Any idea where we're going?" I asked.

"Not a clue."

"That's reassuring."

He turned to smile at me and squeezed my hand gently.

"I wish we'd known more before we came down," I told him. "I wish we could have asked Sloane or Finn or your dad or someone who's actually been down here. Has you dad been down here? He can get really grumpy sometimes. I talk a lot when I'm sleepy," I confessed. "And when I'm nervous."

He smiled at me indulgently. "Are you sure you don't want to stop?"

"I'm sure. I won't be able to sleep."

"You'll let me know when you do need to stop?"

I nodded and yawned.

"Where's the light coming from?"

"I'm not sure."

"Do you think we're under Ireland somewhere?"

Before he could answer, he stopped abruptly, frozen in place on the path where we'd been walking. "Shh," he commanded forcefully.

I followed his line of site to see what made him stop. In the middle of the path, about twenty yards in front of us, was a pack of five dogs—ugly, dirty, scarred, junkyard-type dogs. They were staring at us, and they were growling and I think they were picturing us as dinner.

"Don't run," Ian told me slowly and quietly. "I'm going to pick you up and fly with you."

I nodded.

"Ready?"

I nodded again and Ian scooped me up and started to take off into the air. He wasn't fast enough, however, and one of the faery dogs grabbed at Ian's ankle and we fell to the ground.

"Run to the tree and climb!" Ian commanded. "I'll be right behind you."

I reluctantly left Ian on the ground and ran to the tree he had indicated. The branches were low so I was able to jump up pretty easily. Ian was right behind me, but so were the dogs. One of them grabbed Ian's arm in its mouth and I scooted down and tried to kick it. It bit my ankle and I felt the painful sting shoot into me, but it didn't feel like a deep gash.

"Climb, Maggie!" Ian ordered loudly. "Climb."

I climbed up a few more branches, then took the backpack off my shoulders and opened it. I threw pieces of beef jerky away from the tree, trying to distract the dogs, but they didn't budge. One of them was still nipping at Ian as he tried to climb and I saw that blood was dripping from his arm. I threw my flashlight at the one trying to turn Ian into a Scooby snack. It hit him on the shoulder. Not enough to do any damage, but enough that Ian was able to get away.

"Are you okay?" Ian asked.

"Yes. I'm fine."

"Did they bite you?"

"Just a little bite on my ankle. I'm not sure if it broke the skin."

"Let me see."

I balanced as best I could on my tree branch while I showed Ian my ankle. Meanwhile, the dogs continued to bark and growl furiously—angry, I'm sure, that we had deprived them of a meal.

"You're bleeding a bit," Ian reported.

"You are, too," I told him, pointing to the blood that was seeping through the tear in his jacket.

He nodded grimly in confirmation.

"At least we don't have any injuries that'll slow us down too much," I said, trying to look on the bright side. "Once Cujo and the gang leave, we can start out again."

"Maggie," Ian said grimly, "those are faery dogs."

"I figured as much," I told him. I remembered that the first time I'd met Jake, Simon had told me that faery dogs weren't very friendly. He wasn't kidding.

"You don't understand," Ian continued. "Without a healer, the venom will kill me."

"Venom? They're dogs. They don't have venom."

"Faery dogs do. And it will kill me."

"I was bitten, too," I said, struck by the full force of what Ian was saying.

"I'm not sure if it will kill you," Ian explained. "You're still in that grey area between human and faery. The venom doesn't affect humans. Plus, you have the ring. I think that'll protect you."

I took a moment to let what Ian was saying sink in. We'd both been bitten. Ian would surely die if we didn't get to a healer, and I might die because of the bite, or because Ian died and left me to fend for myself in this completely alien world. The dogs were still yapping furiously below, preventing us from leaving the tree. Even if we were able to get down and away from the dogs, we had no idea how to find a healer. We were screwed.

"There's a cave not too far from here," Ian said, cocking his head in the direction he wanted me to look. "I think the entrance is far enough off the ground that the dogs won't be able to get to us. Get on my back so we can fly there."

"Shouldn't we find a healer?"

"We're not going to find one out here," he said. "We're better off hiding ourselves until things run their course."

"Run their course? You mean until you die, Ian?" I was starting to get hysterical.

"I need you to stay calm, Maggie," he said as he walked away from the path and into the thickest parts of the forest. "I'm really going to need you to stay calm because the venom is starting to work it's way through my body and I'm not going to be much help to you once that happens. We'll get to the cave, then we'll figure out what to do next."

I climbed on Ian's back and we flew to the small cave. It was only about three feet wide and four feet deep, but it would keep us save from Cujo and the Cujettes. We also had a view of the path and could see if anyone walked by.

"Can't I suck the venom out or something?" I asked Ian as we sat in the cave waiting for the venom to take its toll.

He shook his head. "How do you feel?"

"Petrified."

"You don't feel dizzy or hot or anything?"

"No. You?"

"Yes."

"What's going to happen?" I asked, trying my hardest not to cry.

"I've heard that you get a fever and you start to hallucinate and eventually you lose consciousness and—" he didn't finish. He didn't need to.

I took both of Ian's hands in mine and focused everything I had on healing him. It hadn't worked with Jane, but maybe I hadn't tried hard enough. Maybe I needed more of an incentive.

"Anything?" I asked.

He shook his head with a knowing look. He knew

what I had tried to do, and he knew it hadn't worked.

His fever started within an hour, and then the rain started. It was so heavy at times that I couldn't see the trail from our spot in the cave. I opened both of our backpacks and handed Ian a bottle of water and insisted that he drink, knowing the fever would be taking a toll on his body. And that was all the help I could give Ian—a drink of water. I couldn't save him. I couldn't heal him. I was useless.

Ian pulled me to him and I hated that the warmth created by his fever helped me to warm up. He gave me everything so unselfishly, even when he was dying.

He seemed to skip the hallucinations part of the sickness and went straight to drifting in and out of consciousness. Or maybe he hallucinated, but kept it to himself. I tried to sift through my limited arsenal of information regarding first aid to figure out what to do for him. Should I try to keep him awake or was that only for head wounds? Should I wrap a tourniquet around his arm? The bleeding seemed to have stopped, so that seemed pointless. He was sitting up and that seemed like a good idea. Would that keep the venom from moving to his heart?

I fell asleep listening to the sound of the rain and to the erratic beat of Ian's heart. I woke up because Ian was mumbling. I couldn't make out what he was saying, but I could feel that his fever was worse. I took off one of the cotton shirts I was wearing and poured water from one of the bottles on it. I could have held it out to the rain, but I didn't trust faery rain. Maybe faery rain was just as bad as faery dogs.

Ian opened his eyes when I ran the clothe over his face. He smiled weakly and reached up to hold my hand.

"I love you, Maggie," he whispered.

I started to sob, but pushed it down. His words sounded like goodbye. I couldn't say goodbye. Not again. Ian had been the only thing standing between me and death when Simon had gone. I needed Ian.

"I know. I know," I choked out. "I love you, too." And it was true. I did love Ian. Not the way I loved Simon, but I did love Ian.

"It would have been enough, you know," he whispered. "I would have been happy, as long as you were a part of my life. Even a small part."

I couldn't stop the tears. I didn't bother to wipe them away.

"Leave me here when I'm gone," Ian instructed. "You need to find your way out of here."

"Don't you dare die, Ian," I commanded. "If you die, I'll....I'll..." I couldn't think of a punishment that could possibly matter to someone who was already dying. "I don't know what I'll do, but you won't like it."

He smiled again and I tried to soak it up—to remember that smile forever. "I can't believe you ever thought you weren't Irish with a temper like that."

He leaned in to kiss me and I let him. He was weak, but his lips felt so good and I wanted to hold on to every piece of him that I could. His eyes closed when he pulled away.

"Ian," I said urgently. "Ian, don't go to sleep. Please don't go to sleep."

He didn't respond and I decided to take the ring from my finger and put it on his. It did me no good to stay alive without Ian. I would die on my own in the Underworld. I didn't know if it would help, but I pushed it as far as it would go on his index finger.

I kissed his forehead and noticed that he was no longer hot. Was his fever coming down? Then it occurred to me that mine might be going up. The venom may have moved more slowly in my body, but now that the ring was off my finger, it looked like I might be headed toward the same fate as Ian. That fact was confirmed when I saw Brandon walking in the woods below the cave, chatting away with a six-foot cat.

I felt myself drifting into unconsciousness, the feel of Ian's arms around me so distant, but comforting.

"Maggie, come to me now," I heard Grandma Margaret beckon. "Maggie. Maggie."

I couldn't go to her. I couldn't let myself die. If I went to her, I'd be dead.

"Maggie, come to me child. Let me help you."

It was a trick. If I went to her I'd die.

"Maggie. Maggie." It was Simon calling me.

"Simon," I tried to call out. Did I say it out loud or in my head?

Brandon was back with the cat.

"Do you remember that song mom used to sing, Mags? You know, the one about the watermelon on the grave?"

We started to sing together. "Oh, plant a watermelon vine upon my grave and let the juice run down." The cat joined in and sang harmony. He was good.

"Do you want me to plant watermelon on your grave, Maggie?"

I tried to nod.

"Maggie, come with me. Let yourself go. Let me keep you safe."

"Maggie! Maggie!" Simon was back, and he sound frantic.

"Open your eyes, Maggie," Grandma Margaret insisted. I was afraid.

A hand brushed against my cheek and it felt like Simon's hand and I did as Grandma Margaret told me to do and I forced myself to open my eyes. It took every ounce of energy I had, but I was able to open them just enough to see Simon kneeling over me.

"Simon," I breathed. "Am I coming with you, Simon?"

"Yes, Maggie," he said softly. "You're coming with me. Everything's going to be okay now. I'll keep you safe."

"Thank you, Simon."

And he lifted me in his arms and carried me away.

Chapter Sixteen

I was thirsty—thirstier than I'd ever been in my entire life. I found a convenience store and went in to get some grape juice. I felt like that was the only thing that would quench my thirst. I got a bottle and paid for it before ripping off the lid and taking a big swig, but it wasn't cold enough to take away the sandy desert that was setting up residence in my mouth and throat. I went to the ice machine by the fountain drinks and started to put ice in a cup.

"Hey," the store clerk yelled at me, "what do you think you're doing?"

"I just want some ice for my grape juice," I explained.

"You can't get ice unless you're getting a fountain drink," he barked.

"I'll pay for the drink. I just want some ice."

"Are you going to put soda in that cup after you put in the ice?"

"No. I just want the ice, but I'll pay for the soda."

"Sorry. No soda, no ice."

I was beyond caring what the clerk was saying to me. The thirst was unbearable and I started to fill the cup with ice, ignoring his anger.

"Hey! I said no ice unless you get the soda. Weren't you listening?"

I kept ignoring him and started to pour my grape juice into the cup.

"Hey!" the clerk yelled again. "Maggie!"

How did he know my name?

"Maggie," it was Simon saying my name this time. Softly. Sweetly.

"Maggie, wake up," he said to me.

I forced my eyes open and for a brief, fuzzy moment, I saw Simon standing over me. Then my eyes started to focus and I knew it was Finn. Not Simon. I closed my eyes.

"Maggie, open your eyes. It's time to wake up."

Ugh. I didn't want to wake up. I was tired and I was thirsty and I wanted to go back to sleep and dream of a large cup of grape juice, filled to the brim with ice.

"Maggie, take a drink," Finn urged. He had something to drink? Okay, maybe I could wake up. I opened my eyes and he supported my neck while he held the cup to my lips. It wasn't grape juice, but it was ice-cold water and I drank the entire cup before Finn let me slide back down onto the pillows of the bed.

"I had the freakiest dreams," I croaked out, my throat still parched.

"I bet you did," Finn said with a slight smile.

And then it all came back to me in one big rush. The forest. The dogs. Ian.

"Where's Ian?" I asked frantically, bolting to a sitting position, the blood rushing to my head and making me dizzy.

"He's with Erin," Finn told me. He was still sitting on the edge of the bed and he took my hand in his. I noticed that my ring was back in place on my right index finger. "He's going to be fine, Maggie."

I let myself breath again. Ian wasn't dead.

"I thought we were going to die."

"We found you in time."

"It was you? Not Simon? I thought it was Simon that came and got me."

"No, it was me."

"How did you know we were there?"

He sighed and I could tell he was debating whether or not to tell me the truth. "Your necklace," he finally said.

"My necklace?" I fingered the necklace Simon had given me on my last birthday—the Celtic shield knot.

"Simon had it fitted with a tracking device," Finn admitted.

"But Simon wouldn't need to track me down. He'd be able to see where I was just by using his faery skill."

Simon had the awesome ability to find lost people and things. It had come in very handy one time when I'd lost a Western Civ paper that was due.

"When Balor kidnapped you last spring, Simon could see that you were in a cinderblock cell, but he couldn't see where the cell was. Having a tracking devise was a backup to his natural ability."

That made sense. If Balor ever nabbed me again, he'd be able to find me with the tracking devise. I didn't think Balor would let me live long enough for them to track me down, but it was a nice thought.

"Why didn't he tell me?" I asked.

"I'm the only person he told about it. He was worried you'd want to take it off if you felt too smothered by your guards."

"Yeah. That does sound like something I'd do."

"When you and Ian left, I was keeping tabs on you,

but I didn't want to swoop in unless you needed us. When I lost the signal at Newgrange, I knew you'd found the tunnel to the Underworld. By the time we got there, you and Ian had already been attacked by the dogs. We saw the blood and a water bottle and knew you were probably nearby. We finally found you in the cave and brought you here."

"Where are we, exactly?"

"My mother's home."

"We're still in the Underworld?"

He nodded. "We want to give you and Ian some time to heal. The venom had spread pretty far in both of you by the time we got there."

The mention of the faery dogs exhausted me and I suddenly couldn't keep me eyes open anymore. I was aware of Finn pulling the blankets around my shoulders. Then I was aware of complete nothingness.

৸৹ଔ

Ian was sitting next to me on the bed when I woke up again. He held my hand in his and rubbed it gently with his fingers.

"Hi, Sleeping Beauty," he whispered when I opened my eyes.

I was so grateful to see him. He hadn't died. I hadn't lost him. Against impossible odds, we'd been saved in time and we were both alive.

I reached my hand up and ran it along his cheek. "I thought you were going to die."

"Me too."

"But you didn't."

"No. And you didn't."

"No."

"We're both alive."

"Yes."

"So, now that we've covered our continued ability to breath, I am warning you right now that if you ever take your ring off again, I'll kill you myself."

"If you died, there was no way I was going to make it out there on my own. My only chance was for you to live, so I put the ring on you."

"I don't care how good your reasons, I want you to promise me right now that you won't take it off again."

"No."

"What do you mean 'no'?"

"I mean, I'm not going to promise you that. I have a good head on my shoulders. Let me use it."

He started to open his mouth to reply, but Finn knocked on the open door.

"How are you two feeling?"

"Great," Ian and I said simultaneously.

"Well, that's good to hear," Finn said, "because my mother wants to see both of you."

"Crap," I said out loud before I could sensor myself. Finn's mother was a goddess in the faery world and she scared me almost as much as Balor did.

Finn laughed. "I wouldn't worry too much, Maggie. My mother still believes that the fate of the world rests in your hands so she probably won't kill you. Ian's chances of survival, however, aren't looking so good."

I looked at Ian and noticed he'd turned a scary shade of gray.

"You want that ring *now*, don't you?" I teased.

He shot me a scathing look, but didn't answer my question. "Let's get it over with," he mumbled to Finn.

We followed Finn out of the room and down a long hallway. Green and white floral wallpaper lined the walls and a light brown carpet ran along the floor. Sconces spaced every few feet provided the hallway with cheerful, bright light. The whole effect seemed contrary to the dread Ian and I felt at meeting with Danu.

Finn opened the door to what looked like a large office or library. Bookshelves lined the walls and a large wooden desk sat in the middle of the room. Danu was looking out a massive window behind her desk when we walked in, and turned when she heard us enter.

Don't worry. I've got your back, I told Ian silently. *If she tries to kill you, I'll use compulsion on her.*

Yeah, I wouldn't try that if I were you. You're getting powerful, but you're still no match for her.

"Ah, my two explorers," Danu said with forced enthusiasm. "So glad you could join me." *Had it been a choice?*

"Sit, please," she said, motioning to two leather seats in front of the desk. Ian and I sat down, and she sat in the chair on the other side of the desk. Finn took a seat a little further away from us. I wondered if he was staying in the room to make sure she did not, in fact, try to kill us.

"Do you realize how lucky the two of you are to be alive?" she asked. Ian hung his head, but I couldn't bring myself to feel shame. Instead, I was surprised to feel anger rising inside of me. Where was the anger coming from? Why would I be angry with Danu?

"I'm disappointed in you, Maggie," she went on, "but I'm particularly disappointed in you, Ian. You should have known that Newgrange is the entrance to the portion of the Underworld occupied by the Tuatha Dé Danann—the people of *Danu*—*my* people. Why would you think it was a good idea to go through with your plan to find Balor by entering through Newgrange?"

Why did she think we were looking for Balor and not Simon? Had Ian told someone that story in an attempt to cover the true purpose of our little adventure?

"I thought we could still find Balor if we found the tunnels."

"Well, you're right. It is possible to get to Balor through that entrance. Eventually. Which means it's also possible for him to get to you. You're both very lucky *we* got to you first."

Ian hung his head again and Danu turned her attention back to me.

"And why on earth would you think it was a good idea to leave behind all of the people protecting you to go in search of Balor yourself? The fate of the world rests in the hands of such a foolish girl? I thought you were smarter than that, Maggie."

The anger kept pushing its way up from deep inside me.

"I wasn't searching for Balor," I corrected her tersely. "I was looking for Simon." I saw the shock on her face. After a three second debate with myself, I decided to tell her the truth. "I heard Simon after he died. I haven't heard him for a while now, but I think he's still alive."

I watched as the color drained from her face, and out of the corner of my eye, I saw Finn stand and walk toward the desk.

"Alana saw him, Maggie," Finn reminded me. "She said he was definitely dead."

"I know what she said, Finn. I've been reminded of it enough. But what if she was wrong. What if someone who has powers like yours convinced her that she saw something she didn't actually see?"

Nobody responded.

"I heard him, Finn," I said.

"Maggie, dear," Danu cooed, "I know how hard it's been for you to lose Simon. It's been hard on all of us. But I think you're really grasping at straws here."

"I heard him," I insisted fiercely. "Can you sit there and tell me you're one hundred percent certain he's not alive? Because if there's even a one percent chance I'll find him, *I'm* going to keep looking."

"He's my son. Of course I would keep looking if I thought there was a chance, but there's not. He's gone, and the fact that you insist on looking for someone who's been dead for months is a dangerous delusion to be acting upon. You have a greater responsibility to this world Maggie and you need to stop acting so irrationally."

"My first priority is to find Simon," I told her, fighting to keep the calm in my voice. "I don't care what other priorities you have, nor do I care how you rank them. I make those decisions for myself."

I felt Ian gasp beside me at the same moment Danu stood up. I'd broken through her calm demeanor. She was mad.

"I would ask that you remember to whom you are speaking, young lady," she said slowly and deliberately.

"I know exactly to whom I am speaking. I am speaking to Simon's mother, which is why I am at a total loss for why you won't even consider the possibility that Simon's alive. *He's your son.* I thought the love between a mother and a child went deeper than that."

The color drained from her face and I could see the anger, but she remained silent.

"I'm going to keep looking for Simon. You can get on board and help me, or not, but don't even think about getting in my way."

I turned to Finn. "I want to leave. I'm assuming that

can be arranged within the hour."

I didn't give Finn an opportunity to respond. If he wasn't ready to leave, I'd go on my own. The possibility of an encounter with a faery dog couldn't keep me from leaving. I'd made this horrible journey to find Simon. Instead, I came up empty in the lost boyfriend department, and walked away with a growing resentment that nobody but Ian and me believed he was alive. How could his own mother not want to do everything she could to find him, even if there was only a one percent chance that he was alive? In that moment, I hated Danu. I hated her for not believing me and I hated her for not helping to bring Simon home.

I walked down to the room I'd been staying in, and Ian came in right after me.

"Do you realize whom you were talking to in there?" he asked. I heard frustration and awe and exasperation in his tone.

"Simon's mother," I told him. I knew he wanted me to acknowledge the fact that Danu was a goddess and a leader among the faery community, but at that moment, she was just Simon's mother and she was letting me down.

"People have lost their lives for talking to her the way you just talked to her," Ian said.

"Yes, well, when all the humans I love are dead, I don't think I'd be able to take much solace in the fact that I had been polite to Danu," I fumed, transferring my anger to Ian.

"You're lucky she didn't kill you on the spot."

"I'm lucky it wasn't the right time to sacrifice my life for the greater good."

Chapter Seventeen

The entire trip had been a massive disaster. We didn't find Simon. We didn't find Balor. I'd annoyed Danu. We were attacked by faery dogs. I can't say I was sorry to be leaving the Underworld and I would be happy never to return.

On the way home, Finn told us the faery dogs that attacked us belonged to Balor. Finn said he thought Balor found out I was in the Underworld at the same time the Guardians found out and had sent the dogs to kill me. That led me to one conclusion. Whoever was feeding information to Balor had been with the Guardians when Finn told them that the signal on my necklace had been lost at Newgrange.

"Who knew I was headed to the Underworld?" I asked as he drove us to Ballecath. We decided I might as well move back to Ballecath since Balor was going to try to have one of the Fomorians get to me at Slan Lathair. It was suddenly no safer than anywhere else.

"All the usual people were there when we noticed it," Finn said.

"Who, specifically?" I pressed.

"I told Erin and Sloane right away. We brought in Keelin, Aidan, Alan and Quinn to come with us to look for you."

"Did you tell anyone else?"

"I notified my mother so she could be on the lookout for you. I also called the Dream Team and asked them to meet us there in case we needed any help."

So about twenty people that Finn knew of, but who had those twenty people told? Who was betraying us? Betraying *me*?

⊱⊰

"Who do you think it is?" I asked Ian when we were alone in his apartment.

He shrugged and shook his head. "I'm at a loss. He listed people I've known my whole life. I can't imagine one of them being so evil."

"Me either," I admitted. "But, I've been thinking about something." I hesitated, not wanting to give a voice to the thoughts that had been running through my mind. Ian looked at me expectantly. "Simon said Aidan and Alana were working with the Fomorians in order to feed information to the Guardians. What if one of them has turned from double agent to triple agent?"

He didn't look surprised with my suggestion. It was something he'd thought about, as well.

"But which one?" he asked.

"I don't know," I admitted. "Neither of them seems like a likely choice. Alana's daughter was there that day in the field. I don't think she'd risk Gracie's life like that. But Aidan and Simon have always been close. Simon told me that Aidan's worked for his family and lived at Ballecath since before he was born."

"So, maybe it's not either one them."
"Then who is it?"
He shrugged again.
"Let's keep thinking about it," he suggested.
"Okay."
"In the meantime," he said, looking very weary, "I could use a little down time. Do you want to watch a movie with me and do your impression of a normal teenage girl?"
I smiled. "Sure."
Ian switched on the television set in his living room and I cuddled against him to watch the movie. My mind wasn't with him in that room, however. It was with Simon and with the unrelenting suspicion that either Alana or Aidan was the traitor.

ഇരു

Sloane fired Ian the day after our return. She presented him with a long list of Guardian rules and human laws he'd broken and told him he was lucky she didn't kick him out of the Guardian organization altogether. As it was, she was replacing him as my primary Guardian. While there had been a time when I had begged Simon for just that, things had changed, and I couldn't imagine having anyone but Ian by my side.

I went to Sloane and insisted she reverse her decision. She gave me some crap about how I didn't really understand how these things worked and that her decision was made with my best interest at heart.

"I understand more than you think I do, Sloane," I told her.

"I'm not trying to minimize your intelligence, Maggie, but you're not a Guardian. You don't know how these things work."

"I'm not a Guardian?" I asked, incredulous. "Correct me if I'm wrong," I continued, "but my understanding is that the Guardians' primary role is to protect humans from the Fomorians."

"That's correct," she said with an indulgent tone.

"And it's up to me to kill Balor and save every one of them," I reasoned. "I think I'm more of a Guardian than anyone else. I make the sacrifices. I risk my life. The life of every human is in my hands. Whether you want to make it official or not, I'm a Guardian."

She was silent. I knew she didn't have an argument.

"And I want Ian by my side. I trust him."

"This is something I thought about long before you guys went to Newgrange. I've seen the two of you together. It's no secret that you're developing feelings for each other. He can't protect you if his feelings for you are clouding his judgment."

I blushed, the thought that Sloane knew about my love life embarrassing me, but I persevered. "The only person who would work harder to keep me alive is Simon. *Because* he loves me, not in spite of it, and you seemed to think it was fine to have Simon guarding me."

Another silent pause.

"I'm not looking for your permission, Sloane. I'm beyond asking for anyone's permission or approval for the decisions I make. Whether it's official or not, Ian will remain at my side until *I* send him away."

Before she could think of an argument, I turned and left the room. I wouldn't have even considered talking that way to Sloane a year ago. Simon and Ian and so many other people had told me I'd find the strength inside of me when I needed it. I guess I needed it, because it was flowing out me faster than I could staunch it. I worried that I had passed that fine line between asserting my authority and being downright bitchy, but it didn't matter to me anymore. There was too much at stake.

༄༅

Balor was standing in the middle of the football field where the team at Castlewood High School practiced, looking calm and relaxed. His eyes were bright and he had the beginnings of a smile forming on his lips. He looked at me, then looked toward the sidelines where a line a people stood placidly. I knew each one of them. Brandon, my mom and dad. Lexie and all of the faeries who were now so important to me. On and on, at least a hundred people I cared about. And, one by one, Balor went down the line and killed each of them. He started with Brandon. Balor raised his arm as he had with me when we were at Red Rocks and Brandon fell to the ground, screaming with the agony Balor was inflicting. With Brandon still screaming, Balor went down the line, moving next to my parents. On and on he went with each person in that line. They would fall to the ground, screaming in pain. The silence when their screams stopped was even more painful to hear.

When each person had been silenced, Balor turned to me and winked. I started to run after him. I wanted him to pay for what he had done, but he just vanished and I was left with the bodies of everyone I cared about most in the world. I started to walk toward them, but knew there was nothing I could do. Nothing could change what Balor had done. I sank to my knees in the damp grass of the football field, my arms falling limp at my sides, and started to wail for their loss.

When I woke up, I couldn't breath. I sat up, trying to

get a breath in, but nothing was coming. A light flicked on and I saw Nessa standing in front of the bed. She must have been the guard on duty that night. Since I no longer had the protection of Slan Lathair, the Dream Team had returned to twenty-four hour duty.

"Maggie? Are you okay?"

I shook my head. She left to go into the bathroom and came back with a glass of water.

"Drink this." I took the glass from her and swallowed a few gulps. "Concentrate on taking slow, deep breaths."

I handed the glass to her and did as she said. I was able to calm down enough that I could breath freely. I was shaking and sweat was dampening my entire body.

"Nightmare?" Nessa asked.

I nodded.

She sat next to me on the bed and took my hand in hers. "You want to talk about it?"

I shook my head.

"You want me to get Ian?"

I shook my head again.

"You want me to sit beside you while you go back to sleep?"

I nodded and fell back against the pillows, falling easily into sleep. The nightmare had exhausted me.

༺ஓ༻

"Oh. Goodie. You're back," Keelin said in a bored voice instilled with more than her usual amount of sarcasm when she saw me in the kitchen at Ballecath. Ian's sister had never been my biggest fan. In fact, she was downright hostile toward me for reasons that had to do with her perception that I hadn't loved Simon the way he deserved to be loved. Although they were twins, the only things Keelin and Ian had in common were their dark hair, green eyes, and tall build. In personality, they couldn't have been more different.

Unfortunately, there was some truth to what she believed. I had kissed another guy while dating Simon, and that was certainly part of it, but I also felt that I could never love Simon enough to justify the joy he had brought to my life so unselfishly.

I decided to take the high road with Keelin—even if it was a false and sarcastic high road. I walked over to her and reached my arms up to hug her. I was trying to figure out how to embrace her in such a way that made my sarcasm obvious, but she batted my arms away before they made contact.

"Get off, you freak!"

Ian walked into the room, looking like a deer caught in the headlights when he saw the two of us. I'm sure there was a moment when he thought about turning around and leaving in order to avoid the obvious conflict brewing, but he stayed rooted to a spot near the door and watched us, waiting, I'm sure, for a battle to break out.

"I'm going to go check my email," I said. Ian let out the breath he'd evidently been holding as I passed him on my way out the door.

I was hoping to find an email from Lexie, but I was once again disappointed. Instead, there were several emails from Jane, Gertie and Albert asking where I was and why I had left Slan Lathair without saying goodbye. I replied with a group email telling them about Balor's threat to send his people to Slan Lathair. I explained that I would be just as safe at Ballecath, and had decided to stay there in order to keep the students safe from a Fomorian attack.

After I was done, I sat at the desk in Simon's room and tried to decide what to do next. I got up and pulled Simon's journal from my backpack and took it with me to sit in a chair by the window. Returning from the Underworld without him had hurt almost as much as losing him in the first place. I had been so convinced I was right. So convinced I'd find him and bring him home. My conviction that he was still alive started to waver and I felt my heart constrict painfully with the thought that I might never see him again.

I opened his journal and started to read, wanting to feel some sort of connection with him.

...Maggie can't do it. I won't allow her to be the one to kill Balor. Not only will it put her in unspeakable danger, it will also leave her with the guilt of taking a life. She's talked with me about her concern over killing. I know how much it will tear her apart. I am more convinced than ever that I will have to be the one to do it. I tried before, and failed. I need to be careful this time. I need to get close to Balor and figure out how best to do it. If I fail a second time, Balor will make sure it is the last...

...I'm working every day to figure out how to get to Balor, but getting to him will be the easy part. Pretending, even for a moment, that I could betray Maggie will be the most difficult thing I've ever had to do in my life. I've been working every day on lying without visible physical pain, but it is the emotional pain that will be unbearable. I love her more than I love myself. Even if I do manage to master the ability to lie, the pain will always be there, unseen and silent.

Chapter Eighteen

"Do you think we could go to my Grandma Margaret's cottage today?" I asked Ian. I'd woken up before the sun and was restless and edgy. I hadn't given a visit to my grandmother's cottage much thought, and didn't know if going would be helpful, but it would beat spending the day beating my head against the wall in pursuit of the answers to my many unanswered questions.

"Sure," Ian said, looking like he was a little taken aback with my request. "Any particular reason you want to go today?"

I shrugged. "It's something to do. Maybe we'll find some sort of clue, or maybe it will just calm me to be there. I don't know."

"I'll get it arranged," he said as he stood to leave.

Three carloads of faeries were loaded and ready to make the trip within the hour. Simon had taken me to the cottage the first time I had visited Ireland. It was a long drive, much of it along some very bumpy dirt roads, and the longer I sat in the car, the more I wondered what had made me want to take this trip in the first place.

The cottage hadn't been lived in for a really long time.

There were holes where windows and doors should have been, and the roof had long since fallen away. Plants clung to the stone walls, both inside and out, and the walls were crumbling in many places. It was hard to imagine anyone living in the small cottage.

I walked to the stone fireplace and ran my fingers along the shield knots that had been carved along the sides and top. Ian came and stood beside me. A ray of sunshine shot through the clouds and sent a beam to light up the room where we stood.

"Why do you think they carved these?" I asked Ian.

"I don't know. Maybe they thought it would protect them."

"Do the shield knots do any good at all?"

I was thinking of the one I gave Simon for his birthday. It hadn't protected him at the one time when he most needed protection.

"It's no better than wearing a pair of lucky pants," Ian said. "It's just superstition."

Pants, I knew from a prior humiliating experience, were actually underwear in Ireland.

"You have lucky pants?" I teased Ian.

He shrugged. "Everyone has a pair of lucky pants."

"I don't."

"Well maybe that's the crux of our problem. Get yourself a pair of lucky pants and all will be grand."

"If only it were so easy."

"If only."

The clouds overhead shifted and the beam of sunshine moved to focus on a point inside the fireplace. I looked down on the now illuminated bricks and felt my heart skip a few beats when I saw a passageway symbol—the same symbol we had seen at Newgrange that had opened up the tunnel to the Underworld.

"Ian," I said urgently, "Look!" I pointed to the symbol and Ian looked down, a shocked expression exploding on his face. He looked back at me for a moment before kneeling down and placing his hand on the symbol. Nothing happened. He tried again, but nothing opened up. Nothing moved. Nothing changed.

"Maybe they just carved it for decoration," he suggested.

"It seems sort of weird to decorate something people wouldn't see. It's carved in a place that isn't very visible."

"It doesn't make sense," he agreed. "I'll get Finn and Sloane. See what they think."

All of the Guardians who made the trip with us were waiting outside, giving me some privacy to do what I needed to do. Ian walked through the hole where a door had once stood and came back with Finn and Sloane. They looked at the symbol and each of them touched it, but nothing happened.

"It might have opened up to something at some point, but someone must have removed the spell," Finn said as he knelt beside the fireplace and inspected the symbol.

"Why?" I asked. "And what would it lead to? Why carve it in the first place?"

Finn stood and brushed the dirt from his jeans.

"Would someone make it to take them to the Underworld?" I continued.

"Not necessarily," Sloane said. "If there are two symbols connected through magic, they become a sort of portal. Faeries used to make them to travel long distances in a short time. Now that we have cars and airplanes, they aren't really used anymore."

"Why not?"

"A portal can shorten the distance, but it's still going

to be a journey. It's just easier to get on a plane if you're going to cover a long distance."

"The symbol at Newgrange wasn't like that," I reasoned. "We still had to walk the whole way."

"No," Finn corrected, "you didn't. You walked only a fraction of the real distance between Newgrange and the Underworld."

I found that hard to believe since we walked for literally hours.

I slumped onto the hearth and wrapped my arms around my knees. For a moment, I'd had hope. I'd come to my grandmother's cottage wanting to find something—anything—that might help me, and for a moment, I thought I'd found it. But it was nothing. I was leaving her home with nothing.

"If this were a movie, it would have meant something," I grumbled. "If this were a movie, and a beam of sunshine drew my attention to a passageway symbol, it would have meant something."

Finn sat beside me and wrapped an arm around my shoulders. "I'm afraid the real world isn't quite so tidy."

☙❧

I was sitting at Simon's desk, typing an email to Jane, when I noticed that I had a new email. I didn't get too excited, knowing it was probably from Brandon and knowing he probably just wanted to tell me about his new high scores from all the video games he played. I finished my email to Jane before I opened my inbox to see that the email was not, in fact, from Brandon. It was from Lexie.

I opened it, eager for a long explanation of where she'd been and what she'd found, knowing my best friend would certainly have something that could help me find Simon or take down Balor. If I'm being honest, I was also looking for an apology. I wanted her to say how sorry she was for worrying me and for leaving me at a time when I really needed her support. What I got, however, were three measly words.

Can we meet?

I walked to Ian's apartment and told him about the email.

"It could be a trick," he said. "Someone could have hacked her email."

"Yeah, I'm not even going to entertain that as a possibility because that would mean someone has her—someone we wouldn't want her to be with."

He sat down on his sofa and I sat down beside him.

"Not necessarily," he said, taking my hand in his. "They could have hacked her email without ever seeing her. If someone knows her email address, it wouldn't be that hard to hack into her account."

He was right, and my mind went back to the traitor. If Lexie had given her email address to someone at the house, they could hack in and send an email.

"We can't not meet her," I said. "I mean if it is her that sent the email, we have to go to her."

Ian suggested that we all meet in a town south of Ballecath in a park the following day. That way, we would be able to see Lexie, but we'd also be out in the open and it would be easier to escape if it wasn't her.

Lexie—and I wasn't able to consider that it was anyone *but* Lexie—emailed back to say she was okay with that plan. We let Finn and Sloane know where we were going, but decided it would be best if Ian and I drove there alone, followed by a car filled with the Dream Team. They could stay close in case there were any problems, but I didn't want to scare Lexie off with an army of Guardians.

"Do you think it's a trick?" I asked Ian as we made the drive south.

He was silent, and his silence said so much.

I had to hope Lexie would be waiting for us in the park. I'd missed her so much since she'd gone, and I'd spent a lot of time worrying about her. The thought of seeing Lexie again gave me a thrill that was second only to the thought that I might see Simon again.

When we pulled up to the small park, I didn't see Lexie. A few moms and dads were in the park with toddlers and preschoolers, but since it was a school day, all of the older children were in class. It was a cold and grey day and I knew the clouds were going to start relieving themselves of the rain building inside of them at any minute.

"She's over by that tree," Ian said. I followed his line of site to a large tree at the edge of the park. Lexie was standing with her back to us, but it was definitely Lexie. Her long black hair was pulled into a ponytail, and she leaned against the tree, her long legs crossed in front of her. I started to get out of the car, but Ian stopped me.

"Wait for the Dream Team to get out. I want to make sure she wasn't escorted here." I didn't like the sound of that. Had Lexie been kidnapped and brought here as bait to lure me in?

The Dream Team positioned themselves behind me and to my sides when I got out of the car, and Ian walked beside me as we headed toward Lexie. She turned when we were a few yards away and a smile spread across her face and glinted in her eyes. She ran forward and threw her arms around me, hugging me tight. I returned the hug and tried to fight off the happy tears that were pooling in my eyes. It was Lexie and I didn't care if it was a trap because it meant I got to hug her.

Ian cleared his throat discreetly. "Maybe we should head back to the SUV," he suggested. "You might have been followed."

Lexie pulled away and smiled. "He hasn't changed much." She stooped to pick up her backpack from the ground and we walked arm and arm to the car. If only she knew how much he had, in fact, changed. He'd broken about a thousand rules to take me to the Underworld, and he'd paid a heavy price for it. The old Ian wouldn't have done that.

"You do know that I'm furious with you, right?" I told her when we were in the car. I couldn't bear to separate myself from her, so we sat in the backseat together and Ian sat alone in the front seat.

"I know, and I'm sorry. I just didn't see any other way."

"Are you coming back to Ballecath with us?" I asked, hopeful.

"Only if you promise that nobody will alter my memory in any way."

I thought about that for a moment and wondered if it was a promise I could keep. If altering her memory meant that she'd be safe, I'd do it without hesitation.

"Would you be satisfied with a promise that I would only allow your memories to be altered if it's the only option to keep you safe, and if I tell you ahead of time?"

After thinking it through for a moment, she agreed, and we started the drive back to Ballecath.

"So, did you learn anything valuable during your time as a teenage runaway?" I asked once we were on the road.

She looked pointedly at Ian in the driver's seat.

"I'll tell him later anyway," I said. "We might as well talk in front of him."

Lexie and Ian's relationship was rocky, at best, and I knew she'd rather have her feet boiled in lard than have to take Ian on as a confidant, but she only hesitated a moment before telling me everything she wanted me to know.

"So, I've been doing some research,"—*of course*—"and I think maybe you've got things all wrong."

"What things?" I asked.

"I don't think you have to kill Balor," she said with pride. I knew she was happy to have uncovered that fact for me, but I also knew it wasn't an accurate piece of information.

"Lexie—"

"Hear me out. I've been talking to this guy who teaches Irish folklore at Trinity College and he says the prophecy actually says that Balor's grandson will kill him. Not you."

I looked expectantly at Ian.

"Is that true?" I asked him.

"There *is* a prophecy that says that Balor's grandson, Lugh, would be the one to kill him, but Balor had him killed as a baby so that couldn't happen."

"This guy at Trinity introduced me to a grad student who said he thinks Lugh is still alive and in hiding."

"How would this guy know about it?" I asked.

"He knows a lot of stuff about faeries, and he doesn't think it's folklore. He thinks it's real. Which it is—obviously." She waved her hand in Ian's direction, then toward me, as proof that she was stating the obvious.

"But how would *he* know if Lugh is still alive, but none of the Guardians know?" Ian asked. "It seems like something that would have leaked out at some point.

Lugh would be about four hundred years old by now. That's a long time to keep a secret that big from Balor and every other faery."

"What if Balor *does* know?" Lexie suggested. "What if he's been looking for him this whole time but he's so well hidden that he hasn't found him?"

I mulled that possibility over in my head.

"There's more," Lexie announced. "There's a sword—the one mentioned in the story about Maggie and Simon—and the grad student thinks he knows where it's hidden."

"There's an actual sword?" I asked. I guess I always thought it was just part of the story, but not something I'd actually have to use.

Lexie nodded. "I think it's at Tara."

"Tara?"

"The Hill of Tara?" Ian asked her.

"Tara was ruled for centuries by the UiNeills. It gets a little complicated here, but some descendants of the UiNeills actually have the name O'Neill. It's so close and sometimes people would change it themselves to make their name more modern, and sometimes they had it changed for them when they immigrated to other countries because people just assumed they were saying 'O'Neill' when they said their name."

"Simon mentioned the UiNeills in his diary," I said.

"What did he say?" Lexie asked eagerly.

"Nothing. He just had a list of words and stuff in the back. He did say something about the UiNeills ruling Tara or something."

"He was right, and you're a descendant of the UiNeills—at least the grad student at Trinity thinks you are. There's this stone—the Stone of Destiny—and he told me the stone roars when it's touched by the rightful king of Tara. I think Maggie's the rightful king and I think that if she touches the stone it'll reveal the sword."

"I can't be the rightful king. I'm lacking the necessary anatomy."

"King. Queen. Whatever. They were pretty closed-minded back then. They thought only men could rule."

"But wouldn't my dad or my grandpa be the rightful king? Isn't that how it goes?"

"Maybe. But it's also possible that you'll be able to stake that claim since neither of them have, and if you do stake your claim, you'll be able to get the sword."

"Why would I want the sword?"

"To kill Balor," she said in a "duh stupid" sort of way.

"I'm thinking there are much better ways to kill Balor. I haven't figured them out yet, but I'm sure it's going to have to involve magic."

"Actually, the sword in the Stone of Destiny is the only known way to kill Balor. I'm not really sure about the specifics, but I definitely believe you're going to have to have the sword if we want to kill him."

"But you said I wouldn't need to kill him. Why would I need sword?"

I'd spent the better part of the last year worrying about how I could possibly kill a faery as powerful as Balor, so I was relieved to finally discover a way, but I'd be even happier if I found out I wasn't actually the one who would have to do it.

"To give it to Lugh so *he* can kill Balor. The sword belongs to you. You can do whatever you want with it, but if you're the King or Queen of Tara, you're the only one with access to it."

"This is all a little far fetched," Ian interjected.

"You have a better theory, Faery Boy?" Lexie asked him with derision.

"I told you not to call me that," Ian said. I'd never heard her call him that before, and wondered if it had been one of the many points of contention between the two when they'd gone to prom together.

"I'm sorry," Lexie told him sarcastically, "my itty bitty human brain can't remember things as long as you."

"Knock it off, you two. Your bickering doesn't help us."

"But it's so much fun," Ian said wryly.

"There's more," Lexie said, ignoring Ian and moving back to super sleuth mode. "I think I know where Simon is."

Chapter Nineteen

Lexie's announcement filled me with several conflicting emotions. I was excited because we had a new lead. The well of ideas had run dry after we'd returned from Newgrange and it felt good to have the possibility of something else to try. I was apprehensive because I didn't want to get my hopes up, only to have them smashed against a brick wall. And, if I was honest with myself, I was worried about the dangers we would face if we chose to pursue any leads that Lexie might have dug up.

"Where do you think he is?" I asked Lexie, trying not to get my hopes up too much.

"Tory Island," she said with pride. "According to mythology—which we all know is based in truth—Tory Island was the ancient home of the Fomorians. And Balor. He supposedly imprisoned his daughter in Tor Mor, a rock formation on the island, to keep her from getting pregnant because he knew about the prophecy saying that the son of his only daughter would end up killing him. It makes sense that he'd keep Simon there. It also makes sense that the entrance to his home is on Tory Island. Newgrange has always been seen as the home of

Danu's people, so I think the entrance to her home is there, and the entrance to Balor's home is on Tory Island."

"We could have really used that information a week ago," I said wryly.

"Why?"

I told her about our failed trip to Newgrange. When I'd finished, she looked at Ian impatiently.

"You should have known better," she told him, obviously making no attempt to conceal her disappointment in him.

I leaned back in my seat and stared out the window.

What do you think? I asked Ian silently.

I don't know, he admitted. *She does make some good points, though. I just wish it hadn't been her to make them.*

ಸಿಂಡಿ

"So, you want to tell me what's going on with you and Ian?" Lexie asked when we were sitting in Simon's room together at Ballecath. My first thought was to pretend I didn't know what she was talking about, but I felt a deep blush spread across my cheeks and down my neck and I knew denial would be a wasted effort.

"It's complicated," I mumbled.

"I bet it is," she said conspiratorially. "Spill."

I took a deep breath and tried to figure out how much to tell her. "I love him," I began. "And he loves me, but we both know that it's not the same as the way I love Simon. I think we just have so many common bonds. We both love Simon. We're both trying to find him. We're both working to bring down Balor. And we spend almost every waking hour together. I don't know how we could avoid falling in love."

"So what happens if you manage to bring Simon home?"

"I don't know," I admitted. "I think Ian would back off if that happened."

"You really think that's true?"

"He kissed me," I reasoned, "and he said that he only kissed me because he believed that Simon was alive and he knew that once we brought him home, he wouldn't have the chance again. That tells me he really does understand. He knows how I feel about Simon."

"I hope so," she said. "Ian's not my favorite person, but I hate to see anyone with a broken heart."

"I have no doubt he'll back away when we get Simon back, but I worry that I'm hurting him—and that I'm just going to keep hurting him—and I owe him so much. He doesn't deserve this—to love someone who can't love him back completely."

She shook her head and looked amused. "This is the lamest love triangle ever! If you're going to have a decent love triangle, there needs to be at least a little bit of doubt about which guy you'd pick."

"Then maybe it's not a love triangle, because everyone—including Ian—knows I would always pick Simon."

"But what if we don't get Simon home? What then?"

"I can't even think about that possibility."

"But what if?" she persisted. "What if there was no chance of a relationship with Simon. Would you pick Ian then?"

I thought about it for a moment, picturing Ian and me together, kissing, holding hands, spending our lives together.

"He deserves better," I decided as the images formed in my mind. "He deserves to be with someone who isn't wishing they could be with someone else."

ಸಂಡ

Ian and Lexie and I spent the better part of the next week pouring over all of the evidence she had gathered in her time with the grad student at Trinity College. We looked at maps and old documents and handwritten notes. We tried to develop a plan, but after our disastrous trip to Newgrange, I was hesitant to embark on any new adventures.

"It can't hurt to go and check it out," Lexie reasoned. I reminded her that I said the same thing about going to Newgrange, and Ian and I had come very close to dying on that "harmless" venture.

"Well, sitting here isn't going to get us anywhere," she said, folding her arms across her chest and flopping down on the sofa in Ian's apartment.

"You two could be twins," Ian mused. "If I'm not looking right at you, I bet I can't figure out which one of you is talking."

"That's helpful, Ian. Making fun of us is going to bring Simon back for sure." Lexie's sarcasm wasn't at all subtle when it came to Ian.

"I'm not making fun of you. I'm just saying that you think alike. I heard all of the same statements coming out of Maggie's mouth a couple of weeks ago."

"Well, if you don't like what we're saying, contribute something of your own. You've lived with faeries for two hundred years, yet you have nothing to contribute. Are you *completely* clueless?"

"Are you a *complete* bitch?"

"Ugh!" I interjected. "Knock it off! You are not helping. Either of you."

They both looked contrite and I took that as a good sign.

"I think we should go, Ian," I told him gently, but firmly.

"Maggie, did you learn nothing at Newgrange?"

"I learned a lot at Newgrange. One of the things I learned is that it would probably be better to let Sloane in on our plans. She might even decide to help us."

"And if she doesn't?"

"I'm still going," I told him.

"Me too," Lexie piped in.

"Jaysus!" Ian said sharply as he stood up. "Now I have two of you to look after. One wasn't enough. No. Now I have to follow two of you around. I don't know what I did in my past lives, but it must have been really bad to bring on this amount of bad karma."

He'd stopped talking to us and was just rambling to himself. In the end, we convinced him to come with us to present the idea to Sloane and Finn.

⁂

"I know about the legend of the Stone of Destiny," Sloane said after we gave her all of the information and told her our plan. "It's always been dismissed as pure myth, but I think it's worth looking into."

I about fell out of my seat because of the shock at hearing Sloane agreeing with our plan. I was at a complete loss for how to respond. I had come up with a whole list of arguments I could give, and had even practiced how I would tell her that I was going, with or without her. It never occurred to me that Sloane might actually agree that it was a good idea.

"You think we should go to Tara?" I confirmed,

wondering if maybe I had misunderstood her response.

"I do," she confirmed. "I think we should go with a few carloads of faeries, though. If Balor knows about the sword, and knows it might be at Tara, he's going to make sure someone is watching out in case you show up."

"I think a few carloads of faeries would be a good idea," I said. I really wanted to avoid a situation like the one we had at Newgrange and liked the thought of having so many Guardians there to help out in case something went wrong.

"So, we'll go in, you'll touch the stone, see if the sword appears, then we're out of there," Sloane laid out. "Any sign of trouble and we leave immediately. Agreed?"

"Agreed," I told her.

ഇരു

My family and friends were lined up again on the sidelines of the football field behind Castlewood High School. This time, however, they weren't standing. Each of them was lying on their back, their dead eyes staring upward at nothing.

I turned to see Balor standing in the middle of the field. He was at least thirty yards away, but I could hear him clearly, despite his quiet tone.

"I can make this a reality, Margaret O'Neill," he said with a light in his eyes and a smile on his cruel lips. "Oh, how I want to make this image you're having real for you. I can kill them one by one, or I can kill them all at once. How would you like it done? What is your preference?"

Simon appeared next to Balor. "I'll help you, father. I'll help you kill them."

I knew it wasn't really Simon. I knew, with complete

certainty that he wouldn't side with Balor.

"He's with me now, Margaret. My son is with me."

"Only in your imagination," I said with force and determination.

The fake, dream-induced Simon reached out to strike me and I forced myself to wake up before his hand could make contact with my face. He wasn't real. The real Simon would never hurt me.

I'd had plenty of nightmares about Balor, but the ones on the football field left me so shaken. The addition of Simon to those dreams rattled me to the core. All of my family and friends were at risk of being harmed or killed by Balor and there was certainly a part of me that just wanted to walk away—that wanted to hop on the next plane to Denver and forget about Balor and the faeries and the prophecy. But I couldn't. It was too late. Balor would come after me and find me and he'd kill anyone who got in his way.

The nightmares that kept me awake also reminded me that Grandma Margaret hadn't been coming to me in my time of nocturnal need. She was normally there with me in my nightmares, ready to comfort and defend me against the imaginary monsters, but she had been conspicuously absent during my nightmares with Balor. Why wasn't she coming to me? Was something wrong on her side of the universe, wherever that may be? Was she able to choose when she visited me and when she didn't? I hadn't realized how much comfort she'd been to me until she was no longer there.

ഏൟ

A few days after we talked to Sloane about Tara, we loaded up six carloads of faeries and Sloane told me another thirty would be on standby in the area in case we needed them. We'd spent the better part of three days planning this trip, knowing that it might turn out to be nothing more than a worthless myth. Sloane was actually more concerned that it would turn out *not* to be a myth.

"If Balor thinks there is even the slightest possibility that the sword is there, he'll have his people watching the area. We might be setting ourselves up for an attack."

"But if that's the case, if the sword really is there, all the more reason to go," Alana pointed out.

"I'm not saying we shouldn't go," Sloane said. "I just want to make sure we're being cautious."

So, we planned for every possibility before we left on our trip to find the sword hidden at Tara.

Parking six black SUVs in the visitor center would probably raise concern among the humans, so we parked in different locations to meet at the Stone of Destiny. Ian carried me, Aidan carried Lexie and Sloane carried Quinn.

We waited until well after dark to approach the area so that we wouldn't attract attention, and it took me a few moments before my eyes were adjusted enough to see the large stone in front of me. It was about three and a half feet tall and a foot across, and it looked like...well, it looked like a giant penis.

"I knew the pagans were really into phallic symbols, but this thing isn't even subtle," Lexie remarked.

"You have a problem with phallic symbols?" Ian bated her.

"As long as the phallus isn't attached to a jerk with half a brain, I'm good," Lexie countered.

"Give it a rest," Alana, Keelin and I said simultaneously.

Ian and Lexie quieted down and I noticed that everyone was looking at me expectantly.

"Should I just touch it then?" I asked.

"Wait," Lexie said. "We need a control group."

"A what?" Ian asked with irritation.

"Well, we want to make sure that if the stone does roar, it's because of Maggie and not because of something else."

"What else would make it roar? If it roars, it's because Maggie is the king—or whatever—of Tara."

"Indulge me," Lexie told him, and she went to the stone and touched it. The wind shifted slightly, but there was no other change, and certainly no roar.

"Maybe a faery should try touching it, too," Lexie suggested.

Ian slapped the stone impatiently and turned to Lexie. "There. Happy?"

Lexie shrugged.

"So I'm going to touch it now," I told everyone. A part of me wanted someone to stop me. The night I tried on the ring came to mind and what had happened when I'd slipped the ring on my finger was pounding on the doors of my brain. It had turned out okay that night, but what if it didn't turn out okay at Tara? What if something happened to make our situation worse, and not better? Unfortunately, there was only one way to find out.

I took a step toward the rock and held my hand against the cold stone. For a moment, nothing happened and I felt disappointed and relieved and tired. So tired. Tired of not having any answers. Tired of getting no closer to finding Simon or Balor. Tired of not seeing the end of this very dark and morose tunnel I'd been living in.

Then I felt the rock tremble. It was subtle at first, and I wasn't sure if I was imagining it, but the tremble turned into a rumble and the rumble turned into an unmistakable roar. The stone started to crumble and a light shot through the cracks, piercing the sky and blinding everyone standing nearby. I tried to take a step away, but an invisible pull kept me anchored to the spot, my hand still extended toward the stone. Rock was falling at my feet, but I still felt the cold of the granite on my palm. When it didn't look as if there was a single piece of rock standing, I looked up to see a sword in my hand. A large, heavy, cold sword. I gasped, the enormity of what had just happened slowly sinking in. And then I heard him.

Maggie? It was Simon. Unmistakably Simon. I felt tears of happiness spring to my eyes and I looked around to see where he was.

Simon? I called out silently.

Maggie! Get away! They know you're here!

Chapter Twenty

I spun around to face the others, the sword hanging at my side.

"I heard him!" I told Ian urgently. "I heard Simon!"

"What? Now?" Ian looked confused, but the other faeries looked shocked.

Talk to them, Simon. Talk to the other faeries. They're all here with me.

I waited for a moment to pass, then watched as the shock intensified on the faery faces surrounding me.

"He must be nearby," Ian reasoned. "*You* could hear him from far away, but the rest of us couldn't."

"He can't be here," Lexie said, dumbfounded. "I really think he's at Tory Island."

"He says the Fomorians are here," Sloane interjected. "He wants us to get Maggie out of here."

"I'm not going anywhere," I told her firmly. "But someone needs to get Lexie and Quinn out of here if there's going to be a fight with the Fomorians."

Maggie, leave! Simon yelled in my head.

"Quinn can fight," Sloane said with pride.

"I'll take Lexie," Alana said.

"You sure you want to stay?" Sloane asked me.

I nodded decisively.

Alana pulled Lexie away and I was grateful when I saw that Lexie wasn't protesting. I figured she was in shock about the fact that one of her theories was wrong. She didn't have much experience with being wrong and she probably didn't know how to handle the very foreign concept.

When I saw that Lexie was safely in the air with Alana, I turned to Sloane. "What's the plan?"

"I contacted the backup Guardians that we had nearby. They're sending out an alarm to get as many Guardians as we can to come here and help us fight."

"We need to find Simon."

"Agreed. We don't have much time, Maggie. I'm sure the Fomorians are on their way. Are you sure you don't want to leave?"

"I'm sure."

As soon as I said it, I saw the faeries surrounding us, charging at us, ready for a fight.

I grabbed Ian's arm. "Help me find him," I pleaded.

He took my hand and ran toward Keelin, the heavy sword still in my other hand, weighing me down and slowing our progress. "Come with us," he told her.

Keelin can open locks. Faery ability. We might need her, Ian explained as the three of us ran around the side of a small burial mound near the Stone of Destiny. Ian led us to the three-foot high opening, but it was blocked by an iron gate. Keelin grabbed the lock holding the gate and it clicked open. She pulled the gate out of the way and the three of us entered the very cramped space inside. Once we were all in, she turned and replaced the gate and the lock.

"Where are we?" I asked.

"Mound of Hostages," Ian answered. "Look for one

of the passageway symbols that we saw at Newgrange, or any symbol that's glowing."

Simon, where are you? I called out silently as we started to look around for the symbol. He didn't respond. Dread and a sense of urgency started to pound against my heart.

"He's not talking to me," I told Ian and Keelin. "Is he talking to you?"

They both shook their heads and as they did, I heard the fighting begin outside of the mound.

"Keep looking," Ian ordered.

"Here!" Keelin said, leaning down toward the bottom of a rock at the side of the structure. It was the same passageway symbol and it was glowing just as the one at Newgrange had. Three faeries were at the gate, rattling it, trying to get in. A dagger flew past me and nearly hit Keelin. Ian dove toward the symbol and slapped his hand against it. An opening formed in the rock at the back and the three of us went through to the long tunnel that was revealed. We ran as fast as we could, hoping to outrun the Fomorians before they managed to break through the lock.

Unlike the tunnel at Newgrange, this tunnel had several options as to which way to go. Keelin and I blindly followed Ian, but I was pretty certain he didn't know where he was going either. Eventually, we ended up in a small opening at the side of the tunnel that was partially blocked by a large rock. It was a tight space, but we squeezed in, pressing against each other as we did.

"Have either of you heard Simon since we were at the Stone of Destiny?" Ian asked breathlessly.

We both shook our heads.

"Me either," he admitted. "Try again, Maggie. Your connection's stronger."

Simon! Talk to me! Tell me where you are! I mentally

screamed it as loud as I could, but he didn't reply.

I looked at Ian and Keelin and shook my head.

"I say we keep looking," Keelin said. "Even if—" She didn't finish her sentence. She didn't need to. We were all thinking the same thing. Was he dead? Had somebody killed him after he warned us of the attack? It didn't matter. I wanted to keep looking, even if the only thing we had to bring back was a body.

Ian and I nodded and we left the safety of our little nook. Before we started to walk again, I pulled Bob out of his sheath at my waist. I had a dagger in one hand, and a sword in the other, but I still didn't feel very confident.

We were in the tunnels for what seemed like hours. At one point, Keelin suggested we make an "X" with one of our daggers along the walls periodically so we could tell if we were going in circles. As it turned out, we were. The markings helped us to avoid going down the same section of tunnel twice and I felt like we were finally making some progress. When we came upon a large, thick, steel door, I knew we were probably on the right track. Keelin held her hand against the lock and I heard a click before the door opened wide. The tunnel continued on the other side, but there was also another door up ahead. There were three faeries standing in front of the door.

All three faeries reached for their daggers, but Ian was faster. He had his out and thrown in their direction before I even remembered that I had a tight grip on Bob in my right hand, the sword in my left. I threw Bob right after Ian threw his dagger, and Keelin wasn't far behind with her throw. One faery went down. One of us had made a hit. I was pretty sure it wasn't me. When I called Bob back to me, he had some dirt along his blade, but no blood or guts.

Ian pushed Keelin and me down to the ground just as I saw three blades fly over our heads. Two faeries were approaching us, coming closer step by step. I threw Bob again, hitting one of the two remaining faeries in the leg. Then I drew back the sword and swung at the other faery. Given the heaviness of the sword, I wasn't sure if I would be able to lift it enough to actually use it, but it seemed to be helping me out. Not only did it feel lighter, it also seemed to decide which direction to go and at what angle. I was grateful for the help. The sword sliced through the shoulder of the third faery. He fell to the ground and Keelin threw her dagger at his chest. If he wasn't dead, he was doing a really good impression of it.

We ran to the door and Keelin did her magic with the lock. She was the first one through the door and for a moment she seemed unsteady on her feet, almost as if her knees had buckled under her. I looked over her shoulder and saw four more faeries, but I also saw someone else. He was lying on a bed, unconscious, his hands and feet chained. Simon.

Chapter Twenty-One

My knees buckled and I started to fall to the ground, but I felt a hand grip my elbow, supporting me and keeping me standing. I looked over and saw Ian at my side—always at my side—helping me to stand, despite the shock of the moment. It was Simon. He was dirty and bruised and emaciated, and wearing nothing but a torn pair of jeans, but there was no doubt it was Simon. I wanted to go to him, to see if he was alive, but I had to fight off the four other faeries in the room that stood in my way.

I made a split second decision to put Bob back in the sheath that was clipped to my belt. I thought I'd have better odds with the sword—especially since it seemed to do most of the work for me. I didn't think Bob would mind.

I swung forward with the sword and pushed through the chest of the faery nearest me. He fell to the ground, but I didn't have time to check whether he was dead or not before the second faery approached. She was small, like me, but she was fast. I swung at her neck, hoping to take her out with one hit, but she jumped down and back, effectively avoiding the strike. I managed to block her against a wall, but as I swung, she dodged down and ran behind me. When I turned, I saw another faery lying on the ground, and Keelin and Ian were double-teaming a faery that looked a whole lot like Lurch from the Adams Family.

The little faery I'd been pursuing lunged at Keelin with her dagger, and I took her moment of distraction to drive the sword into her back. She fell quickly, and the three of us concentrated our efforts on Lurch.

As I started to lift the sword to use it against him, he put one massive hand around my neck and lifted me off the ground. I couldn't breath, and as I tried to free myself, I dropped the sword to the ground. Keelin tried to get close enough to stab him with a dagger, but he kept deflecting it.

"Give me permission to use the sword!" Ian yelled after picking it up from the ground.

I tried to nod, but Lurch's grip was too tight.

Do I have your permission to use the sword? Ian asked silently, frantically.

Yes! I told him. *Yes!*

He lifted the sword above his head and drove it into Lurch's chest. He loosened his grip around my neck and I fell to the ground, gasping for air. He fell on top of me and Ian and Keelin pushed him off before pulling me to my feet.

"You okay?" Ian asked.

I nodded, still not certain whether I had enough air to talk.

"Check to see if Simon's still alive," Ian told me. "Keelin and I will check this lot."

I walked toward Simon, terrified that I would find him dead—terrified that we had come so close for nothing. I put the palm of my hand on his bare chest and silently pleaded with him to be breathing. I felt a slight movement, but I wasn't sure if it was my own shaking hands, or the breath moving in and out of his chest. I moved my fingers to his neck to feel for a pulse and looked closely at his face for the first time. It was bruised and cut and dirty, dried blood caked to his lips and temple. It made we want to cry to see him like that, but I didn't have time. I'd have to wait until later. I stopped breathing for a moment in order to better detect the movement in his neck, and had to hold a hand to my mouth to keep myself from screaming when I felt the thu-thump of the blood pulsing through his veins.

"They're all dead," Keelin said when she and Ian joined me next to Simon. They both looked at my face and assumed the worst.

"Is Simon?" Ian asked, fear in his voice for the first time that night.

I shook my head vigorously, the lump in my throat preventing me from talking.

"He's alive?"

I nodded, and Keelin reached down and hugged me.

"He's alive," she breathed. "Simon's alive. I didn't think it was possible."

She reached across his body and held each of the locks in her hands, releasing his limbs, one by one, from the chains that imprisoned him in that room. Had he been here since Balor had taken him that day in the field?

"I can't get a response from any of the other Guardians," Ian told us. "We might be too far away from them."

"Do you think you can carry Simon?" Keelin asked. Ian nodded. "Let's get to that little nook we found earlier," she suggested. "It might be faster if we try to fly."

"I can't fly," I remind her. I didn't do a very good job of keeping the shame out of my voice.

"I'll carry you on my back and Ian can carry Simon."

I nodded and we both helped Ian lift Simon off the bed, then I jumped on Keelin's back and we flew through the tunnels. It didn't take nearly as long as the trip in. The marks we had made on the walls really helped, and flying with a faery was typically faster than walking.

Ian stopped at the little nook and gently laid Simon on the floor.

"I can hear Sloane now," he told us. "They're still fighting. She thinks we should stay here until they get the upper hand."

"What about Lexie?"

"Alana's back and she said she checked Lexie into a hotel nearby."

I felt a small speck of relief and walked into the nook to be with Simon while we waited for the others. Keelin and Ian waited outside in the tunnel.

I lifted Simon's head gently and placed it in my lap.

"Simon," I whispered while I brushed my fingers against his brow. "Simon, please wake up."

He remained stubbornly asleep and oblivious. I was still fighting to keep the tears from streaming down my face. When Simon was safe, I could let the emotions flow freely, but not yet. Not until he was safe.

I obsessively brushed his neck with my fingers to feel the pulse running through him. I wasn't sure what had happened to him, but I wasn't going to let him die. He couldn't die. Not now.

Simon, I love you, I told him silently.

His eyes fluttered for a moment, then opened slightly.

Cushla macree, he whispered weakly. Even his silent

voice was faint.

I'm here. You're okay.

He closed his eyes again, and those few seconds of consciousness gave me hope that he might recover.

Ian peaked into the nook. "Finn and Erin and some of the others are on their way down."

It was only a few short moments before I heard them. Finn came to the entrance of the nook first. He squeezed his arm into the small space and took Simon's hand in his, pressing it to his cheek. He held it there for a moment, his eyes closed tight. When he opened them again, he looked at me. "You okay?"

I nodded.

Erin was right behind him and Finn stood to let her get nearer to Simon. She took his hand in hers and rubbed it gently.

"He's been poisoned," she told us softly, "but I think he's going to be okay."

I breathed a sigh of relief

"We need to get out of here," Finn said. "The Fomorians are still fighting on the hill, but if they come down here after us, we'll be trapped. Don't stop to fight. We need to keep going until Maggie and Simon are safe at Ballecath."

Finn put Simon over his shoulder in a fireman's hold while I picked up the sword I had put down while kneeling next to Simon. We ran the short distance in the tunnel that remained before we were at the locked gate to the Mound of Hostages. I wondered how Finn and Erin had gotten past the gate, but didn't have time to ask before we were swarmed by Fomorians. Ian grabbed me and tried to pull me into the air, but we were brought down by the massive hand of one of the Fomorians. Before he could inflict any damage, several Guardians I recognized surrounded him and pulled him away. Ian grabbed my hand and ran with me to a low stone wall, the sword gripped tight in my hand. As we were jumping over it, I saw a group of Fomorians running toward the fighting—toward us. I pulled Ian with me to a space between the wall and a small cluster of bushes. Keelin was right behind us. I crouched between her and Ian and the three of us watched the fighting, waiting for an opportunity to escape.

Did either of you see if Finn and Simon got away? Ian asked silently. Keelin and I both shook our heads. Neither of us had seen anything.

We were still hunkered over in our hiding spot when Sloane started to run in our direction with several other Guardians. They were running straight for us and I knew Ian or Keelin had called out to her silently to tell her where we were. She was about thirty yards away when a group of Fomorians caught up to her. Daggers started flying and faeries started falling, one by one. Quinn saw what was happening and ran toward Sloane. I wanted to scream at him to stay away. He was human and he wouldn't be able to fight against the Fomorians, but because he was human, I couldn't communicate with him silently, and yelling would give away our hiding spot. I watched helplessly as he tried to defend himself and Sloane. Then I watched as a dagger flew toward Sloane. It seemed like the dagger—or the faeries, or the whole world—was in slow motion. I wanted to reach out and grab it because I could see the direction it was going. Sloane didn't see. She was too busy fighting. Quinn saw, but he couldn't stop it. He couldn't get to it in time and it hit Sloane in the chest, sending her tumbling to the ground. She didn't get to her feet. She didn't move. Her eyes stared, lifeless, up to the sky. Just like my dream.

Quinn dropped to his knees beside her, and I fell back on my heals, my hands pushing tight against my mouth to hold back the screams. He didn't have time to mourn his wife. The Fomorians were still there, fighting against the Guardians that surrounded Quinn and Sloane. One of them pulled Quinn from his knees and summoned his dagger from Sloane's body. He was going to kill Quinn, and I couldn't let that happen.

I rose from my knees with fury in my chest and took the sword with me as I bounded over the stone wall. Ian called after me, but I wasn't stopping. I ran toward the faery holding Quinn and rammed the sword through his neck. He fell to the ground, and Quinn was free—for a moment. Another faery raised a dagger to throw at me, or Quinn, or one of the other Guardians in the small fight at the edge of the field. I ran toward her, my sword held high, and plunged it into her chest. I was showing no mercy. I had just watched as one of my friends had died, and I wouldn't let another fall with her.

Ian and Keelin joined the fighting, and we unleashed our anger, showing no forgiveness, until there were only a couple of Fomorians left standing. Then Keelin flew with Quinn and Ian flew with me, away from the fighting. The battle we were involved with was a small drop in the bucket compared to the fighting that was happening on the other side of the Mound of Hostages. Hundreds of faeries continued with their fight as we flew away and I didn't know if Simon and Finn were still there, or if they'd managed to get away.

We found one of the SUVs that we'd driven to Tara and the four of us jumped in, Ian taking the spot behind the wheel. Part of our planning for this trip had included the instruction that every driver leave the keys in the ignition in case someone needed a quick get away, so we knew we'd find them, even though it wasn't the car we'd come in. Ian turned the key and drove quickly away from the fighting.

"We need to find Lexie," I told Ian. I didn't want to abandon my friend in a hotel, leaving her to wonder if we were okay.

"I talked with Alana as we were running away. She said she was already on her way to Ballecath with Lexie."

I didn't have the energy to respond. I sat back and let my mind fade away softly.

Everyone was completely silent for the four-hour trip to Ballecath. We all seemed shell shocked, unable to speak or think or move. I was worried about Simon and the others, and the image of Sloane falling lifeless to the ground was playing in a never-ending loop in my head.

When we pulled to a stop at the front door of Ballecath, I sprinted out of the car and toward the house. Finn opened the door before I could grab the handle and hugged me to him. I could see Lexie standing behind Finn, her eyes rimmed red from the tears she must have shed.

"He's safe," Finn assured me. "He's upstairs in his room."

I started to go to him, but my legs collapsed under me and I fell to the ground sobbing. The full impact of the night started to hit me with a brutal force. We'd found Simon, but at a great cost. Sloane and countless others were dead. And I had killed so many Fomorians without even thinking twice.

Finn pulled me to stand beside him and walked with me up the stairs, his arm wrapped around my shoulder. I fell onto the bed without bothering to change out of the clothes that were stained with the blood of my friends and enemies. Finn took off my shoes and covered me with a blanket.

"You're safe now," he whispered. "You're both safe."

Chapter Twenty-Two

When I woke up, Simon was lying beside me, completely still, his eyes closed. I was worried that he was just a dream, but it was really him. He was safe and we were at Ballecath, and I wasn't going to let anything bad happen to him ever again.

I ran my fingers along his battered and bruised face. Erin had been able to reduce the damage he'd endured, but the marks were still there.

"Who did this to you?" I asked him quietly as he slept. He didn't answer. He didn't need to.

I curled myself into him and laid my head on his chest. I thought my heart would burst with happiness when I heard his heart beating robustly. He was alive. My Simon was alive and he was lying next to me.

I felt his fingers brush along my arm that was draped across his torso, but when I looked at him, his eyes were still closed. I reached up and grazed my lips against his, breathing in his smell—his earthy smell. His wonderful, earthy smell. I brushed his lips again, and his eyes fluttered open.

"I love you, *cushla macree*," he whispered faintly. Then

his eyes closed again and I cuddled back into him, my head resting on his chest, and fell asleep to the beat of his heart.

※

When I woke again, I was alone in Simon's bed. I rolled over, and in the darkness, I could see him standing at the window, staring off into the distance. It was foggy and dark and I couldn't tell what time of day it was, but it didn't matter. Simon was there and everything was okay.

"Simon," I murmured dreamily, wanting him to come back to me in the bed.

He turned around and I saw that it wasn't Simon. It was Ian. Had I dreamed it all? Had something happened to Simon in the middle of the night? Panic shot through me and I bolted to a standing position.

"Where's Simon?" I demanded.

"He's okay, Maggie," Ian assured me.

"Where is he?" I asked again. I looked at Ian and saw a fierce cut on his lip and a black eye that I hadn't noticed on our ride back to Ballecath. "What happened to you?"

He hesitated and looked uncomfortable.

"Ian, tell me what happened to you."

"I got in a fight," he said without looking at me. "With Simon."

"What? How could you, Ian? How could you after everything he's been through? What could he possibly have done that would make a fight with him even remotely appropriate his first night home?" I couldn't believe Ian could stoop so low and I was angry. "Where is he?" I asked yet again.

"He moved into the caretaker's cottage. Aidan moved

up to one of the apartments behind the house."

"What made Aidan want to move?"

"Simon requested it." He seemed reluctant to elaborate.

"You need to explain what's going on, Ian. Now."

He folded his arms across his chest and looked down at the floor before answering.

"Simon went downstairs a few hours ago and told Aidan that he wanted some separation. He asked if Aidan could move into one of the apartments so that Simon could move into his cottage."

"Where's the cottage? Take me there."

Ian hesitated again, and this time, he looked toward the ceiling as if he were asking the heavens for assistance.

"He doesn't want to see you, Maggie," he said sadly.

"What do you mean?"

"He specifically said that under no circumstances are we to take you to him. He doesn't want to see you."

"That's not possible," I protested. "He loves me."

I saw tears pooling in Ian's eyes. "He asked me to tell you that he's very sorry, but he had a lot of time to think while he was away and he said it would be better if you didn't date anymore."

"He's just confused. He's obviously been through a lot in the past few months."

"He said he thought that you might say that, and he said that he's not confused. He's thought through this decision very carefully. He said," Ian hesitated, his voice cracking. "He said he doesn't love you anymore."

Ian's words blew through the core of me and I felt a burning ache in my chest and in the palms of my hands. How could Simon not want to be with me? He loved me. I loved him. I had never felt so right as I did when I was with Simon.

"I don't believe you," I told Ian, the rage starting to build inside of me.

"I can't lie, Maggie," he reminded me.

"He told me he loved me last night."

"He said he doesn't love you anymore," he repeated. "He said it would be best if you would just move on and leave him alone. He said that maybe, in time, he'll want to see you again—as friends, but not now. Not anytime soon."

I couldn't wrap my mind around what Ian was saying. It had never occurred to me that Simon would stop loving me. How could he? I knew my love for him wasn't something I could just turn on and off at will, so I assumed he couldn't either. What had happened? What had changed his feelings for me?

Simon? I called out silently. *Please talk to me.*

Nothing. No response.

I know you can hear me. Tell me what happened. Why are doing this?

Nothing.

Well, you might have stopped loving me, Simon, but I'll never stop loving you. Never.

Nothing. He was shutting me out completely. He was making a choice to exclude me from his life. Through everything I'd had to face since the faeries came into my life, there was one thing I knew I could depend on, no matter what. Simon would love me. He would always love me. Even when I thought he'd died, I imagined that his love for me went on living. What had changed? How could something so wonderful and real stop existing? How could he stop loving me?

I sat down on the floor and the tears started to fall. He didn't want me. For several months, I thought my life wouldn't be whole again until I found Simon, but when I did find him, he didn't want to have anything to do with me. He was hiding from me. It hurt when I thought Simon had died. I didn't think anything could be worse than that hurt, but the pain caused by the knowledge that he had made a conscious choice to leave me after we'd brought him home was unbearable. When I'd thought he'd died, I knew it hadn't been a choice he'd made. He was making a choice this time and the rejection stung worse than any pain I'd ever felt.

So I cried. I cried for the happiness that had built up inside of me at the sight of Simon in the tunnels, and for the anger I felt toward Balor for hurting his own son. I cried for the pain of the rejection that Simon had inflicted. I cried because it felt like I was never going to be able to have a happy moment in my life again. I had been bottling up so much for so long and letting it out felt dangerous and scary, but Ian stayed with me. Loyal, dependable, sweet Ian.

He rubbed my back while I cried myself out. He brought me a cold washcloth to soothe my swollen face. He brought me one tissue after another, and finally brought me the whole box. He brought me a glass of water when the crying brought on the hiccups. He brought me a caring embrace at a moment when I felt completely unlovable and unwanted. He brought me an island of calm in a raging storm.

And I had nothing to give him in return. I was tapped out. I didn't feel capable of loving anyone ever again.

༄༅༅

"I can't let you slip away," Ian said a few hours later. "I can't let you fall apart like you did last time."

He was leaning against the headboard of the bed, his

arms wrapped around me as I rested my head on his shoulder.

"I'm not going to fall apart," I told him.

"I'm here if you do."

"I know."

He squeezed me closer to him and I felt comforted and safe.

"Ian, did you and Simon fight about me? Is that what happened to your face?"

Yes, he whispered silently.

"Do you care to divulge specifics?"

He shifted his weight and pulled my hand to his, moving his fingers in and out of mine, running the tips back and forth and along my palm. "I got the black eye because I told him he was an insensitive ass for even momentarily entertaining the idea of breaking your heart a second time. I got the cut on my lip because I called him an ignorant bastard."

"Yikes! That was harsh."

"Not as harsh as what he's doing to you."

"Did you hit him back?"

"No."

"Why not?"

"He's in enough pain already."

I knew that was true. I'd seen the cuts and bruises all over his body. Erin was great, but she couldn't take away all of his pain. Her healing powers only went so far toward healing the wounds Balor had inflicted.

"What happened to Simon at the battle in the field last November? Why did Alana say he was dead?"

"I don't know. Simon's refusing to talk to anyone about what happened to him that day, or about anything that happened while he was with Balor."

"Why?"

"I don't know, Maggie. I think maybe he needs time to come to terms with it himself. Our best guess at this point is that someone with powers similar to Finn's convinced Alana that he was dead."

"Is he going to be okay—physically?"

"Yes," he assured me. "I think his physical wounds will heal a lot sooner than his emotional wounds."

"And Lexie's okay?"

"She's fine. She's downstairs—anxious to see you."

"Why didn't she come up?"

"I told her I need some time alone with you."

"Are you being nice to her?"

"As nice as she's being to me."

"So, not very nice then."

He chuckled. "I don't know what it is about that girl that gets under my skin."

"I know the feeling's mutual."

He kissed my forehead and pushed a strand of hair behind my ear. It was an intimate gesture –something Simon had done so often. I tried not to let the feelings of dread and hurt push their way into my heart, but I could already feel the heaviness of those emotions pushing against my ribs.

"So," he said teasingly. "What will it be? King Maggie or King O'Neill."

"Yeah," I said forgetting about the legend of the Stone of Destiny and the sword, "What's up with that?"

"You're King of Tara," he said matter-of-factly. "High King, to be more precise."

"First of all, I can't be a king. I can only be a queen. Second, what does any of that even mean?"

"We're not sure. Finn's looking into it."

"I really don't need another destiny to fulfill," I told him. "I have too much on my plate already."

He chuckled. "It may mean nothing more than you get to use the sword against Balor."

"Why did you ask me to use the sword when we were in the tunnel?" I asked him. It seemed odd at the time. We were facing death, but he'd taken the time to ask my permission.

"It wouldn't work for me," he explained.

"What do you mean?"

"It was fighting against me. If I tried to move it up, it pushed down. I thought maybe if it belonged to you, it was waiting to get permission from you."

"You know, it's really weird how you guys all think that your weapons are capable of feelings and have innate decision making abilities."

He chuckled and we were quiet for a while and he started to rub my back, slowly and rhythmically.

"Ian, is Sloane really dead?"

His hand stopped its journey along my back momentarily. "Yes," he whispered.

I knew it was true. I'd known it when I saw her fall to the ground, but I was still holding out hope that I was wrong.

"Who's going to take her place as leader of the Guardians?" I asked, choosing to focus on the practical aspects of her death rather than the emotional ones.

"Finn. He's already taken the vows."

Of course. That made sense. It wouldn't be the same, though. I couldn't imagine the Guardians without her.

"I lost track of how many people I killed," I confessed. "I hate who I've become, but I didn't even think about it. I couldn't let them hurt any of the people I cared about."

"No one will fault you for what you did last night. As a mater of fact, you were sort of a bad ass. You had a look in your eyes that was really scary."

"That doesn't help."

"You're a warrior, Maggie. Whether you want to be or not, you are. And a damn good one."

Ian and I stayed wrapped in each other's arms for a long time. It had been an emotionally draining couple of days and I needed some quiet time to process everything before I went downstairs to face the rest of the Guardians. As I thought about how difficult the hours and days ahead were going to be, I felt a sudden stab of anger toward Simon. This would have been so much easier to deal with if he were by my side.

You promised I wouldn't have to do this without you, I admonished him. *You lied to me. I thought faeries couldn't lie, but you lied to me. You're making me do this without you.*

I was determined not to cry anymore about Simon's decision. I was determined to be satisfied with the comfort I found in Ian's arms.

Chapter Twenty-Three

I was back at the Hill of Tara, but it was quiet. Too quiet. The sun was shining and I knew that if it were daytime, the place should be swarming with tourists. And that's how I knew it was a dream. I sat down on the damp grass near the Mound of Hostages and waited for Grandma Margaret to join me.

"Nice of you to visit," I said grumpily when I saw her walking toward me.

"I tried to come to you after you'd been bitten by the faery dogs, but I couldn't get through."

"Whatever," I said with enough attitude to leave little doubt that I was, in fact, still a teenager. "It was almost three months before that. You told me you would be there for me when I needed you, but you just abandoned me."

"I'm here now."

"Well I needed you before now."

"Seems to me that you're still alive."

"So that makes it okay?"

"Who are you really mad at, Maggie? Me or Simon?"

"Both. I'm mad at you both. You're both abandoning

me."

"I'm not abandoning you, and neither is Simon."

"Really? He won't even talk to me. Or tell me where he is."

"I think Simon is going through a bit of an existential crisis right now. It's not a reflection on you."

"What does that even mean?" My voice was starting to rise and I wanted to bring it down a notch, but yelling at Grandma Margaret felt good.

"He's questioning the value and meaning of his life. He's trying to figure out whether or not he's a good person and whether or not his life is worth living."

"And how do you know this?" I demanded. "You couldn't tell me whether or not he was alive, but you know he's going through some sort of crisis? You seem to be pretty choosy with your information."

She sat down beside me on the grass. She was pretty spry for a super old lady.

"It was the same when I was alive," she explained with more patience than I deserved. "I could see things others couldn't see, but I never knew why I would see one thing, and not another. Why was I able to see that my neighbor down the road was feeling bad about the fight he'd had with his wife, but I couldn't see that my own grandson was going to fall in a pond and die? I just don't know, Maggie Girl. Things just come to me, or they don't."

"It's your fault that Simon was taken in the first place. You're the reason he went after Balor."

"Why is it my fault?" she asked calmly.

"Because of that dream. You said he had to go to him, but you didn't stick around to explain and Simon assumed you meant that he had to go to Balor."

"I never said anything of the sort."

"Yes you did. In my dream. It was during the blizzard last spring."

"I didn't come to you during that blizzard. I tried, but I couldn't get through."

"You were there," I insisted.

"Maggie, sweet girl, I didn't come to you during the blizzard and I never said Simon had to go to him. Is it possible you just had a regular dream with me in it?"

I'd thought that too. That dream had been distorted and surreal like a regular dream. My dreams with Grandma Margaret were usually very real and vivid.

I took a deep breath and tried to calm myself down. It wasn't her fault that Simon was rejecting me. I should have been yelling at Simon, and not her, but I didn't know where Simon was and he wasn't responding to my telepathic pleas for him to talk to me.

"I'm sorry," I mumbled.

She wrapped her arm around my shoulder and pulled me to her. "I've endured much worse, sweet girl."

We sat together in silence, the warmth of her embrace radiating through me in a way you just wouldn't expect from a dead woman.

"So what's your take on this whole High King of Tara thing?" I asked when I was certain my anger toward Simon wouldn't seep through to our conversation.

"Funny thing, isn't it?"

"Is it?"

"I don't know. I suppose it's funny that they didn't make a provision for a queen. I say we make an executive decision and change the title to High *Queen* of Tara."

"Okay," I told her, "but I still don't know what that means. I got the sword, and that was useful, but does it mean anything else?"

"It means you have *control* of the sword. It will do as

you command, and only as you command."

"Then I don't have to rule over some unknown lost continent or anything?"

She chuckled. "My expertise in that area is a bit muddled. The people of Tara are an extinct group, but I suppose it could be that you're in line to rule the Tuatha De Danann—Danu's people. I guess that would make you fourth in line—if that's true, that is."

"But maybe that's not true," I said, holding out hope that I wouldn't have to rule over anyone but Brandon during my life.

"Maybe it's not true," she conceded.

I sat with Grandma Margaret on the Hill of Tara for a long time that night. She told me about some of my ancestors, and stories about her life. I told her about Brandon and the rest of my family and about Lexie. I needed that break from reality. I needed a little girl-time to chill with my great-great-grandmother.

෨෬

It had been over a week since we'd brought Simon home and he still wouldn't see me. The faeries at the house were pretty tight lipped about where he was and what he was doing with his time. He didn't attend Guardian meetings or come to the house for meals. I didn't know if he'd talked to anyone or not. It was awkward and depressing and weird. Simon had been the sun that kept my world in orbit just a few months before, and now he wouldn't even talk to me.

I saw Erin walking into the courtyard with a grim expression one afternoon and knew she'd probably been to check on Simon.

"Did he talk to you?" I asked her.

She looked up, startled to see me standing in front of her.

"Oh, Maggie, you gave me a start," she responded.

"Is he okay, Erin?" I persisted.

She nodded. "He's going to be okay—eventually. Balor left some pretty deep wounds, both physical and emotional, but I think he'll recover in time."

"Balor must have really done something pretty horrible to him."

"It's not just what Balor did to him, it's what he's done to himself."

I looked at her, horrified. "What's he done to himself?"

"He's made promises he didn't keep."

I shrugged. "Who hasn't?"

"It's different with us. You know that."

I did know, but always seemed to forget that lying and promises were a whole other ballgame with faeries.

"What promises did he break?"

"He promised to keep you safe and to never leave you."

"I'm safe, and he leaving me wasn't his choice."

"He doesn't see it that way, and until he does, it's going to be painful—physically and emotionally."

She rubbed her hand up and down my arm.

"I'm working on him, Maggie. He's going to get better."

"Does he ask about me?" I asked shyly.

She shook her head and looked apologetic. It wasn't her fault that Simon was behaving the way he was. I thanked her and walked toward Ian's apartment.

Lexie and Ian and I met every day to go over the research Lexie had done and compare it to information Ian had gathered. I didn't have much to contribute in the information department, but I would talk out any theories we might have about Balor and how to bring the sadistic blowhole to his knees.

"I really think we need to figure out where Lugh is," Lexie told us for about the hundredth time. "I think he's the key to killing Balor."

"Great idea," Ian said with mock enthusiasm. "Has anyone had an epiphany about how to do that since the last time you suggested it twenty minutes ago?"

"Well, I don't see you coming up with anything better," Lexie defended. "I've dug up more information about the faeries in three months than you did in over two hundred years of living with them. Maybe you shouldn't have spent so much of your time at faery school flirting with all the girls."

"Where did that even come from? I didn't flirt with girls. No more than any other guy."

This was a part of life with Lexie and Ian. They fought. No matter what, they fought. About everything. And I do mean *everything*. I learned to ignore them and ride out the wave. If I tried to stop the bickering, it just built up in both of them and came back a million times worse than if they'd just gotten it out of their system in the first place.

"Maggie," Ian asked impatiently, "are you even listening to a word we're saying?"

Oh, yeah. That was the downside to tuning them out and riding the wave. When they were ready to get back to business, they got snitty with me if I wasn't hanging on their every word.

"Sorry," I told them. "Just preoccupied, I guess."

Lexie sighed impatiently. "I was just saying that we should make a list of possible places Lugh could be."

"That list could go on forever," I said before Ian

could. I knew it's what he was about to say, and I also knew Lexie wouldn't take it well coming from him, but she'd be okay if I said it.

"What about the encrypted email?" Ian asked instead. "Maybe it's time to see if the contacts on the other end have any clues."

"Maybe," I said with hesitation. "Simon told me those contacts were working within the Fomorian organization, though. I don't think Lugh would be hiding out with the Fomorians."

Thinking about Simon sent a prickle up my spine. He should've been there with us, helping us to figure this out. He knew so much more than we did, but he refused to talk with anyone.

"Maybe you should ask Simon," I suggested to Ian.

"I doubt that'll get us anywhere," Ian said, the frustration clear in his tone. Ian was just as angry with Simon as I was and he didn't attempt to hide those feelings.

"So, let's table that for the moment," I suggested. "We also need to figure out who's feeding information to Balor. We're not going to be able to accomplish anything if our every move is being reported."

"Any ideas?" Ian asked.

"You know my idea," I told him.

"I guess I should have been more specific. Any *new* ideas?"

I shook my head.

"Aidan or Alana," he clarified.

I nodded. "I just can't wrap my head around either of them betraying the Guardians, though."

"If you had to pick one of them, which would it be?" Lexie asked. "What's your gut tell you?"

"My gut says Alana wouldn't have done anything to put her own daughter in danger the day we were attacked in the field. If she's the traitor, she would have figured out a way to keep Gracie away."

"Well, that leaves Aidan then," Ian said, stating the obvious.

"I just can't believe it would be Aidan, though. Simon told me once that Aidan's been at Ballecath since before Simon was born."

"I asked Aidan about it," Ian said. "He told me he came to live here when he was a child. His parents died when he was too young to remember and Danu took him in. He stayed in the Underworld until he was old enough to work at Ballecath."

"Well," Lexie reasoned, "I guess that would make him a perfect spy, actually. Nobody would suspect him."

"I think it has to be someone on the fringe of the Guardian organization though," Ian said. "When we go through the ceremony to become Guardians, we have to take vows. One of those vows is to protect Maggie at all cost. If a Guardian were to do anything to harm her, it would be like a lie and it would cause pain."

"But if they pass on the information when they're alone, nobody would see that they're in pain," I pointed out.

"They've also put their lives on the line time after time for the sake of the Guardians. Not only do they fight battles with us, they also work as double agents. That's very risky for them."

"Unless they're triple agents, then working for the Fomorians wouldn't be risky at all."

There was a knock on the door and when Ian opened it, Alana was standing on the other side.

"Sorry to interrupt you guys," she said. "Danu's here. She wants to see you, Maggie."

"Crap," I said out loud, again unable to sensor myself

before expressing my dread at being summoned by Simon's mother.

Ian laughed and hugged me. "As long as the fate of the world is in your hands, she's not going to hurt you."

"I wouldn't be so sure about that," I mumbled.

Chapter Twenty-Four

"Hello, Maggie," Danu said kindly as I walked into the drawing room.

"Hi," I said, trying to manage a smile. I hadn't completely forgiven her for not believing me when I told her that Simon was alive. "Have you been to see Simon?"

She nodded, but the look on her face told me that it hadn't been a good meeting.

"Did he talk to you?" I asked, desperately wanting for someone to be able to break through to him.

"No," she admitted, the sadness deepening as she spoke.

"What happened to him?" I asked with consternation. "What did Balor do?"

"I don't know, Maggie."

"But you know Balor. You know what he's capable of doing."

"I have met Balor. I have spent time with him. I don't think I could say I know him, however. I imagine there's not a faery alive that really knows him."

"You had a child with him," I said. "How can you not know someone you had sex with?"

Her face reddened, but I wasn't sure if it was from embarrassment or anger.

"Balor is a very powerful man. He can make people see things that aren't real. I will not defend my choices, or expound on the details, but please be assured that our brief time together produced nothing more than a child."

I tried not to lose my patience with her—again.

"I do know Simon, however," she offered. "And I know he'll come out of this eventually."

I had to hold out hope that she was right. Even if Simon never wanted me back, I wanted him to be happy again. It was obvious to us all that he was so very unhappy.

"I'm sorry I got upset with you when I saw you in the Underworld."

"No apology necessary," she offered. "But please know, Maggie, that things are rarely what they seem. Sometimes our actions are motivated by goals that may not be immediately obvious."

Well that wasn't ambiguous or anything.

"I asked to speak with you because I want you to know that you can trust Finn as much as you trust Simon or Ian. It's been difficult for all of us knowing that someone close to us is betraying us, but Finn is definitely someone you can trust."

"Okay," I told her. I actually already knew that and wondered why she would want to take the time to tell me.

"I know you would like to talk with Simon about some of your next steps, but seeing as he's not talking to any of us, I think you should share your ideas with Finn. He and I talk on a regular basis, so I'll be able to share knowledge with you through him."

I shrugged. "Okay."

"There's one other *situation* we need to talk about," she continued. "When I thought Simon was dead, I transferred his powers to you. That leaves him at something of a disadvantage."

I had forgotten that she'd given me Simon's powers. Was that what was making him such a grouch since he'd returned?

"Give them back," I insisted without hesitation. I didn't want Simon to be at a disadvantage—especially not because of me.

"It's not that simple."

"Yes it is. Give them back."

"Maggie, think with your head, dear. Not with your heart. You're going to need those powers to help you as you move forward. Let's both take some time to think this through and come up with a solution that will work for both you and Simon."

"You said that if Simon and I got married, you would have transferred some powers to me anyway."

"I transferred more than I had originally planned. When I thought Simon was dead, I didn't see any reason not to. He's also being a little obstinate about the whole situation." No surprise there. "He's refusing to take them back."

It was so frustrating not knowing how to help Simon. I wanted to knock him upside the head and tell him to stop being such a jerk, but since I had no idea how to find him, knocking sense into him would be difficult.

"I also want to apologize to you, Maggie," Danu continued. "I should have believed you when you said you thought he was alive. Maybe if I had, we could have found him sooner." She walked to me and took my hands in hers. "Thank you for loving him as much as you do, and thank you for bringing him home. He's here because of you."

There was a knock on the door and before either of us could respond, Finn opened it and walked into the room.

"I'm sorry to interrupt," he told his mother. "I thought you'd both want to know that there's been a tornado in Denver."

"When?" I asked, a little confused given that it was the middle of the winter.

"It just happened. The Guardians protecting your family called to let us know."

"Are they okay?"

"Yes. They're all okay."

"But it's February. How could there be a tornado in February?"

"We think it was Balor's doing."

"You think? Why don't you know for sure?"

My question made Finn look slightly uncomfortable. "Normally Simon is able to tell us."

"He's not able to tell you now?"

"We haven't asked him."

"Well, go ask him."

Danu intervened. "His ability to hear communications from his father might be diminished because he lacks those powers."

"So *I* should be able to hear Balor then," I reasoned. "Since I have Simon's powers now."

"Do you remember when I gave you those powers? I told you that your own powers would increase only in quantity. The powers already inside of you are stronger, but I did not add any powers that you didn't already have."

"Finn, please go ask Simon if he knows anything," I suggested as politely as I could. "My best guess is that a tornado in Denver in February would have to be the result of Balor's handiwork, but I'd like to know for sure."

He nodded.

Before he left the room, I asked him to stop by Ian's apartment and ask Ian and Lexie to come into the house. Then I went to the television and turned it on. After switching through all of the channels, I realized that a tornado in Denver didn't merit more than two minutes on the news in Ireland. Even then, the only detail that made the event newsworthy was that the tornado occurred in February. There was little info on damage or locations affected.

I ran to my room—Simon's room—and grabbed my laptop. When I walked back into the drawing room, Lexie and Ian were there and Danu had filled them in. Lexie was on her cell phone trying to call her family. Ian was trying to call the Guardians in Denver. Danu was talking with Alana, Aidan and Erin. Finn, presumably, was off talking with Simon.

I logged on to a local news channel in Denver. There were pictures posted of places I had been to many times. The grocery store near my home was a pile of rubble, recognizable only by the sign that was standing unscathed at the entrance to the parking lot. Our high school was damaged enough that I knew it would be quite a while before anyone would be attending classes in the building. So many houses had been completely flattened. The number dead stood at nine, but I knew it was still early. Bodies would be pulled from beneath the rubble and the death count would rise.

"I can't get through," Lexie said in frustration. "How are you able to get through?" she asked Ian with an accusatory tone.

"The Guardians in Denver have satellite phones," he explained after he finished his call.

Lexie nodded and started to sob. Ian walked to her and put his arms around her, pulling her close to him.

"I'll send one of the Guardians over to check on your family," he told her when she finally pulled away. He called one of the Guardians and told them to make their way to Lexie's house.

Huh. Lexie and Ian being nice to each other? The world really was going crazy.

Finn came back in the room and I put away the computer so I could listen to his report.

"Well?" I asked expectantly.

"He said he doesn't think he can hear you *or* Balor over long distances anymore," Finn said. "He's been able to hear you from here when he's at the cottage, but he doesn't think he can hear any farther than that."

"I don't think it matters," I told him. "I'm pretty sure this is Balor's doing. Not only is a tornado in February unheard of, but look at this." I turned the laptop around so he could see the picture I'd pulled up. "This is an aerial photo that was just posted. It shows the path of the tornado. This is my house here," I explained, pointing to the middle of the screen. The destruction of the tornado made an almost perfect circle around my house, extending about a quarter of a mile on each side. "I'd say Balor is trying to send a message, albeit a very unoriginal message since he's already pulled the tornado-in-Denver stunt."

Finn sighed heavily and sat down. "He's not happy that we took Simon."

"But why not just kill my family?" I asked. "If he's angry with me for taking Simon back, why not just kill them? He certainly could if he wanted to, so why didn't he?"

"Because he can," was Danu's simple response. "He's trying to tell you that your fate is in his hands."

※

We all stayed up through the night trying to connect with the people close to us in Denver. Lexie had discovered that a few of our friends had been able to get an Internet connection, even when they couldn't get a phone connection, and were posting updates and pictures on Twitter. We had yet to hear of the death of someone close to us, and we felt the ebbs and flows of anxiety as we waited to account for everyone.

There had been little warning leading up to the tornado and people had scrambled to find a safe place before it hit. Katie Hill had run to a closet with her little sister, only to be ripped out with the force of the wind. They ended up on the foundation of a neighbor's house after it had been blown away, bruised and bloody, but alive. Cameron and Connor Martinez had a neighbor's truck sitting in the middle of their living room. They posted pictures on Facebook and I thought it was bizarre to see pictures still hanging on the one wall in the room that was still standing. Brandon and my dad had been at home when it hit, but my mom had been at the grocery store that had been turned into a pile of rocks. She and several other customers had taken shelter in a walk-in freezer.

I wanted to be home with my family and friends. I wanted to protect them from whatever Balor slung their way.

"Call them," Lexie suggested. "You might feel better if you talk to them."

How lucky am I that I have a best friend who can not only tell that I'm upset, but also knows what, specifically, I'm upset about, and what will make me feel better?

"It's crazy, Maggie," Brandon said. I'd talked with both of my parents and was assured that everyone was uninjured before they put Brandon on the phone. "I mean, we just had that tornado last year, and now we have another one. Plus, this tornado made a big circle around our house. The guy on the Weather Channel said he'd never seen a tornado make a big circle like that."

I did feel better after talking with my family, but I also had a new worry. People noticed how unusual this tornado was, and they were talking about it on the television and on social media. Finn was an amazing guy, but he couldn't alter the memories of every person on the planet. And they couldn't find out—I knew that for certain. If the world knew about Balor and his intentions for humanity, everyone would spiral into chaos, and Balor would win.

అంఙ

I didn't sleep well in the days following the tornado. I was anxious to get updates and information, and worried about what Balor might do next, but I also think I needed less sleep as I moved further away from my human existence. I missed sleeping. It was a good eight hours of oblivion that I could look forward to every day. Eight hours when I didn't have to worry and fret. Eight hours when I didn't have to feel the weight of the world on my shoulders.

After several nights of tossing and turning, I surrendered to my inability to sleep and went outside for a walk. It was three in the morning, so I didn't expect to see anyone.

I found myself walking toward the section of beach where I had spent so much time with Simon. It was normally too painful for me to be there without him, but I found myself inexplicably drawn there on that night.

I stopped cold when I saw someone sitting alone in the sand looking out over the water. Simon. He had lost so much weight and his shoulders were hunched in a way that expressed defeat, but it was Simon. Even in the darkness, even with his altered physical state, I knew it was Simon.

I couldn't decide what to do. I knew he didn't want to see me and I knew he'd want me to turn around and walk away, but I wasn't able to move myself from that spot. I wanted so badly to go to him and wrap him in my arms and tell him that everything was going to be okay—that *he* was going to be okay. But he wouldn't want that. He'd want me to leave, so I focused every bit of energy I had and forced myself to turn away from him.

Don't go, Maggie, I heard Simon whisper in my head as I took my first steps toward the house. *Please stay.*

Chapter Twenty-Five

I turned and looked at him, not certain if I had actually heard him, or if I had just imagined I had because I wanted it so badly. He was still sitting on the beach, his back to me, but as I turned around, he stood and turned to look at me.

"Don't go," he said out loud. My heart pushed it's way into my throat and pressed against my chest in a painful, constricting way. He looked so vulnerable—tired and bruised and ragged. But he was Simon and I loved him. No matter what he'd gone through, or how much he rejected me, I loved him.

"Ian warned me that you were walking this way," he said. "He wanted me to leave so I wouldn't upset you. He really looks out for you, doesn't he?"

I nodded.

"I couldn't bring myself to leave, though," he continued.

"Why?" I whispered, afraid that if I spoke too loud, he'd realize that it was me and want to leave.

"I wanted to see you. I know it's wrong, but I wanted to see you."

"It's not wrong Simon," I said, keeping my voice quiet as I took a tentative step toward him. He looked like a scared rabbit and I didn't want to spook him and send him running away from me.

"I don't want to hurt you anymore than I already have." I took another step and I could see the tears forming in his eyes.

"Then stay," I said as gently as I could while I took another step. "Stay here with me." I was close enough to reach up a hand, slowly, gently, to rub his cheek. I sighed deeply, the feel of his skin against my hand washing away all of the tension and worry and fear. Simon sighed too, and pulled me to him. He reached down as if he was going to kiss me, but backed away. I knew he was struggling, trying to decide whether or not he should. Before I could reach up to him, he leaned back down and pushed his lips against mine, his hand moving to the back of my head, holding me in place as he kissed me. I could feel his neediness and hunger in the kiss—or maybe it was my own neediness and hunger. It wasn't a soft kiss, but forceful and demanding and rough and it felt better than anything I'd felt for three and a half months.

I moved my hand under his shirt and found the skin at the small of his back. He shuddered and I heard him moan softly as he moved his lips to kiss my neck, his own hands pushing off the coat I was wearing, reaching under my shirt and caressing my back, pulling me to him until all of our curves and indentations molded and fused us together.

"Oh, *cushla macree*," he whispered when his lips found my ear, his hand tangled in my hair.

"Simon," I breathed. "I love you Simon."

He stiffened and pulled away from me.

"I'm sorry," he said softly. "I'm sorry."

I'd scared the rabbit. He hadn't run away yet, but I knew he would.

"Don't, Simon," I pleaded. "Don't."

"I'm sorry," he said again. "I don't want to hurt you."

"Then don't push me away."

"I know it hurts now, but it's the best thing I can do for you."

"What did he do to you, Simon?" I asked him. "What did he do to make you hate yourself so much?"

He turned away and was silent for several painful moments.

"I think you should move on," he said without looking at me.

"What does that mean?" I asked, the anger and hurt taking over for the love I'd been feeling a few moments before.

"You and I aren't going to be together—ever," he said, once again turning to face me. "You need to accept that and move on. I think you should be with Ian."

"What?" I asked, stunned at the suggestion.

"I think you should be with Ian. I know you've been holding back because you think there's a chance you and I will get back together, but we won't. You need to move on, Maggie. You need to give Ian a chance."

"Are you pimping me out now, Simon?"

"I'm not creating anything that's not already there."

"What exactly do you think is there?"

"He showed me pictures," he said, a tinge of anger and bitterness in his voice. "He showed me pictures of the two of you."

"Who showed you pictures?"

"My father," he said, his voice rising, the anger overtaking the hurt. "He showed me pictures of you and Ian. Of you hugging each other. Of you kissing each other."

"Oh, Simon," I breathed. How could I respond? He was right. I'd kissed Ian. I'd betrayed Simon and I deserved the hurt he was flinging at me. "I'm sorry."

I saw a single tear slide down his cheek. "You and I don't have a future," he said, his voice softening slightly.

"Simon, I'm sorry I kissed Ian. It was wrong, but are you going to destroy our future together because I made one mistake?"

"It's not the first time, Maggie," he reminded me harshly. "You kissed Luke, too."

"Simon, that's not fair. You know I could never love anyone the way I love you."

"We don't have a future together," he repeated slowly and deliberately. "My feelings for you aren't what they were before."

"What does that mean?"

"Don't make me say it out loud."

"You don't love me anymore? Is that what you're trying to say?"

"I think you should go now. I think you should be with Ian."

"No. I'm not leaving you."

"Then *I'll* leave." He turned and walked away without saying another word. I watched his back until I couldn't see him anymore, then I sunk down in the sand and prayed for lightening to strike me dead. I couldn't bear the hurt of his rejection anymore. I honestly believed the intensity of that hurt was going to kill me. I couldn't imagine feeling worse than I did at that moment.

When I was walking back to the house, I saw Simon standing with someone near the stables. As I got closer, I realized that it was Keelin. He leaned down and kissed her, long and deep, his hands moving along her body and her hands rubbing his back. I felt like the world was crumbling from under my feet. He couldn't be with *me*, but he could be with her. It really was over between us. He wanted to be with Keelin and there was nothing I could do about it. I'd lost him. I'd hurt him one too many times, and I'd lost him.

I ran toward Ian's apartment, wanting to be as quiet as possible as I passed Keelin and Simon and their love fest. I was crying by the time Ian opened his door and he wrapped his arms around me as he pulled me inside.

"You okay?"

I shook my head. "He really doesn't love me anymore."

He made a sympathetic sort of grunt and kissed the top of my head.

"I don't know how to stop loving him, Ian."

He pulled back and wiped away the tears on my cheeks.

"Balor showed him pictures of us together," I said.

"Yes. I saw them."

"You did?"

He nodded.

"How did Balor get pictures of us?"

"I've been wondering about that, too. I have to assume that whoever is betraying us took them. I don't think anyone else would have been able to get that close."

"When I figure out who the traitor is, I'm going to kill him myself, slowly and painfully."

Ian chuckled. "Your sadistic tendencies are shining through."

"Yes, well, the faery community seems to bring out that ugly side of me."

Ian rubbed his thumbs under my eyes, wiping away the last traces of my tears.

"He told you he wants us to be together?" he asked, sadness in his voice.

"How did you know?"

"He keeps telling me the same thing," he admitted. "Every time I try to talk with him about you."

"I think he's hoping that if you and I are together, he won't have to feel guilty about leaving me."

"Is that what you really think?"

"Why else would he do this?" I moved away from Ian and flopped down on the sofa, slamming my open palm down on the cushion beside me. "How can he be so cold? How can he not care anymore? How did he turn it off so easily?"

Ian looked like he was dying to say something.

"What, Ian?" I asked with impatience. "Tell me whatever it is you're holding back."

"I can't," he said with frustration. "I made a promise, and because I'm a faery, and because we are genetically incapable of breaking a promise without pain, I can't tell you." I could hear the bitterness in his voice.

"Simon broke promises he made to *me*," I reasoned angrily, "and he seems fine."

"Does he?" Ian asked, rising to my angry level. "You think he's fine? You think he's not in a tremendous amount of pain, both physically and emotionally?" He doubled over and cried out when he'd finished his sentence.

"Ian?" I asked, the anger quickly replaced with alarm.

He took a few seconds to breath in and out deeply before straightening back to a standing position. "I guess I just crossed a line with that promise I made to Simon."

"You okay?"

He nodded, and his pain seemed to have receded completely.

"I know I can never replace him, Maggie," he said "I don't even want to try." He doubled over again, and shouted out a choice four-letter-word I'd never heard him use before—and I'd heard him use some pretty colorful four-letter-words in the past.

"What did he make you promise him, Ian?" I asked as I knelt beside him.

He looked at me, his misery so obvious. "I can't tell you. He made me promise that, too." He cried out again, and I decided to use that same choice four-letter-word myself.

"He made you promise to try to be with me. To try to get me to want to be with you," I told him, putting the pieces together.

Ian cried out again.

"What?" I asked, alarmed, "You didn't even say anything. I did."

His breathing was ragged and shallow when he spoke. "I promised not to let you find out." He cried out yet again and ran to the bathroom to throw up. He was kneeling on the floor, hugging the toilet, when I walked in.

"Damn him!" I said angrily. "Some friend he is. He doesn't even care how much pain he's putting you through."

"It was my choice to feel this pain," Ian said, defending his friend. "I chose to go against the promises I made."

"He shouldn't have asked you to make those promises in the first place."

He looked again like he wanted to say something, but refrained. I didn't ask. I didn't want to cause him more pain.

Ian stood and took his toothbrush and toothpaste

from the counter beside the sink.

"Can I stay here for a while?" I asked when he'd finished brushing his teeth, not wanting to go back to Simon's room in the main house

"Oh course," he said sweetly.

We sat together on the sofa and Ian turned on the television. I had too much on my mind to pay attention, though. What exactly had Simon made Ian promise that was causing him so much pain? Why would he do that to his best friend? I couldn't ask Ian about it. I couldn't risk having him in pain again.

What did you do to Ian? I asked Simon silently. I was angrier than I had ever been with him. He'd rejected me and caused Ian to experience horrible pain. And he'd kissed Keelin. I wondered if whatever had happened to him while he was with Balor had changed him so much that I'd never get the old Simon back. Could I love the new Simon? I knew I couldn't—not because I was incapable of loving who he had become, but because he wouldn't let me.

What promise did you make him give that's causing him so much pain? I continued, wanting him to feel the full force of my anger. *How could you be so cruel to him? How could you be so cruel to me?*

I didn't expect him to respond, but he did.

Forget about me. I don't love you anymore.

I wanted to cry. He'd never come right out and said he didn't love me before. He'd told Ian to tell me, and he'd implied it when we were at the beach together, but he'd never come right out and said it and the pain of those words, in Simon's voice, was unbelievable.

"Maggie?" Ian asked, pulling me away from Simon and his words. "What's going on?"

I shook my head and he reached a hand up to brush

my hair behind my ear and I leaned in to kiss him. Not because Simon told me to, and not because I wanted to, but because I needed to. I needed him to take away the pain I was feeling. Simon didn't want to be with me anymore and I had to move on and I knew Ian was a good person and I could be happy with him if I let myself.

Ian didn't hesitate to kiss me back, and like my kiss with Simon on the beach, our kiss was hungry and desperate. It was like we were both trying to pull something out of the other, but were coming up short.

I knew we were starting down a very dangerous path. I didn't love Ian the way I needed to—the way I loved Simon. The way Ian deserved to be loved. I couldn't kiss Ian until I could do it without wishing it was Simon.

I pulled myself from Ian's arms and stood abruptly.

"Maggie," Ian said, breathless.

There was a knock on the door and Keelin came in before Ian could get to it. I rolled my eyes and shook my head.

"You have *got* to be kidding me," I mumbled under my breath. Keelin was absolutely the last person I wanted to see. "Fun night?" I asked her peevishly.

"Not particularly," she said, obviously trying really hard to act confused and innocent.

"Don't pretend nothing happened, Keelin. I saw you."

"Saw me what?"

"Kissing Simon."

"What?" she and Ian asked at the same time, both of them shocked.

"I didn't kiss Simon."

"*I saw you!*" I repeated.

"I don't know what you saw, but you didn't see me kissing Simon. I've been in my room all night. *Without*

Simon."

"Then Ian isn't your only twin. Someone who looks just like you was kissing Simon about twenty minutes ago by the barn."

"It wasn't me, Maggie."

"She's telling the truth," Ian said.

"How do you know?"

"She's a fairy," he reminded me in a duh-stupid sort of way.

"Oh, yeah. Sorry."

Keelin rolled her eyes.

"Then who was kissing him? I swear whoever it was looked identical to Keelin."

Ian let out an exasperated sigh. "I think maybe Simon used compulsion to make you think you were seeing the two of them kiss."

"Why would he do that?"

Ian didn't answer and I got the feeling the response he wanted to give was all part of the promise he made to Simon.

I sat down on the sofa and rested my head in my hands. Ian sat beside me and rubbed my back.

"Yeah, I'll just leave you two alone then," I heard Keelin mumble before she left.

"He really doesn't love me anymore." I hated that Simon didn't love me, but in making that admission, a new thought occurred to me. I sat up straight and wiped my eyes before I looked at Ian.

"That means I don't have to be the one to kill Balor."

"We don't know if Lugh is really alive, Maggie."

"No that's not what I mean. If Lugh isn't alive, though, then it still won't have to be me."

"Why do you think that?"

"Because Simon doesn't love me. The prophecy says

that the one Simon loves will kill Balor. If he doesn't love me anymore, I don't have to do it."

Ian shook his head at the heavens and said, "Jaysus Crist, Simon." Then he pulled me toward him and I rested my head on his shoulder.

"It will still have to be you. Trust me on that one."

Chapter Twenty-Six

"You definitely had a rough start to your day," Lexie said after I'd filled her on what had happened with Simon and Ian—and what *hadn't* happened with Keelin. I'd gone straight into her room because I still wasn't ready to go back to Simon's room. She'd been sleeping soundly, but I knew she'd want me to wake her up. If she had had a night like the one I'd had, I'd want *her* to wake *me* up. "Well," she said, "at least you got to make out with two hot guys."

I couldn't help but smile. "Are you admitting that Ian's hot?" I asked her.

"I never said he wasn't hot. You can be hot and annoying at the same time."

"Right now, both he and Simon are hot and annoying."

She nodded. "So any ideas on what promise he made to Simon?"

"Well, I think maybe he's pushing Ian to be with me."

"You said that when you were in Ian's apartment it looked like he was having some sort of internal battle with himself. What if it wasn't a battle with himself, but a battle with Simon?"

"What do you mean?"

"I mean that maybe they were arguing silently."

"About what?"

"I think Simon might have been pushing Ian to be intimate with you, but Ian didn't want to."

"Great. Two guys rejecting me."

"Ian's not rejecting you. He just knows you want to be with Simon."

"But Simon doesn't want to be with me."

"But what if he does?" she asked. "Have you noticed that he's never told you that he doesn't love you to your face. He had Ian tell you once and he told you telepathically the other time."

"And he eluded to it on the beach."

"Yes, but he didn't actually say it. Not when you were face to face with him."

"What's your point?"

"My point is that maybe he doesn't say it in front of you because then you would see that it caused him pain and you'd know it's a lie."

I didn't want to let myself hope that it might be true because it would hurt too much if it turned out not to be, but she did have a good point.

"But why would he lie to me?"

"I think, for some reason, he believes that you're better off without him."

"Maybe," I murmured, hopeful, but completely unconvinced that Lexie might be right.

"So, to sum up: Simon doesn't want to be with you because he thinks he's not good enough for you. You don't want to be Ian because you think you don't love him enough. And Ian doesn't want to be with you because he doesn't think he's good enough to replace Simon. Have I left anything out?"

"Nope. I think that sums it up quite precisely."

"You're all pathetic," she concluded. "And, in case you haven't noticed, single."

"Thanks for the reminder."

ಸಿ⋈

I saw Keelin sitting alone in the courtyard a few days later. Jake was sitting next to her on the outdoor sofa, his head in her lap. I pushed his butt out of the way and squeezed myself onto the end of the sofa. Jake wagged his tail at me. He had gone back to his usual exuberant self since Simon had come back. I guess Simon wasn't hiding from Jake.

"I never got a chance to thank you for helping us get Simon home," I told her. "We wouldn't have been able to do it without you."

"I didn't do it for you," she said. "I'm sorry," she continued kindly. "I just mean that I would have done it anyway—for him."

"Well, thanks."

"And you, too. It was a team effort." The other member of that rescue team was keeping his distance. I hadn't seen Ian for more than a few seconds here and there since the night in his apartment. Evidently, we were both avoiding the other, and doing a fantastic job of it.

"And I'm sorry I got upset and accused you of kissing Simon."

"You had no way of knowing that he was using compulsion."

"I'm still sorry. I shouldn't have been mean."

"I'm sorry, too, for so many things. I hated you for taking him away from me and for not loving him enough. But you didn't take him away. It was Simon who made that choice. And I know now just how much you love him. I've seen you risk your life for him and sacrifice so much."

"With Simon, I don't know if I have a choice. I just want him to be okay."

"I know. I really do understand."

"Does he talk to you at all?" I asked.

She shook her head. "Balor really screwed him up."

"Yeah."

Gracie walked out of the back door of the house and went and sat down on Keelin's lap.

"Gracie?" I said, surprised to see her. "Why aren't you in school?"

"I was sick, so my mom came and got me, but she had to come here for a while and I had to come with her."

"You don't look like you're sick."

"I'm not now, but I was throwing up before."

"Well," I teased her with a smile, "since you're a faery, and faeries can't lie, I guess I'll have to believe you."

"Some faeries can lie," she told me as she absently rubbed Jake's ears.

"Only if they want to feel the pain," Keelin said, joining in with my teasing.

"Mommy can lie and it doesn't hurt her," Gracie said seriously. "Nobody's supposed to know, though, so you have to keep it a secret."

At first, I thought maybe Gracie was lying about the fact that her mom could lie, but then I realized that Gracie couldn't lie and the cogs in my brain started to turn faster than I could process the information it was churning out. And once I started to put the pieces together, I felt the hard burn of betrayal shooting through me.

I stood, the smile gone from my face. "Keelin, take Gracie to your room and keep her there until Ian or I come to get you."

What's going on? Keelin asked silently.

I can't talk now, I told her. I was already on my way to Ian's apartment.

I didn't bother to knock. I went through the door and saw Ian sitting on the sofa, his laptop on his knees.

"What's wrong?" he asked, obviously concerned about my agitated state.

"It's Alana," I told him, trying to contain my anger. "Alana's the traitor."

"What? Why do you think that?"

"Gracie just told me that Alana can lie without pain."

I saw the color drain from his face and he stood up and headed for the main house. I followed close behind and hoped that Keelin had Gracie in her room. I didn't want her to see whatever was about to happen.

We found Alana, Erin, Aidan and Finn in the front drawing room, laughing and talking as if they were all friends. But they weren't. Alana wasn't friends with any of them. Ian crossed the room to where Alana was standing, putting his hand around her throat and pushing her against the wall.

"You bitch!" he yelled at her, his face red with anger. "You bitch!"

"Ian!" Finn admonished, seemingly horrified with Ian's treatment of Alana.

"She's betraying us, Finn," Ian told him without taking his eyes off Alana's face. "She's been lying to us."

"Ian," Finn said in a tone that made it obvious he thought Ian was being ridiculous.

"Let her go, Ian," Erin said gently.

He hesitated, then dropped his hand from her neck and took out his dagger.

"This is crazy," Alana yelled as she rubbed her neck.

Ian and Finn looked at each other and I knew a silent conversation was passing between them. Ian took some slow and steady breaths and turned toward Alana.

"Alana," he said soothingly. "I want you to do as I ask." I saw the panic on her face, but I knew Alana was powerless against Ian. He was using his faery power to get her to tell him the truth. "I want you to tell me if you're able to lie without feeling pain."

She looked like she was fighting the urge to speak, but her attempts at resistance were futile against Ian's faery power. "Yes," she said grudgingly.

Everyone in the room gasped, but Ian continued.

"Have you been giving Balor and the other Fomorians information to use against us?"

"Yes."

"Did you help Balor kidnap Simon?"

"Yes."

"Did Balor teach you how to do the spell to cause Maggie pain?"

"Yes."

"Did he tell you to use the spell on her while she was at Slan Lathair?"

"Yes."

"And at Newgrange?"

She looked at me and smiled deviously. "He didn't tell me to do that one," she said, the full extent of her wickedness coming through. "That one was just for fun."

Ian's hand was again around her neck. "*Feicfidh mé tú a mharú.* You evil, manipulating bitch."

"Ian!" Finn admonished again.

"It's all because of her," Ian reasoned, his voice rising.

"It's her fault that Simon is down in the caretaker's cottage instead of up here with Maggie. It's her fault that Sloane's dead. It's her fault that all of the Guardians died at the Hill of Tara."

Liam walked into the room before Ian could say anymore.

"Um, Maggie," he said uncomfortably, "you have company."

"Company?" I asked, not sure what he was trying to tell me.

"A visitor," he clarified.

I noticed someone was standing just behind him in the hallway and had to take a moment to regain my composure when I realized who it was.

"Hi, Dad."

Chapter Twenty-Seven

Talk about bad timing! I had no idea why my dad was standing in front of me in Simon's home, but it was a really inconvenient time for me to have to deal with his sudden and unexpected presence.

"What are you doing here?" I asked him.

"I'm here to take you home," he answered. I *so* didn't have time to deal with this. "I was going to come here to find out where your school was, but you're not even at school."

"We have a break," I told him.

"No more lies, Maggie," he told me firmly. "I *know*."

Nope. *Definitely* didn't have time for this.

"You know what?"

"I *know*. I know who—what—Simon is. What his family is. What all of these people are," he motioned to everyone standing in the room. "I know what they want you to do. I know why you're here."

I didn't know how he'd figured it out, or *what*, exactly, he'd figured out, but I knew it wasn't good.

Finn, I said resolutely in my head. I knew he was going to need to use his special ability to convince my dad to get on a plane and go back to Denver.

Finn stepped toward my dad, but my dad reeled on him. "No!" he shouted. "Enough! I don't know what it is that you're capable of doing to me, but every time you come around, I forget everything I think I know. It won't work this time. I told my father everything, and if I come back not able to remember, he's going to tell me again. And he's going to keep telling me until I get Maggie home."

"Dad," I said as gently as I could, "I'm not going home. I made the choice to be here."

"Go and pack your things," he said, completely ignoring my protest. "We're leaving."

"Andrew," Finn said in a soothing tone, "Why don't we all sit down and talk."

"No talking," my dad said firmly. "I'm sure I'd come away knowing a lot less if I sit down and talk with you."

"I promise you that I will not alter your memory in any way," Finn assured him.

"And I'm supposed to believe that?" my dad scoffed.

"He can't lie to you, dad."

"You might trust him, Maggie, but I don't."

"He's incapable of lying because of what he is," I told him, not ready to say the f-word (faery) in front of my dad.

"Aidan, why don't you take Alana and fill Liam in on the latest developments?" Finn suggested. Aidan nodded and took Alana roughly by the wrist and pulled her out of the room.

"Andrew, please have a seat," Finn said. I saw that my dad was about to protest, but Finn interrupted him. "Maggie is eighteen. I'm afraid she'll have to make the decision as to whether or not to go with you on her own. Maybe talking will make us all feel better about the situation."

My dad made a noise that clearly meant he doubted ever being able to feel better about the situation I was in.

"Please tell us what you know so I can fill in any gaps. I promise to be as honest with you as I'm able to be."

My dad remained silent.

"Dad, please," I begged. "Please just talk with us."

He looked at me with tears in his eyes and came and wrapped me in his arms. "I was hoping, even as I was flying here, that it was all some ridiculous mistake, but it's not, is it?"

"I don't know, dad. Tell me what think you know and I'll tell you if it's ridiculous."

He pulled away and looked me in the eye for a long time before turning to sit on one of the sofas in the room.

"I've been looking for signs in you and Brandon since you were born—signs that you were a faery." My eyes widened in disbelief. "Grandma Margaret was always telling us stories about faeries. She said we had faery blood in us and that we all had the potential to have faery abilities. I always thought she was a little batty. She would notice things that I'd do and tell me it was my faery blood, but I just laughed it off with the rest of the family," he confessed.

"What did she notice?" I asked, breathless with the realization of what he was telling me.

"Just—stuff," he said. "I didn't want you or Brandon to be exposed to that—to her wackiness. I just wanted you to have normal lives—to be normal kids—and I thought you were. Then you started dating Simon and I saw little things in you, but every time I got suspicious, Finn would make me forget. So I started writing things down. I'd find little notes I'd written, but I couldn't remember writing them, and I couldn't figure out what I was trying to say. A couple of weeks ago, Grandma Margaret came to me in a dream and I asked her about my suspicions. I didn't want to believe it. I spent two weeks denying it, but in my heart, I knew it was all true."

The room was completely silent as we all held our collective breath.

"I know what you want Maggie to do. Grandma Margaret filled me in on that, too. I'm not going to let you sacrifice my daughter for this cause," he told Finn firmly.

"Dad, if I don't do this, every human on the planet will die—including me. I'm doing this—with or without your consent."

"You're willing to risk your life for the sake of a high school crush?" he asked, sounding completely incredulous.

"I'm not doing this for Simon. Not completely. I'm doing this because I know that if I don't, every human on this planet will die."

"Because *they* tell you they will," he pointed out as he stood abruptly and started to pace. "Why do you choose to believe them?"

"Because faeries can't lie—at least not most of them." I thought about Alana and wanted to go to her and pump her for information before I strangled her neck.

"So you want to kill this faery—Balor?" His anger was rising again. "What qualifies you to do that?"

"Andrew, I know how frightening this all must be for you," Erin said gently. "We all love Maggie very much and don't want to see any harm come to her, but we don't see an alternative. If she doesn't kill Balor, he will most certainly kill her."

I could see that the words hit my dad like a slap in the face.

Lexie took bad timing to a new level when she walked into the room.

"You're in on this too?" my dad asked, angry and shocked.

"Oh my god," she said when she saw my dad. "Mr. O'Neill, what are you doing here?"

"I could ask the same of you," he said.

I heard Finn gasp and when I looked at him, I saw that his face was stricken.

"There's been a plane crash."

~ ~ ~

The first jumbo jet hit in Northwestern Australia. The second hit in Southern India, and the third hit in Central Italy. Alana had confessed to Ian that Balor had caused all of the crashes.

"They all hit in a line," Lexie observed as she looked at a map online. "If the line continues, it goes toward northern Ireland—toward us."

"Balor's angry that we have Simon," Ian said. "He's making a point."

"And killing a few thousand people in the process," I pointed out, my stomach churning as the number of dead grew.

The three crashes added up to be the second worst plane disaster in the history of aviation, and each crash had been Balor's doing. Ian had been able to get enough information out of Alana to know that all three crashes had been planned out carefully by Balor and the Fomorians. She didn't know what his plans were after the crash in Italy and that could mean that the three were all he had planned. It could also mean that Alana just didn't know about any plans he might have developed after the last time she spoke with someone in the Fomorian organization.

The news was running around the clock with coverage of the three crashes. As a result of 9/11, terrorism was naturally the first conclusion everyone jumped to. In an unprecedented move, all air travel in most of the world was halted until there was some certainty that more crashes wouldn't take place. Political analysts were looking at the common enemies of the three countries, trying to determine who was responsible for the horrific act of terrorism. There was some concern among those in the news media that the unknown nature of the crashes might spark a fire where tensions were already tense, and wars across the world could be the result.

"He really stirred things up this time, didn't he?" Lexie said, making the biggest understatement in the history of the world.

ಌಂಡ

We were on the football field again, but we were alone. My friends and family weren't lying dead at the side. It was just Balor and me. It was February in the real world, but it felt like fall in my dream. I could smell fresh cut grass and decaying leaves, and there was a slight chill in the air that nipped at my nose.

"I will always be in control," Balor said. "It will always be me. I have more power than any of you combined."

I wanted to tell him that I was getting more powerful, but I was pretty sure I wasn't having an ordinary dream. It felt so real and I believed Balor was actually there with me.

"What do you want?" I asked with more calm than I felt. "Why do you keep coming to my dreams?"

He looked amused. "Well, first of all, because I can. Dream walking isn't a common skill, you know. Your Grandma Margaret can come to you, but even she isn't as strong as I am. I've been putting up barriers; preventing her from visiting you as often as she'd like. Oh, and let's not forget the dream I created where she told you that Simon needed to 'go to him.' You drove Simon straight to me. I've never thanked you for that. How very rude of me."

"The dream you *created?*"

"That's right, Margaret O'Neill. I created it. Just like I am creating this one."

"Why?" I kept my voice steady. I didn't want him to know that he was able to get under my skin.

"To weaken you, of course. That's why I do just about everything. It's why I took Simon. It's why I create tornadoes and mud slides and plane crashes. It's why I'm here now. To weaken you."

"You can't weaken me," I said slowly and deliberately. "I am stronger than you'll ever know."

"We'll see about that." He closed the short distance between us and wrapped his hands around my throat, squeezing until I couldn't breath. There was pleasure in his expression. He was enjoying my pain.

Would I really die if he killed me in my dream? I wasn't willing to find out! I commanded every cell in my body to wake up. I wouldn't let him kill me. I wouldn't give up without a fight.

I was starting to feel dizzy because of the lack of oxygen going to my brain, but I couldn't wake myself up. My body was ignoring my pleas to get away from Balor. I couldn't die. I had to wake up. I had to see Simon again. I had to see my family and Lexie and Ian. I had to have a chance to kill Balor before he could get to any of them.

His hands tightened around my throat and I felt myself slipping away. Balor looked triumphant. He was winning.

"Once you're dead, my son will have no reason to stay with the Guardians. He will join me and together we will take over the world." His grip tightened yet again. "You've been a real nuisance, Margaret. You need to die in order for my son to choose to be with me."

Chapter Twenty-Eight

There was no way in hell I was going to let Balor try, once again, to get to Simon. I wanted, more than anything, for him to be happy and healthy, and that wouldn't happen if Balor got to him. It was the motivation I needed to wake up. I needed to stay alive so I could protect Simon.

Balor was gone. I was in Simon's bed at Ballecath, but I was still choking from Balor's grip.

Ian! I called out silently.

"Maggie?" Nessa was there, beside my bed. "Are you okay?"

I still couldn't get enough air through my lungs. My throat stung as I tried gulping in the air around me.

"What's going on?" Ian was through the door and to the bed with just a few long strides.

"Balor," I croaked.

"Where?" he and Nessa asked simultaneously while they looked around the room.

"In. My. Dream," I said between gulps of air.

They both relaxed. "It's okay," Ian assured me. "It was just a dream."

I shook my head vigorously. "No."

"It's okay, Maggie," Ian said as he sat and put his arms around me. "You're awake now."

I pushed him away. "No. It was real. *He* was real. He said he can dream walk. He tried to kill me."

"Is that possible?" Nessa asked.

Ian shrugged, but looked concerned.

"Yes!" I said loudly, my voice rough.

Finn! I need to talk to you! I cried out silently. I wanted to ask what he knew about dream walking, and if he didn't know anything himself, I wanted him to ask his mother. He came into the room a few minutes later. I told him what happened while Ian and Nessa stood by and listened.

"I've heard of dream walking," he told me. "It wouldn't surprise me if Balor had figured out how to do it. He's very—"

"Powerful," I finished for him. "So you guys keep reminding me."

Finn smiled. "I'll ask my mom what she knows. In the meantime, Ian, maybe it's time for you to have another talk with Alana. Get her to tell you what she knows. She might be able to shed some light on what Balor's up to."

Alana had been kept someplace on the estate since the night we had confronted her. The Guardians were still trying to decide on her ultimate fate.

Everyone left the room and I got dressed quickly. There was absolutely no chance that I was going back to sleep now, so I might as well get dressed and do something productive. It was too early to wake up Lexie to see what she thought about the whole situation, so I channeled my inner-Lexie and started a Google search. Before I could even look at one site, Ian was talking in my head.

Can you come down to the kitchen? We need to talk to you.

On my way, I replied.

When I got the kitchen, I saw a room full of somber-looking faeries.

"What's going on?"

"Alana escaped," Ian said.

I sat down in the nearest chair and rolled my eyes. One crisis after another was crashing into me, and I didn't have time to recover from one before the next one was hitting me hard.

"How?" I asked, more than a little irritated. "I mean, I never thought to ask you guys if she was heavily guarded, but I just figured you were taking care of it." I knew it sounded mean, but I was tired and cranky and frustrated.

"We did have her well guarded," Finn said. "She transformed into a raven and flew away."

I probably should have been shocked, but Balor had just tried to strangle me to death in a dream. It was going to be hard to top that one for a while.

"Nobody knew she could do that?"

Finn shook his head. "We think she might be the Morrigan."

"The what?"

"The Morrigan. A very complicated goddess."

"Alana's a goddess and nobody knew about it?"

"There weren't any signs. If she is, in fact, the Morrigan, she kept it well hidden."

"So what makes you think she is now?"

"The Morrigan can turn into a raven."

"Yeah, that would make it a little suspicious all right. But why does it matter so much. I mean, by the look on all of your faces, you'd think it was the worst news ever."

"Well," Finn continued, "it certainly wouldn't be good news. Let me explain about the Morrigan."

"Please do," I said, bracing myself for bad news.

Finn sat down at the table with me before he continued. "The Morrigan is an inherited title. It's passed on from mothers to daughters and it requires a chain of three to make it whole."

"Three what?"

"Three people. The Morrigan doesn't reach full strength unless there are three women who have gathered together their strength as one. They must be related—mothers, daughters, aunts, nieces. Separately, they still have power, but it's only together that they are truly formidable."

"So do you think Gracie is part of the chain?"

"I doubt it. She's not old enough to make that choice."

"So being part of the Morrigan is a choice? You don't automatically become one when you're born?"

"You have to have inherited the title through your family, but you do have a choice whether or not to join."

"So, who do you think the other two are?"

"There may not be two others, in which case, we might be okay. But if the Morrigan has reached full strength and is choosing to side with Balor, it's not good for our side. If there are already three, and Alana chose Balor over the Guardians, we don't have a chance. That would mean that the Morrigan has already chosen."

"Chosen what?"

"Evil over good."

"I don't understand."

"The Morrigan can be a goddess of life, or she can be the goddess of death. Once a group of three has come together to form the Morrigan, those three must decide which they will be. If the three have already come together, and Alana is siding with Balor, that means they've chosen to be the goddess of death. If they haven't yet come together, there is still hope that the other two will choose life over death."

"If not, we're screwed?" I asked, already knowing the answer to my own question.

Finn nodded. "Both Balor and the Morrigan are extremely powerful. If they're working together—"

"We don't stand a chance."

Finn didn't answer, which was an answer unto itself.

It was time to stop playing nice with Simon—he was going to get his powers back whether he wanted them or not. We needed him to tell us what he knew from his time with Balor, and we needed his help moving forward. I wanted to comfort him and let him ease his way back into the world of the living, but we didn't have that luxury. Every day that Simon spent wallowing in his misery was another day that Balor grew stronger.

"Please contact your mom and ask her to come to Ballecath," I told Finn. "She needs to give Simon back his powers."

Finn nodded and left the room, followed by all the other faeries that were gathered. Once everyone had gone, I saw that my dad was standing across the room near the fireplace. I went and stood next to him.

"This is why I need to stay," I told him. He looked a little pale and shell shocked, but nodded his head.

"I'm staying with you," he announced quietly.

"Dad, it's too dangerous."

"If you stay, I stay. We do this together. Besides, the only way home at the moment is a very slow boat and cross-country train ride. Planes still aren't flying."

I hesitated, but nodded. I knew that if I was in a similar situation, I'd insist on staying, too. Besides, he had a point. It would take forever for him to get home.

"What did you tell mom? About why you're here?"

He blushed and looked a little sheepish. "She thinks I'm on a ski trip with some potential clients in Vermont."

"Lying to mom," I said while shaking my head. "That's a new low."

He folded me into his arms. "Only my love for you and your brother could make me tell a lie of that scale to your mom. She deserves better, but I think telling her the truth would be worse."

I pulled away so I could look at him. "When this is over, I promise never to tell you another lie. I've had to tell you guys so many lies and I hate it."

"Let's start that promise now. There's no need to wait."

I nodded and pressed myself against his chest. He hugged me so hard that I thought I might pass out, but it felt good. For the first time in a long time, I felt a miniscule sliver of safety. My dad knew, and somehow that made everything more manageable.

ഌര

Danu arrived at Ballecath later that morning. I explained to her what I wanted to do and she agreed that it was the only option. Simon had to have his powers back. We desperately needed his help. I walked with her, Aidan, Finn and Ian to the caretaker's cottage. She didn't knock before she went in and Simon didn't look surprised to see all of us standing in his temporary home. He almost looked resigned to whatever fate we'd come to deliver.

Danu walked to him and took both of his hands in hers. They looked into each others eyes and something silent passed between them. I wasn't sure if it was words or feelings or just simple understanding and love.

We'd brought Aidan, Finn and Ian with us in case Simon needed to be held down against his will, but he seemed to accept what was about to happen. I braced myself as the two stood together, holding hands. Danu had told me that the experience for Simon would probably be a lot like frostbite. While a person's extremities are still frozen, there's no feeling, but once they start to thaw, the pain is unbearable. Giving Simon his powers back would thaw out something horrible and ugly inside of him that had grown and developed during his time with Balor, and it was going to hurt. A lot.

It was finished so quickly. After a brief moment, Danu let go of Simon's hands and wrapped her arms around him. He started to sob loudly and tried to push his mother away, but she was relentless. Simon slumped to the floor, and Danu went with him, her arms still surrounding his shaking body. Aidan and Ian turned to walk out of the room, knowing, I'm sure, that they wouldn't be needed. It was done. He had his powers back and the only thing left for Simon to do was to ride the wave of his grief. Finn put his arm around me and started to pull me out of the door with him, but I broke away.

"No," I told him firmly.

"Go away, Maggie," Simon yelled through his sobs. "I don't want you here."

"Too bad," I informed him. "I'm not going anywhere, so you might as well just accept that right now."

"Go away," he yelled fiercely.

I walked to him and crouched down, my hand gently resting between his shoulder blades. Danu looked at me with understanding, rising to leave the cottage with the others. I took her place in front of Simon and wrapped my arms around him, letting him melt into me.

Chapter Twenty-Nine

Simon's pain tore me apart, but leaving wasn't an option. He needed to know that I was willing to support him, no matter what, and I had no desire to leave. As hard as it was to watch him, it would have been harder for me to leave him.

He spent a long time sitting on the floor, his forehead resting on his knees that were pulled up to his chest, his arms draped across his head in a way that made it look like he was trying to protect himself from invisible blows. He sobbed and rocked back and forth and all I could do was keep my hand on his back and assure him that I wasn't going anywhere.

At some point, without me even being fully aware of it, he ended up with his head in my lap, both of his arms encircling my waist, tethering me to him. I leaned against a chair in the room and stroked his hair softly with my fingers until he cried himself to sleep. Even in his sleep, his grip around my waist was firm and I wondered if he was finding any peace at all in his dreams.

It was a cold and rainy day and I could hear the sleet hitting the windows. A fire was blazing in the fireplace, but I knew it would get really cold in the rustic cabin if the fire went out. I hoped Simon would wake up before that happened. I didn't want to move him from my lap and risk waking him up, but I wasn't sure I could keep the fire going without standing up and walking to the fireplace. Before Danu gave his powers back to him, I would have been able to use magic to put more logs on the fire. Without those powers, I wasn't sure. While Simon slept in my lap, I tested my magic and lifted a log off the floor and directed it into the fireplace. Well, as least I knew I'd be able to hurl logs at Balor when he decided to come after me.

Simon slept for a couple of hours, not moving once in that entire time. I didn't know if the worst was over or if it was just beginning. I couldn't even begin to imagine what Balor had done to his only son while they were together, so I had no way of knowing how much healing Simon had to do. I'd never seen Simon in so much pain. I'd never seen *anyone* in so much pain. It was hard to witness, and I thought back to the time when I'd thought Simon was dead and how Ian had stuck by me like glue. I now knew just how difficult that must have been for Ian, and I had a renewed respect for him. He was a good friend. A *great* friend.

When Simon moved one of his hands to rub at the bare skin of my lower back, I knew he was awake. I waited for the sobs to start up again, but they didn't. He sat up after a few minutes and we studied each other for several very long, very quiet moments. He had dark circles under his eyes and his face was so thin. The stubble on his cheeks told me he hadn't bothered to shave for a while, and I knew his messy hair hadn't seen a comb in a few days. My heart broke looking at him, but I reminded myself he was alive. Eventually, the dark circles would go away, and he would put on some weight, and brush his hair, and while he would never be the old Simon I met so many lifetimes ago in Denver, he was alive and he would be okay.

He moved one of his hands to brush along my cheek, his fingers moving across my jaw and to my lips. When he moved in to kiss me, I felt a swirl of conflicting emotions rushing through me. I'd waited so long for Simon to kiss me, but I didn't know what the kiss meant. I no longer had the security of knowing that Simon's kisses were part of the bigger picture that was made up of mutual love and commitment and desire. Now, with Simon, a kiss could lead to regret and self-loathing. It could lead to pain and longing and a release of emotions that were unrequited and shunned. But I still let him kiss me, and I kissed him back. I knew he'd likely pull away at any moment and tell me that kissing me was a mistake, but I decided to live only in that moment, not the possible moments that might come after. I would enjoy the kiss for as long as it lasted, and deal with the fallout when the time came.

But he didn't stop kissing me, and it wasn't long before his hands were searching across my legs and arms, desperate and needy. When he pulled my shirt over my head, I held my breath and waited for the fallout, but it didn't come. He went back to kissing me, his lips moving along my jaw and down my neck, his hands moving across the bare skin of my shoulders and stomach and breasts. I grabbed at the fabric at the bottom of his shirt and pulled it over his head, still expecting him to stop at any moment and realize he didn't want to be there with me, but he didn't stop me. My hunger for him fed his hunger for me, and we took turns removing each other's clothes until we were both sitting on the floor together, completely exposed and vulnerable.

When he finally pulled away, I thought for sure he'd decided he wanted to stop, but he stood and held his hand out to pull me to stand with him, and we walked, hand in hand, to the bedroom in the cottage. I was afraid to say anything, afraid that I might say something that would scare him off and make him pull away from me.

I sat on the soft cotton quilt that was draped across the old iron bed, and he leaned in to kiss me, both of his hands on my hips as he pushed me to lie down. I thought of our first time together, how tender and sweet it had been. It wasn't tender or sweet this time. It was feral and insistent and intense. So intense. The emotions of what we were doing mixed together with the physicality, and I was overwhelmed with it all. It felt good and scary and sad and needy, but I was with Simon and it was okay. It was okay.

When we finished, I still expected Simon to tell me how wrong it was for us to be together, but he didn't. He pulled me to him to lay my head on his chest, and I listened to the thu-thump of his heart and it felt like home in his arms. It felt so right.

"I'm sorry, *cushla macree*," he whispered. I didn't know if he was sorry for what we'd just done, or sorry for the way he'd acted before, or sorry for something else entirely. I was afraid to ask—afraid of his answer—and I fell asleep without knowing.

Chapter Thirty

I wanted to stay in the cottage with Simon and tell him how much I loved him and talk about everything that had happened with both of us during the time we were apart, but there was no time. After a twenty-minute nap, we got dressed and headed back to the main house to start planning with the others.

Simon held a large umbrella and pulled me close, wrapping his arm around my waist while we walked together across the estate.

"Would you rather fly?" I asked. "It would be quicker."

"I'm told you're not able to fly," he said quietly. He seemed shy and unsure and it was a side of Simon I didn't know if I'd ever get used to.

"No. I can't fly. But I can ride on your back."

"That's okay. I'd rather take the slow option and keep you to myself for as long as I can."

My heart swelled with happiness and I wrapped my arm around his waist and hugged him to me.

The umbrella wasn't doing a very good job of covering us both and I was getting wet as we walked. It wasn't long before I started to shiver. Simon stopped and removed his coat, careful to keep the umbrella over me as he did. He helped me pull it on over my own coat, then zipped it up for me before pulling the hood over my head and tying the cord below my chin. He reached both hands up to my cheeks to push wayward strands of hair into the protection of the hood. Keeping his fingers on either side of my face, he coaxed me to look at him and leaned down to kiss me, more tender this time than in the cabin, and even though it was cold, and even though the wind blew so fierce that a piece of sleet would occasionally sneak under the umbrella and sting one of us in the face, I wanted to stay out there forever, alone with Simon.

Before we walked into the door of the main house, Simon pulled me back and held both of my hands in his. He kissed me again and rested his forehead on mine.

"You okay?" he asked tenderly.

"Yes," I whispered. "You?"

He started to answer, then stopped. After a brief pause, he said, "I will be. I know I will be."

He kissed me again, and we walked hand in hand toward the flurry of activity in the main drawing room at the front of the house. I took a deep breath and forced myself to switch gears from what Simon and I had just done to what we needed to do moving forward.

Simon didn't seem surprised to see my dad and I guessed that one of the faeries had alerted him telepathically.

"Mr. O'Neill, I'm so sorry for all of this," Simon said as he stood in front of him. "I'm so sorry that we dragged Maggie into something so dangerous."

My dad looked like he desperately wanted to chew Simon out, but when he finally spoke, he simply said,

"You look like you've had a really rough couple of months."

"Yes, sir," Simon agreed. "It has been that."

"So, what did I miss?" I asked the room at large, wanting to move on quickly before my dad decided he should yell at Simon after all.

Lexie pulled on my elbow. "What happened?" she asked in an insistent whisper.

"I'll tell you when we're alone," I promised.

She nodded and I could see the concern in her expression.

"It's okay," I assured her. "He's better now."

We all sat down and everyone shared the details of any new developments.

The faeries asked me to do what they could not and lie to Gracie about her mom. I told her that her mom had been called away and that we would be taking her back to school the following day. Finn arranged to have two Guardians sent to live at Slan Lathair to protect her because we speculated that Alana might be waiting for Gracie to come of age and become a part of the Morrigan.

"She would still need a third," Keelin pointed out. "Does she have any sisters or nieces or anything?"

"As far as I know, Gracie was her only living family," Erin said.

"Then she'd have to wait for Gracie to have a daughter that came of age," Liam said. "Or, Alana could have another daughter of her own."

"If she and Balor have a daughter together, we're screwed," I said. "That would be one heck of a powerful kid, and without a positive influence, she'd definitely choose evil over good."

"Well, it would be hundreds of years before she was

old enough to make a decision about the Morrigan," Finn said. "I'm hoping we can take care of Balor before that time."

I was hoping the same thing.

Simon was pretty quiet while we were all together, and generally stood staring out a window, his attention far away from the room and the people and the things we were talking about. When Finn asked him to relay what had happened to him when he was gone, he did turn and talk with us, but he offered little information. He said that he remembered leaving our car when we were attacked in the field, but nothing of the battle or being taken. His next memory was of waking up in his cell at the Mound of Hostages. He also told us that he was aware of losing his powers because he could no longer hear me and it became harder for him to fight off Balor and his attempts to bring Simon over to the dark side.

I knew there was a lot more to Simon's time with Balor, but I didn't want to push him. If there were some piece of information that would help us on our way toward defeating Balor, he would have told us. The rest would come out when he was ready.

When we had wrapped up our conversations for the day, I saw Ian head out of the house and toward his apartment. We hadn't had a chance to talk since I'd come back with Simon, and I wanted to check in on him.

I walked into his apartment without knocking and found him lying on his back on the sofa.

"You asleep?" I whispered quietly, not wanted to wake him up if he was, but also knowing he couldn't have fallen asleep so quickly.

He opened his eyes and sat up, smiling when he saw me standing in front of him. He reached out for one of my hands and pulled me to sit next to him.

"He looked a little better this evening than he did when we left you this morning," he said.

I nodded. "He has a long way to go yet."

He nodded.

We were silent. We'd already run out of safe things to say. I could have stood up to leave, but I wouldn't do that to Ian. I'd come to talk about the hard stuff and we were going to talk about the hard stuff. Ian was one of my two best friends, and I would talk about this with him because I knew it's what he needed—what we both needed.

"Simon and I—" I hesitated. "I don't know if it will change anything between us. He hasn't talked to me at all since we came back to the house and he's probably off somewhere making a long list of reasons why it was a mistake, but I wanted you to know."

"I knew," he admitted.

"How?" I asked, incredulous.

"Simon and I talked while we were all in the drawing room—silently."

"What did he say?" I asked, eager to hear Ian tell me something that might give me hope.

"Just that. I asked him directly, and he refused to tell me, but I kept pressing him. I asked him what the status of your relationship was, and he said he didn't know."

I nodded. We were silent again.

After sitting next to each other, listening to the tick-tock of the clock on the wall for what seemed like days, Ian broke the silence. "I'm happy he's back, Maggie—or at least on his way back—and I'd be very happy if you two can figure out how to be together again. I'd say that I want us to go back to the way we were before Balor took Simon, but that's not going to happen. We've developed a bond we can't split, and Simon knows that—and he's okay with that—and I'm okay with being your friend."

"I feel like I've really taken advantage of you," I confessed. "Now that Simon's back, you don't just stop existing and I can't just flip a switch and turn off the feelings I've developed for you."

"We both knew what would happen when we got Simon back. You've never lied to me about your feelings. I will always love you, but I can be satisfied with a platonic love. And someday I'm going to find a woman that makes me wonder what in the heck I ever saw in you."

He smiled, and I smiled, and it felt like maybe things could be okay with us.

Ian pulled me to him and kissed my forehead. I stood to leave, but turned back around before I walked out the door.

"I love you, too, Ian," I told him sincerely. "And it would have been enough."

ಏಡ

Walking up the stairs of the house felt like I was finishing a very long marathon. It had been one of the longest days of my life and I didn't have much energy left. I wanted to sleep, but was afraid Balor would join me and finish what he'd started in my last dream with him. I knew I would have to sleep at some point, but I also knew I needed to go and talk to Lexie, so I had a good reason to put it off a little while longer.

"I've been thinking about something," she told me after I fell face first onto her bed.

"Of course," I mumbled matter-of-factly into the mattress. She was *always* thinking through some problem or another, so it really went without saying.

"I think I should call the grad student from Trinity

College and have him come here. He might be able to help."

I rolled onto my back, the effort feeling monumental. "I don't know if that's a good idea, Lex. We don't even know the guy."

"*I* know him. Besides, this place is teaming with faeries. I think we'd be safe from one human with all of them around."

"I'll talk with Finn," I told her as I fought to keep my eyes open. "He's the head of the Guardians now, so it'll be his decision."

"Well, I was actually thinking that maybe we could just say he's a friend of mine that we're inviting over. We don't have to tell them that we want to bring him here to help us figure all of this out."

I took a deep breath and realized this was a decision that needed to be made only after a considerable amount of thought.

"I'll think it through," I promised.

She nodded and seemed satisfied with my answer.

"So, big change of subject. What happened with Simon at the cottage?"

I rolled onto my side to face her. "He didn't put up a fight when Danu gave him back his powers, but it was really painful for him. It was hard to watch. I kept wondering if maybe we made a mistake—if maybe we should have just let him live the way he was living."

"Do you still feel that way?"

"No. He's doing better now and I think every day will be a little easier. I'm not sure he'll ever be the same, though."

"None of us will," she said kindly. "We've all changed and what we've been through will leave its mark on us for the rest of our lives."

I nodded and knew she was right. I'd changed so much since meeting Simon, and for the most part, I was happy with the changes. I was a stronger person than I had been, but it had come at a dear price.

"At the risk of sounding like a five-year-old, can I sleep with you tonight? I'm afraid of the Boogey Man."

"You mean the Balor Man?" she teased with a smile. "Of course you can sleep in here."

"I should warn you, I usually have invisible faeries watching me while I sleep. You okay with that?"

"Of course, but only because it's you."

I rolled myself off the bed and stood to go change into my pajamas. When I walked into Simon's room, I saw him standing at his desk, looking at a picture of the two of us from another lifetime—from before I knew about faeries and Balor.

"I sort of moved in," I confessed as I stood next to him. He nodded. "I'll move out."

"No," he said quietly, his voice hoarse, "*I'll* move out."

"This is your room. *I'll* move out."

"It's okay. I know Lexie's in your room now, so stay here. You'll want to be close to her."

"Simon—"

"I've already moved my things."

"You're not going back to the cottage though?"

He shook his head. "I'm right next door. We can tap Morris Code messages through the wall," he smiled a little, but I could tell he was forcing it.

It was awkward to be with Simon—unsure of where we stood with each other. It was almost as painful as being apart.

"I'm sorry," he said, a feathery whisper that floated to my heart as he turned away from me.

"For what?" I asked softly, hoping that if I kept my voice calm and quiet, I wouldn't scare him away.

"For so many things," he said, still not looking at me. "For leaving you in the car that day in the field. For not figuring out a way to get away from him. For making you hurt so much when you thought I was dead. For the way I've treated you since I came back. For trying to push you and Ian together." He hesitated. "For what we did earlier today."

I reached out and took his hand in mine. He kept his back to me.

"I'm not sorry for what we did today, Simon, and it hurts me to hear you apologize for it."

"I don't know if we can be together, Maggie. I don't know if I'm ever going to be okay again. I shouldn't have done what I did unless I was certain that we could have a future together."

"I don't know if we have a future, either," I admitted. "And I don't know if we'll ever be okay, and that just makes what we did more precious. When we made love today, it wasn't with the understanding that it was the start of a new beginning. We made love knowing that it might be an ending, and for that reason, we're both going to hold on to that memory a little tighter."

He was silent.

"I'm willing to take it one day at a time, Simon. Are you?"

He turned around and nodded slightly. He pulled me close to him, wrapping me in his arms for a brief moment before pulling away and leaving me alone in his room.

I went back to Lexie's room after changing into my pajamas and climbed into bed with her.

"Do you miss Denver?" I asked her, trying to put off

the inevitable sleep that was closing in on me.

"Every day," she said. "You?"

"God yes! I mean, I love it here. Ballecath is beautiful and everything, but I miss Denver so much."

"Besides the obvious, like family and your old room, what do miss the most?"

I didn't even need to think about it. "Snow. Inches and inches of snow. The snow here is just lame. It doesn't even cover the grass. I miss sitting by a window on a cold, snowy day with a good book and a cup of hot chocolate. I miss playing in the snow and skiing and snow days. I think I even missing shoveling snow."

"I miss freeways," Lexie said. "They have about two miles of true freeway here, the rest of the roads that they call highways are just little two lane country roads. They don't even have a center line."

"I know, right?" I agreed. I told her about the one time I'd driven in Ireland and how I'd nearly made Ian pee his pants with fear. We laughed and she told me some of her own stories about driving while she'd been away and we laughed some more.

"I miss the library, too," Lexie said.

"Of course you do."

"The library at Trinity is absolutely amazing, but I miss going to the local library where I know where everything is and I know all the staff."

"I miss the mountains. They were always just there and I never really paid much attention to them unless I was trying to figure out which direction I was going, but it's weird to look out and not be able to see them."

We started on a conversation about the things we'd miss when we left Ireland and I was surprised by how long both of our lists were. We finally came to the conclusion that we would have to split our time between the two places because we loved them both.

Eventually the conversation died down and Lexie started to drift off to sleep. I thought about Simon. He was back in the main house, just a couple of walls separating us, but it felt like he was miles away. I wanted him there with me, rubbing my back while I fell asleep. I wanted him to be happy and whole again. I wanted us together again. The physical distance between us had shortened significantly, but the emotional distance was massive.

Can you hear me? I asked him from Lexie's bed.

Yes, he responded. It felt so good to hear him in my head again, but I didn't know what to say to him. What was safe to talk about? What would keep him from shutting down?

I can throw and retrieve Bob now. That felt like a safe topic.

I heard.

And I'm king of Tara—or queen or whatever.

Yes.

I have the sword.

Yes.

Silence.

I miss you Simon. I miss us.

One day at a time, he reminded me.

One day at a time.

Goodnight, cushla macree.

The music of those words was enough to lull me into a deep and Balor-free sleep.

Chapter Thirty-One

The first thing I wanted to do when I woke up the following morning was talk with Ian about Lexie's idea to bring the grad student from Trinity to Ballecath. Keep moving forward. That was my new mantra. There was no time to stagnate. Every minute needed to be productive if we were going to bring Balor down.

I walked out of the house and started to go toward his apartment, but saw him playing with Jake in the courtyard.

"I was just coming to look for you."

He was smiling, enjoying the game of tug-of-war he was playing with Jake. "What's up?"

"Can we sit down for a minute?"

He dropped the frayed and knotted rope, leaving a disappointed Jake with nothing to pull, and walked with me to the outdoor furniture surrounding the stone fireplace in the middle of the courtyard. He sat down on the sofa and I sat in the chair facing him, wrapping my arms around my knees as I pulled them to my chest.

"Lexie wants to bring her grad student friend here," I said. "She thinks he might be able to give us some sort of information that could help us."

"I seriously doubt that a human would have any more information than we do."

"I agree, but you never know. What can it hurt? He's one human. There are tons of faeries here at Ballecath so he won't be any sort of a threat. And if he sees or hears something he shouldn't, we can always have Finn mess with his head."

"If I thought there was an actual point, I wouldn't have a problem with bringing him here, but he seriously can't know anything the Guardians don't already know."

"You're awfully sure of yourself."

He leaned toward me, resting his elbows on his knees. "Think about it, Maggie. We've been alive for a lot longer than he has and there are a lot more of us. How could he possibly know anything we don't?"

"Considering we have absolutely no other leads—no piece of information that might help us—he's really our only option for forward progress. Besides, it will keep Lexie happy."

He leaned back on the sofa and crossed his arms defensively. "Well we both know I live to keep Lexie happy."

"What do you guys have against each other?"

"Ours is a bond forged by mutual distaste and loathing."

"Nice," I said with disapproval.

The corner of his mouth twisted into a half smile. "Let's talk to the other Guardians," he suggested. "See what they think."

"Actually, Lexie thinks we should just tell everyone he's a friend she met who's coming for a visit. She doesn't want anyone to know how much he knows."

"And you're pretty determined that we should do

this?"

"I think that if there is even a miniscule chance that he has even the tiniest piece of information that can help us, we should bring him here."

Ian nodded. "Okay. Let's do it then."

I smiled, happy that Ian would trust my judgment enough to go against his own.

I didn't have long to bask in the afterglow of his esteem, however, because Simon came out of the door to the main house and started walking toward us. My first thought was to jump up and run away—fast. I couldn't think of anything more awkward than the three of us sitting alone together, but before I could make a move to leave, Simon had taken a seat next to Ian on the sofa. I still thought about leaving, but decided it would be a total chicken move. I had to face them together at some point. I couldn't put off this moment forever.

"We have to figure out a way to get past this," Simon said. "We need to work as a team right now and we can't do that if we're all avoiding this moment."

Ian and I hung our heads like naughty children.

"We have a job to do and we can't let anything stand in the way of getting that job done," he continued. "We're going to have to put all of this awkwardness aside until after Balor's dead. Agreed?"

Ian and I mumbled, "Agreed," at the same time, still avoiding Simon's eyes.

"Good. Well, to prove your sincerity, I think the three of us should go for a very long walk together."

Ian and I looked at him, confused.

"Ian's filled me in on some of the magic you've developed, Maggie, but we need to find out if you're still as powerful now that my mother has transferred those powers back to me. It might mean that you can't do the stuff you were doing before."

"I don't care," I said as I unwrapped my legs and planted my feet firmly on the ground. "I'm not taking them back. We're better off with *you* having them."

"I'm not asking you to take them back. I just want to know what we're working with. But I also think Ian's right—we need to be careful about who knows, so I was thinking we should take a long walk and test out your magic away from the house."

I was reluctant to show Simon what I could do, worried that he would, in fact, decide I needed some of his power back, but I stood with him and Ian and walked toward the woods behind the house.

We walked for a long time, wanting to make sure that no one would see us. I walked between the two of them when the path would allow us to walk three-wide. Ian kept both of his hands in his pockets, but despite the frigid air, Simon and I both let our hands dangle at our sides. Sometimes, one of us would bump into the other, and our hands would touch and I would think that he was going to grab my hand and hold it in his, but he always moved away. I still left it dangling by my side, wanting so much to hold his hand in mine that I was willing to let it freeze rather than put it in my pocket and risk a missed opportunity.

We found a small clearing in the woods beyond the house and we all stopped and looked at each other. I felt like something of a circus freak on display for the morbidly curious willing to pay a small entrance fee. "Step right up and watch as the defender of the universe shows us the skills that will save all of humanity—or lead to the complete end of civilization, as we know it. It's anyone's guess which way it will go."

I looked at Simon and felt shy. He'd never seen me

do magic before and it made me uneasy to show him. It took me a moment to track down the source of my shyness, but then I realized that I was worried I'd disappoint him. What if he thought I wasn't powerful enough? What if he thought I was too powerful? Simon's opinion of me was so important and I didn't want to let him down.

He came to me and took my hands in his. "Are you okay?"

I am now, I thought to myself, the sensation of finally feeling my hands wrapped in his taking away my anxiety.

"I'm good," I said as I smiled up at him.

I pulled my hands from his and started with the easy stuff, shooting flames out of my fingers. Then I moved on to turning the flame into drops of water, keeping them suspended in the air. I focused on moving the drops together and pushed it to fall on Ian's head.

"Taking this very seriously, I see," he said with sarcasm. I smiled and kept working.

I used compulsion to make a group of birds think that a large stone was actually a pool of water. They dipped their beaks toward the stone and fluttered their feathers as if they were splashing water on them.

"Birds are too easy. They're brains are like the size of a grain of rice. Try using compulsion on me," Ian suggested.

"No. I don't like doing that to you."

"Maggie, we need to know what you can do. We need to know what tools you have at your disposal."

"I don't like that one," I repeated. "I don't like forcing you to tell me something you don't want to tell me."

"Maggie—"

"No, Ian. I'm not testing that one. It's not that important, anyway. If I'm in the middle of a battle, it's not going to be one of my more useful tools."

He didn't push it and I moved on to testing my ability to make myself invisible.

"Well, you couldn't do that one before, so it's not really surprising that you wouldn't be able to do it now that you've lost some of your power," Simon offered when I remained stubbornly visible.

I jumped off a small boulder to test my flying abilities, but wasn't surprised when I couldn't do that either.

"We'll keep working on it," Ian offered.

I nodded and picked up a branch that had fallen from a nearby tree. Several leaves still clung to it, brown and dry and brittle. I turned them into small chestnut birds that took off flying in a low circle. I turned them into pinecones mid-flight, and stacked them in a pyramid at Simon's feet. I reluctantly moved my eyes from the pinecones, up Simon's legs, past his chest, and to his eyes. I couldn't quite make out what I was seeing in them—maybe pride, or shock, or something else.

"Is this about the same as you were able to do before?" he asked.

"I think so."

The barest hint of a smile twitched at his lips. "I'm going to have to be very careful not to make you angry in the future."

"I thought I would be weaker," I confessed. "I thought I would lose all of my magic once we gave you back your powers."

His smile widened. "It would seem that you're strong enough without them."

"I still can't fly or make myself invisible," I reminded him.

"I think it's just a mental block. We'll just need to figure out a way to unblock your mind. Flying without a few layers of steel between you and the ground can be scary."

I had a few ideas about how I could unblock my mind, but since holding hands with me was too much for Simon to take on in that moment, I didn't figure he'd be up for trying what I had in mind.

"You were right not to share this with anyone," he said, splitting his gaze between Ian and me. "It's best if Balor continues to underestimate her."

"But I still don't get it," I said. "I thought the only reason I could do magic before was because I had your powers. I shouldn't still be able to do it—at least not all of it."

Ian and Simon exchanged a look.

"I think the only thing my powers gave you was confidence," Simon said. "Those powers were inside of you all along, waiting for a chance to get out. Having my powers did nothing more than make you believe in them."

෪෬

Lexie's grad student friend, Ronan, arrived at Ballecath the following day. He turned out to be a good-looking, nerdy-type of a guy. He was tall with sandy blond hair that looked like it was a few weeks past needing a haircut, and he alternated between pushing his glasses back to the top of his nose and pushing his hair out of his face. But he was really cute—a sweet, kind face and a nice build. I could see why Lexie might be anxious to have him visit.

Ian suggested that he stay in his apartment while he was at Ballecath so he could keep a better eye on him. We had told everyone that Lexie had a friend coming to visit, but we didn't want to draw attention to his presence, so we kept the details of his visit to ourselves.

"So, Ronan, you're not actually human then," Ian said as the four of us sat in his living room. Lexie looked like she was about ready to fall out of her chair from shock, and I'm sure I must have looked about the same.

"Nor are you," Ronan pointed out.

"No, I'm not."

"But the young ladies are."

"Lexie is human. Maggie is....complicated."

"Oh, I know how complicated Maggie is," he agreed. "I've studied you for a long time, Margaret O'Neill."

"You're not a human?" Lexie asked, the stunned look still dominating her expression.

"Had I known you already hung out with faeries, I would have told you," he explained. "It's not something we go around telling just anyone."

"So, what's your agenda?" Ian asked, the antagonism still trying to fight its way out through his words.

"No agenda," Ronan told him. "I met Lexie when she came to Trinity asking questions about faeries. I didn't know that she actually knew faeries. Until she invited me here, that is. I was more than a little surprised to see that she was inviting me to the Brady estate."

"Is that why you agreed to come? Because it's Finn and Simon's home?"

"No, I agreed to come because Lexie asked me to and I knew she wouldn't have asked unless it was important."

"And now that you're here, what are your plans?"

"I plan to help Lexie figure out whatever needs figuring out."

"And what makes you think you have anything at all to offer in this situation?"

"Knock it off, Ian," Lexie finally insisted. I was surprised she'd let Ian's grilling go on that long, to be honest.

"I don't know why you think you can trust this man," Ian said.

"You didn't seem to have a problem with having here before," Lexie pointed out.

"Because I thought he was a human before," Ian countered. "He's a faery, Lexie. He could be working with Balor."

"I'm not," Ronan interjected matter-of-factly.

"And you brought him *here*!" Ian continued, ignoring Ronan's comment.

"All three of us decided it was a good idea, so don't put this on me," Lexie told him.

"You run away and go off and find this guy and suddenly he knows more than anyone else. Is it his knowledge base you're attracted to, or is it something else entirely?"

"At least he *has* a knowledge base."

"What's that supposed to mean?"

"It means that Ronan didn't lead Maggie to a pack of angry faery dogs on a misguided adventure to the Underworld."

I sat down next to Ronan. "They do this a lot," I explained. "It's best just to let them get it out of their system."

Ronan nodded thoughtfully, then leaned back against the sofa, looking bemused with the situation.

Chapter Thirty-Two

Ronan's appearance at Ballecath made life a little more interesting. When I walked into Ian's apartment the following morning, Ronan was sitting at the kitchen table with a cup of coffee in one hand and a pencil poised above a pad of paper in the other. He had several books strewn across the table and seemed to be taking notes while he was reading. Lexie leaned against the counter, her own cup of coffee held between both of her hands. She had a look of pure adoration on her face as she watched Ronan and I could definitely see why she would be attracted to him. He was Lexie's dream-boy—smart, good-looking, studious. For Lexie, watching a good-looking guy pour over a bunch of books was the same as a normal girl watching a bunch of scantily clad Calvin Klein underwear models playing flag football.

The most interesting part of that scene, however, was Ian. He was leaning against the counter, as well, glaring between Lexie and Ronan. He looked frustrated and hurt and confused and...and...if I didn't know better, I'd say he looked jealous. My first thought was that he was jealous of Lexie's feelings toward Ronan, but that was just crazy talk. After considering it a moment, I decided he must be jealous of Ronan's ability to find answers that Ian hadn't been able to find, despite a lifetime spent with the Guardians.

"So," I said by way of announcing my arrival, "what's new?"

They all three looked my way and were silent for a beat before Lexie started talking.

"Ronan was telling us that Balor's daughter actually had triplets and that two of the triplets drowned, but Lugh survived."

"Which is absolutely ridiculous," Ian interjected.

"Of course you would think it was ridiculous," Lexie countered. "You've been very negative about everything Ronan's had to say since he got here."

"Well if the guy would ever say one thing that wasn't ridiculous, I might not think that everything he said was ridiculous."

"You weren't kidding about these two, were you?" Ronan said quietly.

I shook my head and sat down next to him at the table. He poured me a cup of coffee and explained the triplet theory to me while Lexie and Ian continued slinging verbal assaults at each other.

"Birog is the faery who said Balor's grandson would end up killing him. She also wrote the prophecy about you. Anyway," he continued as he shuffled through some papers on the table, "this is a copy of a letter that was written by Birog saying that two of the triplets died, but that she had rescued Lugh and was hiding him away for his own safety."

"How do you know Birog actually wrote that?" Ian asked, evidently taking a break from tormenting Lexie to torment Ronan.

"Do you want me to go into the specifics or do you want to just trust that I know?"

"I want you to go into specifics."

Lexie shot Ian a dirty look and he shrugged his shoulder in way that made it clear he didn't care if she disapproved of his distrust—or dislike—of Ronan.

Ronan shuffled through his stack of books and papers and pulled a copy of another letter out of the pile. He laid the two letters side-by-side and started with his explanation.

"This letter is a fake," he said, pointing to one. "This one is the real thing," he said, indicating the first letter he'd pulled to show us. "The handwriting in the real thing is fluid and natural. Now look at the fake. You can see where the pen has lifted in unnatural places because the person writing it had to think about how they were writing and the way they were writing it. It's also just a little too perfect. When we write letters, we generally don't think too much about it, and we can sometimes get sloppy. Here, look at the real thing," he held up the paper and we could see the slight messiness to it. "You can also see how the individual letters in the real thing are different. For instance, look how Birog wrote an 'h' here, and compare it to how she wrote an 'h' here." He held the paper up and I could see that one "h" had a loop and the other did not. "Now look at the fake. All of the letters are made exactly the same way every time." We all looked and I saw that he was right. All of the "h's" in the fake had a loop, without variation. "Then there's the paper."

"Okay, we get it," Ian conceded. "But how is it that a letter with information this important went unnoticed by the Guardians? How is that you know about this letter, but nobody else does?"

"Because," Ronan explained, "this letter was written to me. By my mother. I'm Birog's son."

I looked at the top of the letter and noticed that Ronan's name was, in fact, at the top. I definitely hadn't seen that one coming.

"And yet nobody knew Birog had a son?" Ian asked, still a little combative.

"My mother has worked very hard to keep my existence a secret. She has a lot of information about a lot of different things, and there are a lot of people who would want to use me to get to her. She sent me to live among humans when I was a baby so that nobody would know about me."

"And yet you're willing to tell *us* all of these secrets that you're mother was protecting you from," Ian pointed out.

"I was willing to tell Lexie when she visited me at Trinity because I thought she was just a human girl curious about Irish mythology. I'm willing to tell you all now because I know that you're all working with Maggie, and I know that Maggie, given the prophecy about her, wouldn't be working with Balor."

"But you agreed to come here before you knew Maggie would be here. Why would you come all this way for a human girl who was just curious?"

Ronan blushed deeply, leaving little doubt as to what was motivating him. He liked Lexie.

"It's personal," Ronan responded.

Ian scoffed. "Personal? What does that mean?"

"Let it go, Ian," I told him. I noticed that Lexie was blushing, too, but she was also smiling.

"I can't let it go, Maggie. Doesn't this all feel a little suspicious to you?"

"No, it doesn't," I told him.

"How could it not? Why on earth would this guy come all this way just to appease a girl wanting answers about Irish mythology?"

"Because I like Lexie," Ronan explained. "A lot," he quantified as he looked up at Lexie and smiled.

After taking a few seconds to process what Ronan had said, Ian stormed out of the room, muttering, "Jaysus Crist," as he slammed the front door behind him. I followed him, wanting to give Lexie and Ronan some time alone to discuss their mutual crushes.

"Ian, wait," I called after him as he stormed out of the courtyard.

He turned around and faced me, waiting for me to close the distance between us before continuing on his walk.

"Why don't you like Ronan?" I asked.

"It's just all a little hard to believe. I mean, who would come all the way from Trinity College just because some girl he has a crush on asked him to? It's just really suspicious."

I smiled and took his hand in mine.

"Ian, you went all the way to the Underworld and nearly lost your life because of the girl you have a crush on," I reminded him.

"That's different," he said defensively.

"How?"

"It just is," he mumbled.

I gave him a few minutes to calm down before I continued. We walked down the path that led to a stream that wound through Ballecath. It was a nice day—sunny and fairly warm—and it felt good to get a break from everything that was happening at the house.

"I think we should tell Finn and Danu everything Ronan told us," I finally said to Ian, cutting short both of our mental vacations.

He nodded. "I know."

"We should probably introduce Ronan to them."

"Yeah," he agreed reluctantly. I knew Ian couldn't be irrational for too long. It wasn't in his nature.

⁂

Finn took the news from Ronan exactly as I would expect he would—with shocked silence. Danu, on the other hand, had a very different reaction. She didn't seem at all surprised to hear that Lugh might be alive and that Ronan was Birog's son. She just sat at the table in the room and looked at the letter Ronan had produced—the letter his mother had written to him regarding Lugh.

"This doesn't seem like much of a surprise to you," I pointed out to her.

"No," she said reflectively. "No, it's not much of a surprise."

"You knew this?"

"I knew that Birog had a son. I didn't know that Lugh was alive—until now—but I do think I know where he is."

We all looked at her expectantly.

"Why didn't you tell us then?" I asked, incredulous.

"I didn't know it was significant before now. Birog asked me to hide away a child, but she didn't tell me who the child was, or why she wanted him hidden. I had no reason to suspect it might be Lugh."

"Where did you hide him?" Finn asked.

"Here, at Ballecath. I think Lugh's been living at Ballecath for over two hundred years."

Chapter Thirty-Three

Once we'd all pulled our jaws off the floor, Danu continued.

"Birog came to me and asked me to hide a child for her," she explained. "She said she couldn't tell me why, but asked me to trust that the child's life was in danger. I've known Birog since I was a little girl, so I didn't hesitate when she asked me to do this for her.

"I kept the child in the Underworld, living with a servant and his family. I knew that if the child were to live with me, it would put the spotlight on him and make him vulnerable. By hiding him with a servant's family, I was protecting him from whoever might want to bring harm his way.

"When he was older, the child applied for a job here at Ballecath. I felt that it would be a good move for him—a way to keep him hidden away while still in plain site—and I knew he'd be happy here. I knew Finn would treat him well."

"Aidan?" Finn asked, shocked.

"Yes," Danu confirmed. "Aidan."

Well, I definitely didn't see that one coming! Would there be no end to the number of shocking pieces of information I was going to get in one day?

"How can we know for sure?" I asked, not wanting there to be any uncertainty at all in this particular situation.

"I'm sure Ronan can get ahold of his mother and ask her," Danu suggested. "If she understands the situation and how it's playing out, I know she'd be willing to tell us Aidan's true identity."

"I'm afraid that's not possible," Ronan said. "Unfortunately, my mother passed away three years ago. I'm fairly certain it was Balor's doing."

Danu stood and started to pace the room.

"Aidan must be Lugh. There could be no other explanation."

"But we don't know for certain," Ian reminded her.

"No, but it seems there is little room for doubt. How many children do you suppose Birog would hide away?"

Evan Ian had to agree with that. How could it be anyone else? Based on the letter Ronan had produced, and what Danu had just told us, it was a near-certainty that Aidan was Lugh. He was Balor's grandson—and Simon's nephew.

ಐಞ

"Eventful day," Lexie said, seriously understating the current mood. We were sitting together in Simon's room—my room—later that night.

"And then some," I answered.

"Irish mythology is worse than Greek mythology," she said with a chuckle. "You need a color-coded diagram to keep track of all the baby-daddies and baby-mammas."

I laughed.

"So, what's up with you and Ronan?" I asked.

She smiled and blushed. "He kissed me after you and Ian left this morning."

I smiled with her. I was so happy she'd found someone that could make her blush. I'd worried after Max had died whether she'd be able to feel that same way again.

"When I met him at Trinity, I thought he was really cute, but I also thought he was twenty-four and way too old for me. But now that I know he's over two hundred years old, our age difference doesn't seem to matter that much."

"How can twenty-four make a difference, but two-hundred-and-something not?"

She shrugged. "I don't know. It just does. Speaking of our respective love-lives with crotchety old men, how are things going with Simon?"

"They're not," I admitted. "He evidently has a lot of crap to wade through before he's back to his old self again. I'm not even sure he ever *will* be one hundred percent. I'd settle for eighty-five."

"Has he told you what happened when he was with Balor?"

I shook my head. "He won't talk about it."

"I'm sure he just needs time," she offered. I nodded, but I wasn't convinced that time was going to help.

☙❧

Maggie! Maggie!

Simon yelling silently woke me up and I immediately jumped out of bed and ran for his room. I didn't know what to expect when I threw open the door—for all I knew he was being attacked by Balor—but I didn't think about. I didn't hesitate.

Simon was alone, and asleep, but he was breathing rapidly and his brow was furrowed into a deep crease.

Maggie! Come back! Come back, love!

"Simon," I said gently, my mouth close to his ear. "Simon, sweetheart, wake up. You're having a nightmare."

He opened his eyes and when he saw me sitting beside him, I could see the relief. He grabbed my shoulders and pulled me to him in a tight embrace.

"You're here," he hummed. "You're here."

"Yes, I'm here," I assured him.

"I thought you were dead."

"I'm not dead. I'm right here."

He lay back on his pillow and took me with him to lay my head on his chest. I hated that Simon had had a nightmare, but I didn't hate the resulting consequence. I was with Simon and he was willingly hugging me to him.

"Will you stay in here tonight?"

"Yes. Always. I'll stay with you whenever you want me."

"I always want you."

"Always?"

"Always."

ఎఁౘ

I was alone when I woke up and for a moment, I worried that Simon had left me again as he had when he moved into the caretaker's cottage. When I sat up, I noticed that he was standing at the window, looking out at the night sky.

"Star gazing?" I asked, trying to shake my voice of the sleep that wasn't quite ready to leave my body.

He didn't answer, but he did smile as he walked toward the bed and sat down beside me.

"I was worried that you'd left me," I admitted.

"No," he said simply as he wrapped his arms around me. "No."

I cuddled into him, my head on his chest.

"Do you remember what your nightmare was about last night?" I asked.

"No, not really. I know it was about you, but I don't remember the details."

"I didn't know that you could talk to someone telepathically when you were asleep. You were calling out to me, though. Silently."

"Was I?"

"That's how I knew you were having a nightmare. You were calling my name."

"I'm sorry," he said.

"I'm not."

He kissed the top of my head and it felt like warm sunshine wrapping around me.

"Simon?"

"Mm-hmm?"

"I was thinking about something—an idea I had."

"What's that?"

"Well, I know it's really hard for you to talk about your time with Balor, and I was just thinking that maybe you could tell me one thing each day that happened there. It doesn't have to be a bad thing. It could be a really meaningless thing, but maybe if you start by telling me the stupid stuff, you can work your way up to the important stuff. And I really think it'll help if you talk about it."

He didn't answer right away and I thought that maybe the reminder of Balor had upset him and I was angry with myself for even bringing it up.

"I think I could manage three things a day," he finally said.

"Always so competitive," I teased, and he smiled at the familiar joke. Seeing him smile made me smile, but I didn't push him to tell me the three things right away. I knew that if he said he would, he would, and I just needed to give him time.

"One of the faeries guarding me would sometimes sneak me books to read. She risked a lot to do that and it somehow gave me hope that there was a little bit of good in all of the Fomorians—maybe even my father."

I took a deep breath and hugged him tighter, but I didn't say anything.

"The water they brought for me had a funny metallic taste. I didn't like it." He hesitated for a moment before giving me the last piece of information. "And I missed you every single day that I was gone."

"Thank you," I whispered.

He put his fingers beneath my chin and slowly lifted my face to look at his. He bent down and gently kissed me, his lips soft and warm and so, so good. He pulled away, and I thought the kiss was done, but instead he moved his lips to press feathery kisses up my jaw and toward my ear. He nibbled gently on my ear lobe and when he finally pulled away, I was breathless.

"Was that my reward for listening to your three things?"

"I was actually thinking that kissing you was *my* reward."

Chapter Thirty-Four

I found my dad in the drawing room one morning, flipping through a magazine. He was restless. He didn't want to leave me, but it must have been so hard for him to sit around and listen to all of the plans and speculation brought up by the Guardians and Ronan and Danu.

"Have you seen this?" he asked, handing me the magazine he'd been looking through. I took it from him and saw that the cover story was about the mystery of what happened to the Stone of Destiny. The article said that scientists had looked at vandalism, lightning and a variety of other possible explanations, but were still scratching their heads about how a stone that had stood so solid for so many years had just crumbled away.

I sat down on the sofa next to my dad and he draped an arm around my shoulder.

"Yeah," I confessed. "*I* did that."

"I know. Finn filled me in on the stone and the sword and what you went through to find Simon. You're very brave, Mags."

"With some things. Not so much with others. And speaking of bravery, and the lack there of, have you talked to Mom?" I asked.

He nudged my shoulder playfully at my little dig. "I called yesterday and talked with her and Brandon."

"They still don't know you're here?"

He shook his head.

"I'm really sorry about all of this, Dad. I wish it could be easier for you."

"I wish it could be easier for *you*. I get why you feel like you have to do this—I really do—but I just wish I could do something to help. You have no idea how hard it is to watch your daughter plan something so ridiculously dangerous, knowing there is absolutely nothing you can do to help."

"You being here helps," I said. "It really does. I hate that you're so worried and restless, but I'm glad you're here."

He pulled me to him and kissed the top of my forehead. "I saw a copy of *Airplane* in the DVD cabinet the other day. Can you stand watching it again?"

Airplane was my family's go-to movie when we needed cheering up. It was eighty-eight minutes filled with mindless humor, and sometimes that was just what we needed to pull us out of a funk.

"I think it would be great to watch it again," I said.

My dad got up and loaded the DVD into the player and we cuddled together on the sofa to watch. Simon came in after the movie had started and sat with us and I was so glad to see him laugh. Lexie, Ronan and Ian came in to see why everyone was laughing and ended up sitting with us. By the end of the movie, Finn, Erin, Aidan and Quinn had also joined us.

"I think we should watch a funny movie together at least once a week," Erin suggested when the movie had ended. "We all need to laugh a little more than we have been."

Everyone agreed and we made plans to watch *My Cousin Vinnie* a few nights later, then we all started to leave the room, returning to whatever it was we had taken a break from.

"Can I talk with you for minute?" Simon asked when I stood to leave.

"Of course."

"Finn and I have something planned for tonight. Something for you."

"What kind of something?" I asked, wishing he hadn't included Finn in his plans.

"It's a surprise. A good surprise, I think."

"What should I wear?" I was hoping his answer might give me a hint about what we would be doing.

"Anything you wear will be perfect," he said. "But Finn and I will both be wearing suits and ties, if that will help."

༄༅༆

Simon knocked on the door to my room at seven o'clock. He looked so handsome in his perfectly tailored, dark blue suit. He still wasn't back to his old weight, so I knew he must have had some alterations done recently.

"You're beautiful," he said with awe.

I'd had to go to Keelin for help when Simon told me he'd be wearing a suit. Lexie and I had both left our dresses in Denver, and it didn't sound like jeans would be appropriate for whatever we were doing.

Keelin smiled when I told her I needed a dress.

"I know just the one," she said as she walked to her closet.

"You know what we're doing, don't you?"

She nodded enthusiastically. "It's a good thing," she assured me.

The ice that had once encased our relationship was slowly thawing and I no longer felt combative toward Keelin. She, too, was acting more like a friend and less like she was planning to kill me in my sleep.

She pulled a dress from her closet that was absolutely beautiful. The loose-fitting, sleeveless top was made of a shimmery silver material with silver sequins sewn in to make it sparkle even more. The skirt was made of black silk over several layers of black tulle. On Keelin, I'm sure it hit mid-thigh. On me, it stopped just above my knees.

"You're sure this is appropriate for what we're doing?"

"Trust me," she said, and for the first time I felt I actually could, and when I saw the look on Simon's face, I knew she'd made the perfect choice.

"It's Keelin's dress," I told him.

He smiled. "I'll make sure she doesn't ask for it back," he teased. "I'm definitely going to want to see you wear it again at some point."

He took my hand in his without even hesitating, and walked with me to the front door. Finn was there, all of our coats in his arms. After helping me with my coat, Simon put on his, and the three of us walked to a waiting SUV.

We drove for a quite a while, but we didn't go through the main gate, so I was pretty sure we were still on their estate. Finn stopped the car in front of a small stone building and we all walked up the front steps together.

Inside, the building looked like a small chapel. There was one large room with several rows of backless, wooden benches and an alter-like section at the front. Hundreds of candles had been placed around the room, their twinkling glow giving the space a confusingly romantic feel.

We all took off our coats and the two brothers walked with me to the front of the room, standing in the alterish area.

"Sloane talked about doing this before she died," Finn said. "We were actually making plans for it. But then she died, and Simon came home, and our attentions have been elsewhere. But it needs to be done. We owe you at least this much."

I furrowed my brow, still completely clueless about what they had planned.

"You once told Sloane that you're just as much a Guardian as any of us, and you're right. If we were doing this properly, this room would be filled with people watching as we did the ceremony to make it official, but Simon thought you might feel more comfortable if it was just the three of us."

I looked at Simon. He knew me so well. Doing this in front of a crowd of people would have been nerve racking. For a moment, I wondered if I should at least make them wait until we could get my dad to join us, but I knew it would upset him to watch. He wanted me to go back to Denver and resume my normal life, and I knew this ceremony would take me several steps further away from what he wanted.

As it was, the ceremony was beautiful. It passed in a blur, and I can't remember much of what was said, but I do remember promising to devote my life to defeating Balor. It was a commitment I'd already made long ago, so making it again was no big deal. There were times during the ceremony when I knelt before Finn, the head of the Guardians, and there were times when the three of us knelt together, hand in hand, all of us equals. At the end, Finn pushed aside the fabric of my dress just a bit and gave me a tattoo on the left side of my chest, over the symbolic position of the heart. There were no needles involved—just magic—and while it did burn just a bit, it was more pleasant than painful. The tattoo was in the shape of a shield knot and a faint silver color that looked like snow twinkling in the moonlight. Finn told me that all of the Guardians had them and it was a way for us to identify each other. He said that only another Guardian could see the tattoo. It also bound us to each other and sealed our vows. When the tattoo was complete and the ceremony was ending, Finn and Simon both knelt before me, pledging their protection and devotion.

I was happy they thought enough of me to believe that I deserved to be an official member of the Guardians, but it was all just a formality, really. I'd already devoted myself to this cause and each time Balor hurt me, or someone I loved, that devotion grew stronger. I was determined to bring him down, or die trying.

When it was all done, they both hugged me and offered me their congratulations.

"We should have done this long ago," Finn said.

Dinner was waiting for us in a small alcove to the side of the main room.

"We cooked this ourselves," Finn said as he poured wine in all of our glasses.

I figured we'd be eating a cold dinner since they must have brought it out hours before, but Simon waved his hand over each dish as he removed the lid, and a wisp of steam rose from each one.

"You're pretty handy to have around," I teased.

"As are you," he said sweetly.

We started talking and joking around, and it wasn't long before I stopped wishing that Finn wasn't there. He felt like family. They *both* felt like family.

When it was time to go, we pulled our coats back on and headed for the door.

"Hold on," Finn said before we left. "I need to extinguish the candles."

"Let Maggie do the honors," Simon suggested.

They looked at me expectantly and I turned back to the room, pushing soft swirls of billowy air around the open space, blowing out the flame on each of the molten candles.

Simon walked me to my room when we returned to the house.

"Do you have a tattoo?" I asked as we sat on the bed together. I knew Finn said that only other Guardians could see them, but I found it hard to believe that I'd been up close and personal with Simon's chest and had never seen any hint of a tattoo.

He undid two buttons on his shirt and pushed aside the fabric. There, in the same place as mine, was a shimmery silver tattoo. I brushed my fingers along the pattern, still incredulous that I hadn't seen it before. Simon sucked in a sharp breath and pulled away as he buttoned his shirt. We looked at each other and I knew we both wanted to say we were sorry—me for touching him in such an intimate way and making him uncomfortable, and him for pulling away.

※

The next couple of weeks were consumed with strategizing and speculation. Ronan shared all of his theories and documents with the Guardians at the house, and

Finn shared everything the Guardians knew with Ronan. The one thing they hadn't done, however, was tell Aidan their suspicions about his true identity. I think everyone was waiting for some sort of definitive proof before they told Aidan about his heritage and his destiny.

My dad was in the middle of it all, offering suggestions and speaking up when he thought something sounded ridiculous. Simon, on the other hand, was uncharacteristically quiet. He attended every meeting—physically—but his mind seemed a million miles away. He came to his old room every night before I went to bed and told me three things from his stay with Balor, but he was still only able to share insignificant details.

My dad seemed a little on edge one afternoon when we were all in the drawing room, and kept pacing back and forth, alternating his gaze between Simon and the front window.

"Oh, for Christ's sake," he finally said. "Simon, your dog would like to go for a walk with you. He's being very insistent."

Everyone in the room stopped what they were doing to stare at my dad. Had he finally cracked under the pressure of having his daughter involved in such a mess? Was he hearing voices and crap like that?

"Andrew, you can communicate with the animals," Danu stated calmly.

Chapter Thirty-Five

My dad turned his back on the window. "Yes. Yes," my dad said impatiently. "And that damn dog is relentless. Simon, take him for a walk before he drives me insane."

Simon nodded absently, looking confused, and went to where Jake was wagging his tale outside of the front window.

"You can talk to animals?" I asked, dumbfounded.

"Yes."

"How? When? How?" I was more shocked, in that moment, hearing that my dad could talk with animals, than I had been when Simon told me he was a faery. This was my dad. My dad! He couldn't talk to animals. I would have known.

"Are you okay?" Ian asked me, and I shook my head slowly in response.

"You're a faery," Danu said, still very calm. How could she be so calm? My dad was a faery! He could talk to animals!

"Yes," my dad responded unnecessarily. "I'm a faery. I can't do any of the things I could do when I was a kid, though. I fought really hard to make sure I was—normal.

But then Maggie started dating Simon and it all started to come back—everything I knew and everything I'd forgotten."

"And your special faery skill is that you can talk to animals," Danu said.

"Yes."

"Why didn't you tell me?" I asked.

"I didn't want to scare you," he said. "Seems silly now, all things considered, but I didn't want you to think I was insane. I thought if I kept it from you, you'd never realize what you were, or what you could do."

"Why didn't you want to me to be a faery? Were you ashamed of what we are?"

"No," he said, regret in his voice. "I'm not ashamed. I'm just afraid. Grandma Margaret came to me in a dream after you were born."

"Yeah. She likes to do that," I said.

"She told me about the prophecy—about your role in the prophecy. I thought if you never knew who you were, or what you were, you wouldn't have to play your role. I wanted to keep you safe. I even forgot about it myself. I just kept burying everything somewhere in my brain where I couldn't get to it anymore. But now it's coming back."

I nodded. I understood. I'm not so sure I would have done things differently if I were in the same situation. Who wants to know that they're newborn daughter is fated to save the world, or die trying?

"So, I guess I understand why you never wanted us to have a pet," I told him.

"That was one skill I couldn't extinguish—communicating with animals."

"That's because it's your unique faery power. It's stronger," Danu explained.

"And you haven't seen signs that Brandon's a faery?" I asked. Brandon as a human little brother was a handful. Brandon as a faery little brother was too much to even consider.

"I don't know," my dad responded. "He's never mentioned anything, and I haven't seen anything, but it's hard to say."

"Why didn't you ever tell me about any of this?" I asked yet again.

"I actually didn't know a lot. As a matter of fact, the more time I spend here, the more I know just how little I knew."

"But you knew about the faeries. Why didn't you tell me?"

He looked beyond my shoulder and out the window for a long time before he finally spoke. "My father told me that Grandma Margaret's father was beaten for what he knew. For who he was. His parents didn't want to believe that he was a faery, so they beat him. For a while, he believed them. He believed that he wasn't a faery. Then he got married and had children, and he started to see the signs in them—signs that *they* might be faeries. He never beat them, but he was afraid for them, so he forbade them to talk about it. Grandma Margaret grew up believing that faeries were bad and corrupt. She buried who she was for so long that she lost touch of that side of herself. She still believed in faeries, though, and in the prophecy."

He reached a hand toward me and rubbed it along my cheek.

"I started seeing signs in myself when I was younger and I hated it. I hated being different. I didn't want that for you or Brandon. Kids these days are beaten up and ridiculed for wearing the wrong brand of socks. What do you think they would do if they found out you were a faery?"

"Does Mom know?"

Tears welled up in his eyes. "No. I've worked really hard—too hard—to keep it from her."

I fell back into the sofa behind me. It was too unreal. My dad was a faery. He could talk with animals. He was in Ireland with my faery boyfriend and his faery family and his faery friends talking about faery things. I had friends who wanted to disappear off the face of the earth because their dads liked to dance in front of their friends or because they wore clothes that had long gone out of style. *Yeah. Try having a faery dad, then get back to me on how you feel about your embarrassing dads!*

༄༅

"So your dad's a fricking faery!" Lexie said as she walked across the threshold to Simon's room. I had gone upstairs to escape the craziness downstairs. Ian came up soon after me to check to see if I was okay. Lexie came in right after him.

"Thank you, Captain Obvious," I said. It was actually one of her lines, but it felt like a really good time for me to start using it.

"But he's not aging, and he can't fly or do anything faeries can do—well except the whole talking to dogs thing. Even if he did manage to forget that he's a faery, he couldn't stop himself from aging slower than normal."

"The mind is a very powerful thing," Ian told her.

"Yes, the mind *is* a powerful thing, but it can't just make up things that don't exist."

"Danu told me once that if you want so badly to believe something that's true, it would eventually become true," I said, still trying to understand the entire situation myself. "She said that if you're told enough that you have brown hair, you eventually start to believe it and your hair would turn brown."

"That's the most ridiculous thing I've ever heard."

"There are studies to support what she's saying, actually," Ian said.

"I seriously doubt that." She rolled her eyes in a way that said she thought Ian was a complete idiot for even suggesting such a thing.

Ian went to the desk and tapped on a few keys of my laptop before pushing it in Lexie's direction. She took a moment to read through the page before responding. "So that's one study. That proves no—"

Ian pulled away the computer and did some more tapping before shoving it in front of her again.

"So, two studies. That doesn't—"

He tapped again. Lexie took a look and shoved the computer away from her, folding her arms across her chest in preparation for full-on sulk mode. She really hated being wrong.

Before I had to figure out how to break up a brawl between my two best friends, Simon knocked on the open door.

"Can I come in?"

Simon coming to my room every night to share his three things was the best part of my day.

"Of course," I told him, happy to have a reason to end the conversation we'd been having.

"We were just leaving," Ian said while he pulled Lexie by the sleeve of her shirt.

Simon and I went to the bed and sat down beside each other.

"Interesting day," he told me.

"Whenever I think things can't get any weirder, they do. How much weirder are they going to get?"

He shrugged sympathetically before taking my hands in his.

"Pretty cool that he talk to animals, though. I've always wondered what's going through Jake's mind sometimes. Your dad says he mostly thinks about walks with me and sticks."

"Yeah, my dad is a regular Dr. Doolittle."

"Well, at least you don't have to hide anything from him anymore."

He leaned closer to kiss me, then moved to sit behind me, my back to his chest and his arms wrapped around my shoulders. I had noticed that Simon liked to tell me his three things when I wasn't looking at him.

"Sometimes I was afraid I was going to die. I was afraid my dad would get so mad at me that he would kill me, but it wasn't death that I was afraid of. I was afraid of dying because it would mean that I wouldn't be with you. It would mean that I would break your heart."

I rubbed my fingers along his arm and felt the shame rise inside of me. I'd been so upset about finding out that my dad was a faery, but Simon had to worry that his dad would actually kill him. Not in the my-dad's-going-to-kill-me-because-I-stayed-out-too-late sort of way, either, but in a very real and permanent way. It put the situation with my own dad into harsh perspective.

"Sometimes he was nice to me, and those were the times when I was most on guard. I knew he was trying to get me to do something or believe something and when I resisted him, he would be angry."

He hesitated before going on to the third thing.

"I left you that day in the field for no other reason than because he told me to," he whispered softly. I knew he was ashamed.

"Simon—"

"Please don't try to justify it, Maggie. I left you. I shouldn't have left you."

I turned around so I was facing him.

"Finn said that Balor's power over you is stronger than his power over other people because you're his son. He said it's really hard to resist Balor."

He stood abruptly and started to pace.

"He wanted me to kill you," he said from across the room. "And I considered it. I considered it, Maggie. He wanted me to be the one to kill you because then he would know for certain that I was on his side."

"You resisted," I pointed out, hoping I was right. "You've been home for weeks now and you haven't once tried to kill me."

"But I considered it on more than one occasion while I was with Balor."

"Because he was using his faery ability on you, Simon. Not for any other reason. Now that you're away from him, have you thought about killing me?"

He turned his back to look out the window and shook his head.

"And even while you were there, you fought it. You knew it was something *he* wanted—not something *you* wanted."

He kept his back to me and I didn't know what to say. I knew it had been hard for him to share that piece of information with me and I didn't know how to pull that particular demon out of him.

"You said you considered it," I pointed out. "Did you come to a conclusion?"

He didn't answer.

"You knew you couldn't do it. After you considered

it, you knew you couldn't do it."

He whipped around quickly.

"But I considered it," he said, anger rising in his voice.

"But you couldn't do it."

"But I considered it," he repeated.

"Only because your father has an ability to manipulate you in an unnatural way."

He stood before me, silent and vulnerable.

"We need to figure out a way to get you past this. We need to figure out a way for you to see that considering it wasn't an option he gave you."

"I can't get past this because it's not over."

"What do you mean?"

"We're all working very hard to make sure Balor dies—the sooner the better. But when he dies, his powers will all transfer to me."

"Why?"

"Because that's the way it works. When our mother dies, Finn and I will split her powers. It's not something we'll discuss. We won't close ourselves in a room and hash out who will get which power. It will just happen. When my father dies, his powers will all come to me. As far as I know, I have no siblings from my father. My sister died long ago, and there's been no mention of other children, so there is no one to share those powers with."

"Okay, but why is that upsetting you?"

"Because what if having his powers makes me evil? What if it makes me want to kill you, just as *he* wants to kill you now?"

"It won't. When I had your powers, it didn't make me able to do things you're able to do. It just made me more able to do the things I could *already* do. The powers inside of you will be stronger, that's all."

"But I thought about it, Maggie. I thought about killing you. What if having his powers will make me want to do it?"

"It won't. It's not something you're capable of doing."

"How can you not be angry with me about this?"

"Because it's him, not you. I'm angry with him."

He looked at me, and his expression softened just a bit before he walked toward me and put his hands on either side of my face, reaching down to kiss me.

"I love you, *cushla macree*," he whispered as his lips moved toward my ear. "I love you."

I felt a massive release—a huge dam breaking down everything that had been pent up inside of me for months—and I started to cry. Big, fat alligator tears streaming down my face. I cried for all of the times I thought Simon didn't love me anymore—*couldn't* love me anymore. I cried for the pain Simon must have been in when he lied to me and told me he didn't love me. I cried for everything he'd been through when he was with his father and for the wounded soul that now lived inside of him. I cried because I was so happy to hear him tell me he loved me again.

Simon looked at me for a moment, dumbfounded, then pulled me to him.

"Maggie, love, what's wrong?" he pleaded as I cried into his shoulder. I tried to talk, but the emotion was squeezing at my throat, preventing me from saying anything. Each time I tried, it just made me cry harder, so I finally gave up. Simon seemed to understand and he patiently waited out the wave with me, his arms wrapped protectively around my shoulders.

When I felt like I'd calmed down enough that I might

be able to talk, I pulled away and started wiping my tears with the palms of my hands. Simon pulled his shirt over his head and used one of the sleeves to wipe gingerly at the tears on my face. Normally, the site of Simon shirtless would send me into a lustful frenzy, but with his shirt off, I could once again see the bruises and abrasions that still hadn't quite healed from his time with the Fomorians. I felt the tears welling up again when I thought about how horrible that time had been for him, but I concentrated on staying calm, breathing deep and willing myself not to look at the scars that may never heal.

"Are you ready to tell me what's wrong?" he asked soothingly.

"I think it was a lot of pent up stuff actually, and you telling me you love me again just brought it all back up. I feel sad for everything you and I have been through and everything we've lost, and I feel happy that you can tell me you love me again because it gives me hope that we might be okay someday."

He nodded. "I understand. I really do."

"I know you do," I told him as I pulled his hand from my cheek to kiss his palm.

"I want you to be with someone who loves you the way you deserve to be loved."

"I don't want to be with anyone else. I want to be with *you*."

His mouth twisted into a smile. "I was talking about me, actually."

We started to laugh and it felt so natural and real. We needed to start laughing more together.

Simon stopped laughing and looked serious again. "I'm trying, Maggie. I really am. I know we're never going to be what we were a year ago. We can't be. You're not the same person and I'm not the same person, but I love you. At the core of it all, I love you. And I know you love me. And somehow, someday, we're going to figure out how to be with each other, given who we've become. I want to get to know the new you and I want you to get to know the new me, and with any luck, we'll actually still like each other."

"You think I've changed that much?"

"Definitely. Ian's filled me in on a lot of what happened while I was away. You stood up to my mother. You stood up to Sloane. You risked your life to try to find me. I thought you were brave before, but that's nothing to what I see now. You've become a leader among the Guardians. But there are some scars there, too. I can see them. You don't trust me—not completely—and you have a hard edge. You expect things to go wrong. You expect the world to be a bad place."

"You see all that in me?"

"Yes," he whispered as he ran his finger along my jaw.

"And you don't think you'll like me now that I've changed?"

He took in a deep breath and let it out. "It's not that I think I won't like you anymore. I'm worried that you won't like *me*. I'm worried I won't be able to pull myself back to a place where you can like me again."

"I like you now. I like you no matter what."

"No," he corrected. "You love me now, but you don't like me. And that's okay. I don't like myself very much, either. But I'm going to try really hard to work through everything that's happened in the past couple of months so that I can be someone you'd like again."

I wanted to argue with him, but he was completely right. I loved him more than I loved anyone else in the entire world, but I didn't like him. Not completely. Not now. Each day, I saw him inch his way out of the depression that followed him around, but he wasn't there yet.

"I don't like everything about you now. I don't like that you're sad and I don't like that you push me away, but that's okay. I like other pieces of you, and if you end up being depressed for the rest of your life, I'll still be right here, going through it with you. I never want to live without you. I tried it. It's horrible."

"Yes," he agreed, "it was truly horrible."

"So, let's figure out how to get you back from the walking dead—together."

He nodded and kissed me again, and I believed there was happiness in him somewhere. There had to be.

Chapter Thirty-Six

A light breeze blew around me as I stood, once again, on the football field. I turned around quickly, looking for Balor, knowing this was where he liked to set our dreams together. But Balor wasn't there. Grandma Margaret was walking toward me, her grandson's hand in hers.

"Did you choose this setting for our dream?" I asked, unable to keep the panic out of my voice.

"Maggie, sweet girl, what's wrong?"

"*Did you?*" I asked again, more insistent.

"What's wrong, Maggie?" little William asked. "Aren't you glad to see us?"

I looked at his big blue eyes and the ice-cold fear around my heart melted just a little. "Of course I'm glad to see you. Come give me a hug."

I crouched down and opened my arms wide to him. He came to me and hugged me and the panic washed away. I looked over his shoulder and saw Grandma Margaret smiling at us. But then her smile twisted into something sinister. Her face started to contort and a moment later, she was Balor. William went limp in my arms and when I looked down to see if he was okay, I saw that he had become Brandon. I took a deep breath and reminded myself it wasn't real before I placed the fake Brandon on the ground near my feet.

"You!" I said accusingly to Balor. "I *knew* it was you."

"Of course it's me, Margaret O'Neill. It's always me. Every little detail of your life is controlled by me."

"That's not true," I told him forcefully. "You actually control very little."

"I'll control how you die. You can count on that."

"You give yourself a lot more credit than you actually deserve." I knew I was walking in dangerous territory, but this dude pushed all the wrong buttons.

"Did you know that my son once tried to kill me?" he asked conversationally. "Years after his brother took him from me, Simon came back and tried to kill me." He paced around, looking at the black sky above us. "I nearly killed him as a result. He's my son, but if it comes down to a choice between him dying or me dying, I *will* kill him."

"Not if I can help it."

"Oh, you can't. I assure you." He was smiling now—an evil, heartless smile. "Yes, you have the sword now, I am aware of that. I knew you'd come looking for it. That's why I held Simon below the Mound of Hostages. I had plenty of Fomorians there to watch him, and to watch for you. But there was another reason I held him captive in that particular spot. Can you guess it? No, of course not. You are completely ignorant to your own history. The kings of Tara—your ancestors—held their prisoners at that mound until they crumbled into submission. Naturally I saw the irony there and just couldn't resist. But Simon didn't submit. He still refuses to submit. Because he loves you."

He looked at me and smirked. "So you see, my dear

Margaret, you are killing him with your love. Because he loves you, and because you love him, he won't submit to me. He won't fight with me. And that will kill him, ultimately. That is why *you* must die now. Without you, he has no reason to resist me. Without you, my son can live and he can join me without resistance."

He closed the space between us with a few long strides and wrapped his hands around my throat. I reached up and tried to pull him away, but I knew that wasn't the solution. The only way to stay alive was to once again wake myself up.

Balor's face twisted in pleasure and fury. "Funny that I can't use magic when I come to you in your dreams, especially since it is magic that gets me here in the first place."

I closed my eyes and distanced myself from Balor and his hands encircling my neck. I had to stay calm and focus on waking up. I had to push past the wall between sleep and awake in order to survive yet another assault.

Balor laughed. "You can wake yourself up again, but in the end, it won't matter. I'm weakening you. You're afraid to sleep, aren't you? You never know which night I might visit and kill you before you wake. You have the sword, but you will be too tired and emotionally drained to fight me. I'll kill you while you sleep, or I'll kill you when you try to attack me, but either way, you *will* die."

I tried calling out to Simon silently. When he'd called for me in his dream, I'd heard him, and I prayed he would hear me and come to me and wake me up.

Balor was gone. Simon was sitting beside me, saying my name, trying to get me to open my eyes. It worked. Simon had heard me. I sat up in my bed and gasped for air, trying to fill the lungs Balor had emptied.

"What happened?" Simon asked.

I couldn't talk. I couldn't breath.

"Relax. Relax. Take slow, deep breaths." He demonstrated with his own breathing and it wasn't long before I was able to follow his example.

"Did you have a bad dream?" he asked when I was once again breathing normally. I laughed involuntarily because "bad dream" was such an extreme understatement for what had just happened.

"Balor was in my dream again. He tried to strangle me. He said he's going to kill me in my dreams, or he's going to weaken me so I can't kill him."

Simon had my hand in his and started to rub my palm.

"He doesn't know that you're not the one that needs to kill him anymore," he pointed out. "He's going to keep trying to kill you because he doesn't know that Lugh is still alive and will be the one to do it."

"No, I don't think he does know. How could he? So he's going to come after *me* because he thinks I'm the threat."

"We need to tell Aidan. We need to figure this out before he can do anything to hurt you."

༄༅

Putting off the inevitable was not going to alter the situation we were currently facing. We had to tell Aidan about his true identity, and we had to start implementing a plan for him to kill Balor.

"Huh," Aidan responded reflectively when Finn told him. I envied his calm. "So, I guess we better set about figuring out a way for me to kill him."

"Yeah," Finn said with a slight smile. "I guess so."

"I think I need to go back in," Simon said quietly

from his spot near the window in the drawing room. He didn't turn around to face us when he said it, but I didn't need to see his face to know what he was talking about.

"No," I told him firmly.

He turned around and looked at me with sympathy and compassion. "Now is not the time to think with your heart, *cushla macree.*"

I knew he was right, but I hadn't yet been able to develop the skill necessary to separate my heart from my head when it came to Simon.

"Simon, he knows you wouldn't go back to him willingly. He'll know it's a trick," I said.

"Maggie's right," Finn told him. "If I thought it would do any good, I'd take you there myself, but it won't help the situation."

"We don't have a better plan," Simon reasoned. "I might as well go back in."

"I have a better plan, actually," Ronan said. We all turned to look at him, anxious to hear the plan he was developing. "I think Aidan should go in. He's been working as a sort of double agent for the Fomorians for a long time, so it wouldn't be such a stretch for him to show up on their doorstep. He can tell them that he's getting nervous since Alana was discovered as a spy. Then, he can feed us information about how we can get access to Balor and we can bring Maggie as a decoy to kill him."

"But Maggie doesn't need to kill him," Ian pointed out. "Not since we know that Aidan's his grandson."

"No, she doesn't need to kill him, but if Aidan tells Balor that he has news of Maggie coming to kill him, and Maggie shows up, then Balor will be focused on Maggie, and while his focus is elsewhere, Aidan can kill him."

It was very quiet in the room while everyone contemplated what Ronan had said. I couldn't find a hole in his plan, and I was certain that no one else could, either. It made sense. Balor didn't know that his grandson was still alive, so he was only defending himself against me. His guard would be down with Aidan, leaving him vulnerable to an attack.

"Aidan?" Finn asked.

He smiled. "I'll pack my bag, boss."

ೞೆಲ

Aidan left that day to go to the Fomorians, and the rest of us waited around for news from him regarding Balor's whereabouts. We didn't know if it would be hours, days, weeks, or even years. Aidan said he knew how dangerous this mission was, and he knew he could lose his life in the effort of killing Balor, but he said there was no question in his mind as to whether or not it was the right thing to do. The days went by, one after another, with no word from Aidan and everyone was getting restless, all of us ready to move on to the next phase of the plan.

Simon had good days and bad days, and sometimes his moods would switch so quickly that he had good minutes and bad minutes. It was going to take time for him to work through everything going on in his head, and I tried to be as supportive as I knew how, knowing he needed me to be solid and dependable.

Three things? he asked silently from outside of my room a few days after Aidan had gone.

I smiled to myself, happy for the quiet time Simon and I spent in my room each night.

I went to the door and opened it and Simon opened his arms to me. I reached up to kiss him, and he lifted my feet off the floor and carried me toward the bed. I lay down on my back, and Simon lay down on top of me, his fingers brushing the hair out of my face.

"Am I smashing you?" he asked sweetly.

"No," I hummed.

He kissed me softly and brushed his fingers along my jaw.

"He told me that he kept me at the Mound of Hostages because it's where kings of Tara—your ancestors—used to take prisoners to get them to yield. He thought it would be an ironic place to imprison me, and he knew there was a good chance you'd come to look for the sword at some point. He had guards there to watch me, but also to watch for you."

It was the first time he had told me his three things while looking at me, and it made me believe that he was doing better.

"He told me that," I confessed. "When he came to me in my dream."

"That still counts as one of my three things," he said with a smile. I really loved that smile.

"He would watch as the faeries guarding me would torture me. He seemed to enjoy my pain."

I braced myself for what would come next. The last thing would be the worst, and I couldn't imagine anything worse than having your own father take pleasure in your pain.

"When he showed me pictures of you and Ian kissing, I wanted to be angry, but I wasn't. I was happy because I honestly didn't think I was going to make it out of there alive, and I knew that if you could find love with Ian, it would make losing me easier."

I rubbed my thumbs across his temples, my fingers tangled in his hair. "I really hate it when you're selfless,"

I teased. He smiled again. Every day, I was starting to see more and more of the old Simon. Every day, he took a few steps closer to me.

His expression turned serious as he put his hands on either side of my face and rubbed his thumbs along my jaw.

"I've broken so many promises to you," he said. "I promised to never leave you. I promised to never let you go through this on your own. I never want to make another promise to you that I can't keep."

"He forced you to break your promises. It wasn't a choice you had."

"I can't blame him for every one of my failures. I'm responsible for my own actions."

I raised my hands to rest on top of his. "Simon, love, how can you be responsible for your own actions when you were chained to a bed in an underground bunker?"

He moved one of his hands to brush his fingers along my hairline.

"I thought about you ever minute of every day that I was gone. I could hear you, at first, and it broke my heart to know how much pain you were in."

"Why didn't you tell me where you were or that Balor had taken you?" I asked. "I know that after your mom gave me your powers we couldn't hear each other, but why didn't you tell me before that?"

"I tried. You didn't hear me every time I would talk to you. I think it depended a lot on how strong I was, and I was getting weaker every day I was with him. He made sure of that. If he knew we could talk to each other over that much distance, I'm sure he would have found a way to block the messages that we were able to send to each other."

"He thinks you would join him if it weren't for me.

He told me that when he came to my dream. He said the only reason you're not with him is because you love me and you don't want to hurt me."

"If that were the case, I could have gone to him before I met you and fell in love with you. I don't fight with him because he's an evil man."

"As evil as he is, I'm glad I'm not the one to have to kill him," I admitted. "The idea of killing your dad was really messing with my head."

"I'm glad, too."

He ran his fingers along my lips and leaned down to kiss me, gently and cautiously. When he started kissing my neck, the gentleness was very quickly replaced with passion and I felt a nervous excitement in my belly. I pulled at his shirt and moved my hands to rub at his back while he moved a hand to pull under my thigh, encouraging me to wrap my leg around his.

"I love you," I whispered before nibbling at his ear. He let out a soft moan and pulled me to roll onto my side next to him. His hand ran along my hip and to the small of my back. He pulled me closer, every bit of me touching every bit of him. He started kissing my neck again, and eventually pushed my top out of the way to kiss along my collarbone.

"Oh, Maggie, I love you more than I ever thought possible," he whispered into my shoulder.

I pulled away from him, just enough to squeeze my fingers between us so I could unbutton his shirt, pushing it from his shoulders when I was done. I rolled on top of him and kissed his neck and his shoulders and his arms, but when I reached down to pull off my own top, he stopped me and sat up abruptly, forcing me to straddle his legs and sit in his lap.

"I can't," he said, unable to look me in the eye. "I

can't."

I moved to sit next to him while he pulled his shirt back on.

"I'm sorry."

"It's okay, Simon." I knew he could hear the hurt in my voice. His rejection brought me very close to tears.

He finally turned and looked at me. "I'm just not ready," he explained. "I don't want to hurt you anymore and I promised myself I wouldn't do this with you until I could stop hating myself."

It broke my heart to hear him say that he hated himself, but I understood. I didn't agree, but I understood.

"Would it be okay if I stay anyway? I like to hold you when I fall asleep."

"Of course," I said.

Chapter Thirty-Seven

"Balor's at Tory Island," Lexie crowed triumphantly the following morning when she threw open the door to Simon's bedroom. "Oh," she said when she saw Simon and I wrapped in each other's arms. "I'm so sorry."

She turned and started to leave, but I stopped her. "It's okay, Lex. You're not interrupting anything." I was hoping Simon didn't hear the bitter disappointment in my voice.

"Come downstairs, then. We just got word from Aidan and everyone's in the kitchen talking about it."

I kissed Simon quickly, and we both got out of bed to follow Lexie downstairs when a thought struck me.

"Shouldn't you know where your father is already?"

"Why do you say that?"

"I mean, that's your special faery skill. Why did you have to leave me to look for him and why don't you know where he is now?" I felt stupid for not asking this question sooner. Simon could find any object or any person. He should have just known where his father was without going to look for him.

"He blocks me," he said as he led me through the

open door.

"Blocks you?"

"Yes. He knows what I can do, so he blocks me."

"How?" I couldn't imagine ever wanting to hide from Simon, but it would be nice to know how if I ever felt the need.

"I don't know. He's the only one who can do it."

So much for that idea.

"We got word from Aidan and he said Balor's on Tory Island," Lexie explained when we were with the others. "Aidan told him you were planning to ambush him there a week from tomorrow. We're all going to go and pretend we're there for a fight, and when he's distracted, Aidan will kill him." I hadn't seen her this enthusiastic about a project since she started a campaign to encourage composting in the school cafeteria.

"But he'll need the sword," Ronan pointed out.

"I'll take it to him," Simon offered.

"Balor will see you," Liam said.

"What if Aidan pretends to capture Simon and bring him to Balor? Then Simon can give Aidan the sword when Balor's distracted," Finn suggested.

"It's a big sword," I reminded them. "It's going to be hard to conceal."

"I know a way to do it," Simon told us. "I can make the sword invisible."

"How?" Ian asked.

"It's something I saw one of the guards do a few times. She would hide books for me by making them invisible. She taught me how to do it so I could hide the books from the other guards. It's just an extension of the spell we use to make our clothes invisible when we make ourselves invisible."

"Okay," Finn told him. "Work on it before we go."

I was a little overwhelmed by the idea that the time had finally come. The day that Balor would die was no longer an abstract time in the future. It was now. And I felt energized. I was ready to get this over with and move on to the next chapter in my life.

"We'll all go to Tory island and Maggie will be the decoy," Finn reminded us—as if any of us could forget what we had already planned.

"No," my father said boldly from the other side of the room. "She's not going."

"Dad—"

"I'm not arguing about this Maggie. You are not going and that's final."

"Andrew, I'm sure you can understand the necessity of Maggie being there."

My dad turned and faced Finn. "While Maggie's mother and I haven't discussed it specifically, I think I can speak for both of us when I say that we do not allow Maggie to go chasing after sadistic faeries bent on killing her."

I walked over and took my dad's hand in my own.

"I'm eighteen, Dad. I will always listen to your advice before I make my decisions, but they're my decision to make now."

"Don't go," he pleaded. "Don't do this."

"I have to do this. It's the only way."

I could see the resignation in his eyes as they sparkled with tears. "If I go home without you, your mother is going to kill me," he teased.

I hugged him tight. "Then don't go home without me."

"Will you walk with me?" Simon asked the morning before we were to leave for Tory Island. I went with him behind the main house and we walked along the paths that ran through the wooded area on his estate. It was raining and cold and gloomy, but I didn't care, and Simon didn't seem to, either. He didn't say anything for the first half hour of our trip, but it was a comfortable silence.

We stopped along a small stream and he leaned his back against a tree.

"It seems so strange to think that everything my life has been building to is so close," he said. He pulled my hand to rest in his. "I've had over two hundred years to prepare for this, but you've only had one. Are you ready for what's about to happen?"

"I am," I said. "I'm ready. It's easier now that I know I won't have to be the one to kill him. It's not a part of this life that I ever want to get used to, but killing your dad would be worse than killing other faeries. It would be a difficult thing to live with."

"I'm glad you don't have to do it, too, but I wish you didn't have to be a part of it at all. I'm so sorry we pulled you into this life."

I moved closer to him and put my hands on his hips, leaning my body against his. "You didn't pull me into this life. That sword belongs to me and only me. If it truly is the only way to kill Balor, then I would have to give my permission to use it. Without my permission, the sword is useless. My dad or my grandfather could have claimed it, but they didn't. I did. I was a part of this long before I was even born. I was a part of this from the moment my ancestors buried the sword in that block of granite. And when I fell in love with you, my place in the world just solidified, but you didn't pull me in, Simon. I was born to it."

He looked into my eyes and showed me so much of what he was feeling. He loved me—I saw that first—but I also saw his admiration and his confidence in me and I saw his bravery and his strength.

"We're going to get through this—together," he said. "It's the only option I'm willing to consider. We're going to get through this."

I reached up on the tips of my toes and put my hands on either side of his face to pull him to me, each of us reaching across that small space to kiss the other.

"Together," I murmured, my lips still against his. "Together."

Chapter Thirty-Eight

I was ready. I cleaned and dried Bob with great care, infusing him with my strength and determination. I went over every detail of our plan over and over and over again, until it became a part of me. I closed my eyes and visualized everything I needed to do and pictured myself emerging from the battle triumphant. I thought I would be nervous as we set out in the early hours of the morning, but I was ready.

It felt wrong to plan the battle without Sloane. Finn was great as the head of the Guardians, but it just wasn't the same without her. She had worked so hard to get us all to this day, and I wanted her to be able to fly to that island with us. Instead, I would be going to battle with a small piece of fabric from one of her shirts pinned to the inside of my jacket, just over the tattoo on my chest. Quinn had given each of us a piece so that we could take her with us—so we could remember the sacrifices she had made for us.

My dad insisted on going to Tory Island with me. He gave me his word that he would stay out of the way, but it was still hard to let him go. I knew the faeries would do whatever they could to protect him, but I worried it wouldn't be enough. Talking to animals might come in handy in many situations, but I didn't see how it could help him in a battle.

He pulled me aside while we waited for everyone to gather at the front of the house.

"I don't know what's waiting for us after this life, but I *promise* that you will not make the journey alone. If you die tonight, I'll die with you—either because I was defending you, or because I was avenging your death. I won't let you die alone."

"And I promise *you* that we are both coming back to this house alive after Balor's dead." I knew it was a promise that I had no control over, but I figured if I were dead, I wouldn't care. "Besides, we can't die. Mom needs us. It takes a village to raise Brandon, and if we die that poor woman will be on her own with him."

I succeeded in getting him to smile and we hugged each other as if it were our last time. I tried to memorize the feel of my dad's arms around me—just in case.

Lexie stayed behind at Ballecath to wait for us. There was no reason for her to go, and she couldn't defend herself against the Fomorians. Quinn and a few members of my Dream Team stayed behind to protect her.

"Go kick Balor's ass," she said while hugging me. "For Max."

"For Max," I promised before pulling away to join the others.

We flew to Tory Island before dawn. It was only about twenty miles from Ballecath, and I made the trip on Simon's back. I wrapped my arms tight around his chest and enjoyed the closeness for those last few moments before we met face to face with his father. I wanted to believe that we'd all make it back to Ballecath alive, but I knew the odds were against us and I wanted to memorize the feel of Simon against me in case I never had a chance to feel him again.

We landed on the east side of the small island, south of the area known as Dún Bhaloir—Balor's Fort. He'd been hiding in the most obvious spot possible.

The island was home to fewer than two hundred people, and while the village was small, it wasn't far from the section of the island where we would most likely find Balor. When I told Simon that I was worried Finn might have to alter a lot of memories if the villagers saw the faeries in the middle of a fight, he said he suspected they already knew about faeries. The island was the entrance to Balor's home. It would be hard to keep something like that a secret in such a small place. If the villagers did already know about faeries and Balor, they would most likely stay in their homes when they heard the fighting.

We didn't try to keep our visit a secret. We wanted the Fomorians to know we were there. It was part of the plan. Simon landed near a cliff and I climbed off his back. He brushed a strand of my hair that had escaped from my ponytail off of my face and smiled.

"I love you, *cushla macree*—always."

"I love you, too. Always."

He hugged me and kissed me briefly before turning to fly away. I had to believe I would see him again.

I tried to conceal myself as best I could behind a tangle of jagged rocks. Hundreds of Guardians were waiting on the mainland, ready to fight the Fomorians there in order to take the bulk of the battle away from Balor and Aidan and Simon and me. Aidan would pretend to capture Simon, then I would make my presence known, and while Balor was focused on me, Simon would hand Aidan the sword and Aidan would kill him. That was the plan.

I lost track of Simon, but heard him yelling at me in my head.

We're below you. On the rock in the sea.

I looked below the cliff and saw Simon, Balor and Aidan standing on a massive flat rock jutting out of the water a few yards beyond the cliffs. The waves around it were fierce and the only way to get to it would be to fly. Swimming would be impossible since the water around it was churning dangerously.

As I climbed out of my hiding place to make my presence known, I watched as Balor slammed Simon into the rock. The clouds that were twining themselves around the moon weren't enough to keep me from seeing the blood seeping from a gash on the side of his head.

"Si-mon!" I called out. It had been part of our plan—a way to make my presence known to Balor—but instead of flying after me, Balor turned and slit Aidan's throat with his dagger. Aidan fell to the ground and I knew Balor had succeeded in killing his only remaining grandson.

Simon got to his feet and attacked his father with a spell, but Balor deflected it and grabbed his son, his hand on his throat, his dagger ready to strike.

I *had* to help Simon. That was all that existed in that moment. I had to help Simon. The only way to him was to fly, so that's what I did. I was going to fly to him and help him because it was absolutely the only option. I couldn't let his father hurt him any more than he already had.

I ran toward the edge of the cliff and let the air cradle me as I floated toward Simon on the rocky island. Balor threw Simon away from him and cast a spell in my direction, the familiar pain of his spells burning through me. I hit the rocky ground hard, and before I could think of what to do next, I saw Erin, Liam, and Keelin flying toward us. Ian, Ronan and Finn, with my father on his back, flew in right behind them. Our backup plan. The first plan had been for Aidan to kill Balor as soon as he got the sword. I don't think any of us really believed it would happen that easily.

Balor grabbed me roughly around the throat and lifted me off the ground, flying us both back to the island. Simon and the other Guardians followed, but a group of Fomorians blocked them and a fight broke out.

When Balor touched down, we were standing in front of a smirking Alana. Balor threw me to the ground beside her feet and she grabbed my arm, pulling me to stand beside her.

"Keep her here while I convince my son to join us," Balor said as he strolled away.

I made a move to grab Bob, but Alana took both of my hands in hers and squeezed painfully.

"Do you actually believe that you and your pathetic dagger have any chance against me? I'm more powerful that you'll ever know. I'm the Morrigan."

Well, she settled that debate for us.

"If you are the Morrigan, you won't be at your strongest until there are three of you."

"Oh, someone's been doing her homework," she taunted. "But even without the others, I'm more powerful than you, little human."

I wasn't convinced she was, actually. I'd been working on my magic and getting more powerful every day, so I knew it was possible to take her on—and win. I pushed Alana's hands away from me and reached toward my waistband where Bob was resting comfortably in his sheath. Before I could touch him, however, another set of hands was around both of my elbows, pulling them behind my back. I turned my head to see who had grabbed me and was actually relieved.

"Am I glad to see you," I said to Mr. James. "I need to get to Balor."

Alana sprang quickly to her feet and took one of my arms from Mr. James. He went along as she pulled me toward a jagged rock face. It took me a moment to realize that Alana wasn't the only double crosser I had dealt with in my time in Ireland.

"I trusted you!" I yelled at Mr. James. "I trusted both of you!"

"Your mistake, not mine," Mr. James said casually. "Do we kill her?" he asked Alana.

She shook her head. "He wants Simon to do it."

"He won't!" I spat out.

"We'll see," Alana said dismissively as she scanned the barren landscape in front of us.

Rage purred inside of me, loud and vibrant. It had hurt so much when I found out Alana had betrayed us. She was such a big part of all of our lives and knowing what she had done was devastating in so many ways. Finding out Mr. James was also betraying us broke apart my last threads of trust. It made me question every relationship I had with every faery on that island on that cold spring morning. I couldn't trust any of them. Nothing mattered. I didn't want to keep fighting. I didn't know who else would turn on me, and for that reason I wanted to give up.

But I couldn't give up. That wasn't an option. I had to figure which of the Guardians I could rely on and place my faith in them. I trusted my dad. I absolutely trusted my dad. And Simon. There was no doubt in my mind that I could trust Simon. And Finn. And Erin. And Ian. I trusted all of them completely and I could get through anything with those five people beside me.

I felt a renewed strength and I wanted to fight, starting with Alana and Mr. James. I focused on picturing the skin of my arms on fire, all of the heat from within me going to the spots where they held me against that rock. Within seconds, they both jumped backed and yelled.

"What the hell?" Alana asked as she looked down at her blistered hands. It was going to be very hard for her to hold my arms, or her dagger.

Before either of them could work out what had just happened, I ran from them and searched for Simon. I had to get to him so I could get the sword and kill Balor.

Where are you? I called to Simon in my head.

I'm on top of Dún Bhaloir. *I'm surrounded by faery dogs.*

The last thing I wanted to do was come face to face with a faery dog, but I didn't have a choice.

Simon, I'm on my way! I'm coming to you!

I'd spent a lot of time studying the geography of the island before we made the trip. I knew where Simon was, but I also knew he wasn't close. I started to run as hard as I could, the cold morning air stinging at my lungs. A heavy fog shrouded the island, but I was still able to maneuver myself toward Simon. I speculated that the fog probably had nothing to do with the relative humidity in the air and was actually something Balor had conjured to disorient his opponents who weren't as familiar with the island as he was.

Before I could get to Simon, a menacing Fomorian stopped me. She wrapped an arm around my neck and wrestled me to the ground. When I struggled, she reached out a fist and plunged it into the side of my face. I was disoriented for a moment, but when I regained my wits, I used magic to fly her through the air, far away from the spot where I sat on the ground.

I stood quickly and continued to run, knowing I needed to get to Simon as soon as I could.

Are you okay? I asked him in my head. *Can you fly away?*

I tried, but these faery dogs can fly. And they're faster in the air than they are on the ground. I'm trying to use spells to fight them off.

Hang tight. I'm on my way.

Two Fomorians came at me from either side, one of them throwing a dagger that was in his hand. It grazed my arm, but it wasn't enough to stop me. I held out my arms and shot a series of fireballs at each of the faeries. My effort caused one of them to fall to the ground, but the other continued to pursue me. He grabbed at the collar of my jacket and pulled me back, but Liam was there beside us, pulling the Fomorian away.

"Go!" Liam commanded.

I nodded and kept running.

I heard a voice in my head, but it wasn't Simon.

Maggie, are you okay?

Holy crap! My dad could speak telepathically!

Dad? Where are you?

I'm close to Simon. I've talked to the faery dogs. They won't hurt you. I told them to keep growling like they will though. I figured it would throw Balor off if he thinks they're going to attack and they don't.

Dad! That's incredible. I said as I continued to run.

It hurts that you sound so surprised, Mags, he teased.

Stay safe, Dad. You promised.

You too. Go kill that bastard so we can go home to your brother and your mom.

I came upon Ian fighting with three Fomorians. I stopped to help, holding tight to Bob in my hands.

I can handle this, he said. *You need to get to Simon.*

I threw Bob at one of the Fomorians and she fell to the ground, unconscious or dead. I called him back to me and wiped the blood that covered him on my pants.

Aidan's dead, I told Ian as one of the other Fomorians grabbed me around the neck.

Ian elbowed the guy holding me in the face and turned to throw his dagger at the other remaining Fomorian. *I know.*

It has to be me. I'm going to have to kill Balor. I put out my hand and cast a spell that threw the guy who had put me in a headlock back ten feet.

Yes. And you need the sword. Leave these guys to me and go get it.

You're good?

The Fomorian I had just thrown was getting back on his feet. Ian threw his dagger and the Fomorian tumbled back down.

I'm good. Go!

I finally reached Simon and saw that he was surrounded by the faery dogs, all of them barking and drooling and looking ferocious.

They won't hurt you, I assured him. *My dad talked to them.*
I know. He told me.

When I was about thirty yards away from Simon and the dogs, Balor flew down between us.

"Margaret O'Neill," he said as he walked toward me. "How nice of you to join us. This will make Simon's job much easier."

He came to me and grabbed my arm, dragging me toward Simon. I tried to use the burn trick I'd used earlier, but it didn't work. His grip tightened around my upper arm, but he must have felt something because he turned around and slapped me across the face.

"Don't try your amateur tricks with me," he spat out,

his face so close to mine. "They won't work on me and they will only serve to make me angry."

Simon had run past the barking dogs, trying to reach us, but Balor spun around and held out his hand. Simon fell to the ground in pain. I spun on Balor and yelled for him to stop, but he just raised his hand and cast the same painful spell on me as he had on Simon. When he finally stopped, I didn't dare open my eyes for fear he would start again. Let him think I was dead for a few minutes. It would give me time to gather my thoughts and figure out what to do next. I heard Balor go to Simon and lift him off the ground.

"You are my son!" he yelled, the veneer of his calm cracking apart. "You will do this! Do you hear me? You will do this!"

They were both silent, but I didn't dare open my eyes to see what was going on.

Let go of the sword, Simon. I need to call it to me. I wanted to kill Balor and get this over with. I needed him away from Simon—forever.

I'll let go on three. You call out to it as soon I get to three. One. Two. Three

I used my brain to call out to the sword and told it to come to me. As soon as it was in my hand, I stood and faced Balor, ready to take him on. I made eye contact with him and expected him to come after me, but instead he turned to Simon. He grabbed him by the back of his shirt and flew further into the peninsula we were standing on. I followed close behind, the sword still in my hand. When I landed on the ground, I looked back to where we had stood moments before and saw Guardians and Fomorians all trying to get to us. An invisible barrier seemed to hold them back, each of them bouncing away from us when they reached a certain point in the landscape. They met the same obstacle when they tried to fly to us. Balor had done something to create that barrier. He wanted to keep them away from us.

"Let him go!" I commanded as Balor stood with his hand around Simon's throat.

He ignored me, and drug Simon by the neck to a boulder sticking out of the ground. He slapped his hand to the boulder and an entrance opened up in the ground. He pushed Simon through, and went through after him before closing the entrance.

Chapter Thirty-Nine

I ran to where they had been standing and looked for the passageway symbol I hoped would be there. I found it right at the spot where Balor had placed his hand. I pressed my own hand to it and the entrance opened again. I walked through and felt myself sucked into the air for a few seconds before being slammed onto a snowy piece of ground. I looked up to see Balor with his hand still around Simon's throat. We were on the football field at Castlewood High School. Balor had evidently made a passageway between Ireland and Denver and I knew that only he would have been able to make a connection that would take mere seconds to travel.

The three of us were alone on the football field and I'm sure that was Balor's intention. It was probably close to nine o'clock at night in Denver, but the school was deserted. The thick snowflakes and the many inches of snow on the ground told me the reason that nobody was out and about. Balor most likely created this storm to keep everyone away. I was on my own. I was the only person who could kill Balor and the only person who could save Simon.

I got to my feet, the knees of my jeans wet with snow, and turned to face Balor.

"It's not a dream, Margaret O'Neill. This time, it's real, and I can use my magic and we will kill you."

"We" of course meant he and Simon. Balor was a delusional bastard, that's for sure.

"He won't kill me," I said, trying to keep my voice steady. I felt something like an invisible tree trunk hit my chest. The force pushed me back about twenty yards from where I had been standing, the snow doing little to cushion the fall, but I was able to keep my grip on the sword in my hand. I quickly got to my feet, not bothering this time to brush away the snow that clung to my clothes.

"He won't kill me!" I yelled at Balor as I strode toward him. "He won't kill me!" I was rewarded with another push from Balor's invisible tree trunk. This time, I flew farther and hit the ground harder. I lost the sword mid-flight. I gasped for breath, the force knocking the wind out of me. I tried to get to my feet, but I couldn't breath and that made me panic.

Balor turned his back to me and focused his attention on Simon. "Kill her, son. Kill her now. You know it's what you want. You know it's what must be done. Kill her."

Simon gasped for breath, choking as his father's grip tightened.

"Kill her—for me. For us."

Simon shook his head, but seemed incapable of defending himself.

Kill him, Simon told me in my head.

I was still struggling to stand and the sword was several yards away from me. I felt myself failing to do what I absolutely must.

I don't think I can do it, Simon. I don't think I can kill him.

You can do this! You were born to fight this battle and you were born to win! Get to your feet, Maggie, and get the sword. Kill him.

He was right. I had to do it. I had to save Simon from his father, and I had to save the rest of the world from Balor's evil. The decision to kill him had been made long before I was even born.

I'd thought about martyrdom a lot in the past year. I'd seen pictures of a lone student standing in front of a line of tanks in Tiananmen Square. I'd heard of monks setting themselves on fire as a means of protest. They knew their own sacrifice would bring attention to the causes they believed in—causes they were willing to die for. People all over the world would remember them and remember what they were willing to do. Very few would remember me. My death would not make it to the evening news. My actions would not rally people together against a common enemy. The cause of my death would be altered and I would slip away from the world quietly. My family, my friends, would be told a story about my death that they could manage—a story that did not involve evil faery gods and prophecies. But if I died when I stood to face Balor, it wouldn't be for nothing. The world wouldn't know about my sacrifice, but it was still a sacrifice I was willing to make. I would miss my family and Lexie and Simon and the life I'd loved so much, but I honestly didn't want to live in a world with Balor, and I knew I'd never forgive myself if I didn't stand up to him and fight.

So I fought.

I struggled to my feet and summoned the sword before I lifted off the ground and flew at Balor. He kept one hand around his son's neck; the other he reached toward me, his palm facing in my direction. He hadn't made contact with me, but I felt like I'd been knocked over by a line backer. I fell to the ground, but the sword remained firmly attached to my hand.

"Kill her, or I'll do it myself," Balor spat at Simon.

"No," Simon croaked, his father's grip still tight around his throat. Balor growled in fury, then inflicted a spell he'd used twice on me, throwing Simon back twenty feet before hitting the ground. His body was unmoving and lifeless.

"I've killed him, Margaret," Balor taunted. "I've killed my son, and my grandson—the grandson you tried to send to fool me—and now it's just you and me, here on the football field of your high school. Which one of us is going to live, young Margaret? I don't think the odds are stacked in your favor."

He started to come after me and in the split second I had before he reached me, I talked to the sword in my hand.

We need to kill him, I told it. *We need to kill him.*

I felt myself pulled to my feet, the sword bringing me with it as it went toward Balor. It swung in Balor's direction, but he deflected the strike. He moved his hand to send a spell my way, and the sword moved up to deflect it, sending the spell back toward Balor. He fell to the ground, writhing in pain, and I didn't even need to think about it. The sword thought for me. It pulled me toward Balor and helped me lift my arms in the air and bring them down, driving the sword through Balor's chest.

I fell to my knees next to Balor's body, the sword dropping from my hands. I knew we'd accomplished our task, but I moved my shaking fingers to Balor's neck to make sure.

He was dead. Nearly two years of trauma and drama

and fighting and fear, and now it was done. Balor was dead.

I pushed my palms against the cold snow and tried to steady my breathing. I'd done it. I'd accomplished what the prophecy had said I would, but at what cost? So many had died, including the ones I had killed with my own hands.

When I felt steady enough to face what I might see when I looked at Simon, I turned my attention to where he lay on the ground. He wasn't moving and I knew there was a possibility that his father had killed him. I crawled to him slowly, not wanting to confirm my worst fear any sooner than I absolutely had to. When I reached him, I stroked his face with my fingers, not quite ready to reach down to his neck to feel for a pulse. In a moment, his eyes shot open and he took in a deep, unsteady breath.

"Oh, god, Simon!" I pulled him to sit up and wrapped my arms around him. "You're okay!"

He squeezed me tight and when I pulled away I could see that he was looking at his father's body with shock and disbelief.

"He's dead?" he asked.

"Yes," I told him.

"You killed him?"

"Yes."

He pulled his knees to his chest and put his head in his hands. I knew he was grieving for the death of his father—even though his father was sadistic and evil—but I also knew we couldn't stay there. We had to find a passageway symbol and get back to Ireland to help the others and to let them know that Balor was dead—and that *we* weren't.

"We need to get back to Ireland, Simon. We need to

find a passageway symbol."

He nodded and we started to search, but the snow was either covering it, or we were looking in the wrong place, or Balor had created a one-way route.

Simon sunk to his knees.

"We can't give up," I told him. "We have to get back there. We have to tell them."

I didn't even want to think about what my dad might do if he thought I wasn't okay.

"I'm not giving up," Simon said. "I'm going to try to make a passageway symbol in the snow. I have his powers now, so I might be able to do it. And the storm will cover the symbol up so no one else can use it."

I sank down beside him and watched as he used his right index finger—the one with his Claddagh ring—to draw two almost-complete circles, one inside of the other. He then rested his hands on his knees and closed his eyes, and after a few moments, the symbol started to glow and I breathed a sigh of relief.

"I need to get my father," he said as he stood up. I could hear his sadness and his loss.

He picked up Balor in his arms and walked back to where I was kneeling beside the symbol. I placed one hand on the glowing circles, and a three-foot-square space opened up in the field. I stood and put my hand on Simon's shoulder and we jumped in together, landing a few seconds later on the cold, grassy ground in Ireland. Simon let his father's body fall to the ground, but he didn't make a move to leave him.

I didn't have time to celebrate our ability to return to Ireland. Balor's barrier was down and an army of Fomorians was walking toward us.

"We need to get out of here, Simon," I told him.

He lifted his head and shook it slowly, pushing away

his grief. "I'm their leader now," he said. "Without Balor's compulsion, most will choose to follow me."

He stood and reached out his hand to pull me to stand beside him.

Balor is dead, I heard him call out silently. *I will lead the Fomorians now. If you want to fight with me, come to me and pledge your allegiance. If you choose not to join me, you will be shown no mercy.*

I watched as dozens of Fomorians lifted off and flew into the night sky, but even more continued to walk along the cliff to where Simon and I now stood side by side, and knelt down in front of him, their heads bowed. Alana and Mr. James weren't among them. They'd obviously decided not to acknowledge Simon as their leader.

The Guardians at Tory Island flew toward us. We'd won. The fight was over and we'd won.

Chapter Forty

My dad pushed his way through the crowd and pulled me to him for a bear hug.

"Can't breathe, Dad," I rasped.

"Get used to it," he said. "I don't plan to let you go until you're thirty." He pulled back a little and smiled down at me. "You did good, kiddo. I'm so proud of you. It's not every guy who can brag about his daughter saving the universe."

"You did good, too, Dad. The faery dogs would have killed Simon if it weren't for you."

"We both totally rocked," he teased. "But we will not breath a word of this to your mother. Understood?"

"You can take on evil faery dogs and tame them enough to do your bidding, but you're afraid of Mom?"

"Oh, you bet I am." He smiled and kissed the top of my head.

Finn was hugging his brother when I finally extricated myself from my dad's arms.

"I think you guys should walk through the village," he said to Simon and me. "The residents on the island would like to pay their respects."

"They do know about Balor, then," I said.

"Yes. They know. More than any other humans on the planet, they know."

I turned to Simon. "You up for this?"

He took my hand in his. "Absolutely."

We started to walk away, but Simon stopped and turned around. "Finn, my father," he said to his brother.

"I'll take care of him," Finn assured him.

I squeezed Simon's hand and we started the walk to the section of the village nearest *Dún Bhaloir*. We weren't greeted with a raucous celebration. It was very quiet in the village, but people stood outside their homes and bowed their heads, or smiled at us as we walked through town.

When we were at the end of the main street, a weathered old woman approached us, looking somber. "Thank you," she said, looking between Simon and me.

She bowed slightly, then walked away to join the other islanders as they returned to their homes.

"Let's go home," Simon said quietly.

We flew together back to Ballecath. Simon had wanted me to fly on his back, unsure of how strong my flying ability would be since I was so new at it, but I insisted on doing it on my own. Simon was nervous the entire time we flew above the ocean and toward his home. Every time I dipped a little lower, he would reach out and grab my arm and pull me up. Despite his concerns that I couldn't, I managed to fly the entire way without assistance.

Other faeries had beaten us back to Ballecath and given all the details to those who had waited there during the battle. I hugged Lexie as soon as I walked through the door and was surprised to see Jane, Gertie and Albert standing behind her.

"We heard what was going on and wanted to wait here for you," Jane said when I went to hug her.

"You really killed him, Maggie? You really killed Balor?" Gertie asked.

I nodded once, not wanting to be too enthusiastic about the fact that I had killed Simon's father.

"And Mr. James turned out to be on their side?" Albert asked.

"Yeah," I confirmed. "Definitely wouldn't have predicted that one."

We ended up in the front drawing room and everyone talked about what they had seen and heard and done that night. Someone brought in some food for the two-dozen or so who were gathered there, and we shared stories about the friends and loved ones we'd lost. Eventually, pillows and blankets and sleeping bags were brought in and we all found a space on the floor or a sofa and, one by one, we drifted off to sleep. Nobody wanted to go their rooms. Nobody wanted to be alone. We'd won a huge victory, but at such a tremendous cost and, for at least one night, we wanted to soak up the company of others.

My dad managed to stake his claim on one of the sofas. I slept on the floor beside him, one hand held tight in his. Neither of us wanted to let go of the other. Simon slept beside me on the floor, his hand wrapped around mine. I was awake long after I heard the rhythmic breathing of the others that told me they were all sleeping. There was so much to think about. So much to worry about. So much to regret.

When I finally did drift off, Grandma Margaret was there with William.

"It's over," I told her. We were standing on Tory Island, the wind blowing our hair.

She didn't say anything, but came to me and folded me into her arms. William wrapped his little arms around my thighs

"Are you guys going to stop visiting now?" I asked, not ready to face another void in my life.

"Of course not," Grandma Margaret assured me. "Of course not, sweet girl."

She and William stayed with me all night, but none of us said much.

༄༅༄

There were so many funerals, both for the Guardians and Fomorians, and Simon wanted to go to them all. He felt each loss so completely and going to the funerals was his way of thanking each one of them for the sacrifice they'd made. I went with him to all of them, wanting to support Simon and to show my respect and gratitude to the families and friends of all of those we lost.

Simon and I were the only two people attending Balor's funeral. Simon chose to bury him on the cliffs where we had fought—Balor's Fort. It seemed appropriate. Simon dug his father's grave himself, and lowered his body into the ground before pushing the pile of dirt back into the earth. He left the grave unmarked.

"He was my father first," he whispered as we stood at the grave together. I took his hand in mine and squeezed it. "Before he was evil to me, he was my father. He gave me life and he made me who I am—for better or worse. I wouldn't be the man I am today if not for his influence."

"It's okay to grieve him, Simon," I said. "Nobody can blame you for grieving your dad."

He nodded silently and we sat together on the cliff

and looked out at the waves churning in the sea below. We sat like that for hours before we finally stood and flew back to Ballecath together.

The hardest funeral of all for me was Aidan's. He had done nothing but good and was willing to put his own life in danger to help others. He'd never been anything but kind the entire time I'd known him and it felt like we just needed more people like him walking the earth, not fewer. I thought about a toast Finn had once made. "May God grant you many years to live, for sure he must be knowing, the earth has angels all too few and heaven is overflowing." Heaven had another angel, but we really needed a few more with their feet planted firmly to the earth. It was so hard to say goodbye to such a brave man who had put his life in danger in order to do the right thing. But just like the student in Tiananmen Square and the monks on fire, he would never be forgotten. His sacrifice would be remembered long after we were all gone. He had risked his life in order to rid the world of evil, and he would never be forgotten.

Chapter Forty-One

My dad went back to Denver a few days after our trip to Tory Island. Finn went with him to help convince my mom that his absence wasn't something she should be concerned about and to help smooth the way for Lexie and me to return. I wanted to stay in Ireland for the funerals and Lexie said she wanted to be there to support me, but I also suspect she was reluctant to leave Ronan.

I hadn't wanted to move to Ireland and had fought pretty hard against the suggestion, but now I considered it home—almost as much as Denver. The two places were so different and I felt like I needed everything both had to offer in order to feel whole.

"You're not leaving forever," Simon reminded me. "You're a part of this world now and we can't survive without you any more than you can survive without us."

Simon and I hadn't spent any time alone since Balor's funeral. As a matter of fact, it felt like he was going out of his way to avoid me. I wondered if maybe the only thing that had been holding us together was our mutual desire to fulfill the prophecy. Now that Balor was dead, maybe our bond had been broken. But I still loved him. I still wanted to be with him and I still wanted him to be with me.

"Ian said he thinks Simon's afraid to be alone with you," Lexie told me one afternoon after we'd played some tennis at the Brady Indoor Tennis Court.

"Why would he be afraid to be alone with me?" I asked before an even bigger question popped into my head. "Wait. You talked to Ian? Like, on purpose? With no one forcing you to?"

"He's not so bad," she said with a shrug. "I think we just got off to a bad start is all."

"Bad start? You're kidding, right?"

She shrugged again. "Anyway, he said he thinks that Simon's still waiting to see if he turns evil now that he has Balor's power. Maybe he's worried he might snap and decide to hurt you and he doesn't want to be alone with you until he knows for sure."

I shook my head. "He can be such an idiot sometimes."

༄༅༄

I knocked on Simon's door later that night.

Can I come in? I asked silently.

He came to the door and opened it, but he didn't move aside to let me in.

"Can we talk?"

"Yeah, let's go downstairs."

"We can't talk here?"

He looked like he was about to say something, but stopped himself.

"You're not going to hurt me, Simon," I told him softly. "You have his power, but not his emotions."

"I just need to make sure, Maggie. Your life isn't

something I'm willing to risk."

"Simon—"

"Please give me time, Maggie. I love you—that will never change—but I need to know I won't hurt you."

"How will you know? What will need to happen before you're certain you can be alone with me?"

"I don't know," he confessed. "Time, I guess. Please, just give me some time."

I lived a long time believing Simon was dead, and we'd been completely cut off from each other for months. If I could live through that, I could live through anything. Time was all he was asking for and I could give him that.

"Of course," I told him before turning and walking downstairs.

I found Ian alone in the kitchen.

"Hey there," he said when he saw me. "I was just making some tea. Care to join me?"

I smiled. "Tea fixes everything."

"Absolutely. We have fewer therapists in Ireland because we just drink tea and all our problems float away." He flourished his hand in the air to demonstrate what he was saying.

He poured cups for both of us and we sat down near the fireplace. A strong storm had been pounding the house for a couple of hours and the harsh wind seemed to be pushing the cold through the walls.

"He's going to be okay," Ian said—solid, dependable Ian. He knew exactly what was bothering me, and what to say to make me feel better. I knew it wasn't the tea that made problems go away, but the company you shared your tea with. "He just wants to make sure. He loves you too much to risk hurting you."

"He's not going to hurt me. Simon doesn't have even

an ounce of evil in him."

"I know that, and you know that, and eventually, Simon will know that, but right now, he's worried."

I reached over and took Ian's hand in mine. "Thank you," I said. "Even with this ring on my finger that keeps me from aging, I will still never live long enough to thank you for everything you've done for me."

"We're friends," he said. "Friends look out for each other."

I pulled my hand back and wrapped it around my mug, looking intently at the tea inside. "Will we still be friends? Now that this over?"

Ian stood and walked around the table, pulling me to stand with him so he could wrap his arms around me.

"We will *always* be friends, Maggie O'Neill. If you think you can get rid of me now, you are sorely mistaken."

"Thank you," I whispered.

Solid, dependable Ian.

Chapter One of the Rest of my Life

Lexie and I went back to Denver and graduated with our class. I was certain Finn had needed to use his special abilities in order to convince the authorities that we had satisfied the necessary requirements, but we didn't care. We'd learned more in our time away from Castlewood High School than we had ever learned while we were there.

Our graduation ceremony was held at Red Rocks. I hadn't been there since the battle that had taken Max's life, but I wasn't afraid of the place anymore. The one person who had made Red Rocks a bad memory was no longer alive. He didn't have the power to frighten me or make me sad any more.

Finn also used his magic to make sure Lexie was valedictorian. She had been on track for that role since sixth grade, and he didn't think she should lose the title because of her time in Ireland.

"I used to be very driven," she said as she stood at the podium to address the students and their guests. "Being the best at everything I did was the only option for me. I wanted to be the best student and the best tennis player and the best musician. The best daughter. I wanted to get into the best university in the best program and be at the top of my field after I graduated. I wanted so much from my life that I no longer feel is important. I lost someone very dear to me a year ago. He was taken away from us far too soon and in the year since his death, I have seen and done so many things that have caused me to reassess my priorities. Success is important, but happiness and relationships and life are crucial. My advice to all of the graduating seniors is to live your life with balance. Make sure you know what is *truly* important. Whether your life is long or short, end it with no regrets." She looked at me and smiled, tears in her eyes. "Before I leave this stage, I want to have a minute of silence for Max Levy. He should be here with us today, but he's not. I want each of you who knew him to think about Max during our minute of silence, but I also want you to think about your priorities and ask yourself if you're focusing on what is really important."

Thousands of people were in the stands that day, but all of them were completely silent for a full minute. I knew my family was sitting somewhere in the stands behind me. Simon, Finn, Erin and Ian were with them. That's what was most important to me—those people sitting in the stands behind me, and the one girl standing so strong at the podium before me—all of those people who I loved so much. Everything I'd done over the past year and a half had been for them, and everything I did in the future would be for them. I would go to college and get a job, but none of that was as important as the people that surrounded me with their love.

&⃝ℜ

Finn also helped to get us into the University of Colorado in Boulder. Lexie and I both felt a strong need to be close to home, so Boulder seemed like a good option—far enough away from our parents that we would feel some independence, but close enough that they could be to us in an hour if we needed them.

Simon split his time between Denver and Ireland. He took his role as leader of the Fomorians seriously and wanted to devote his time to his people, but he also wanted to spend the time with me that we needed in order to repair the damage that had been done to our relationship. We had spent our entire relationship focused on something other than each other. Would we still like each other—love each other—now that we could focus only on us? Balor was dead. Our mission was complete. It was time to find out.

I'd offered to stay in Ireland until school started in the fall, but Simon insisted I go home and graduate with my class and live the life of a normal teenager for a while. I went to movies and parties and baseball games—sometimes with Simon and sometimes without. I reconnected with old friends. I didn't worry about their future or my future at the hands of Balor. I laughed and I relaxed and I allowed myself to re-rank my priorities. I was no longer responsible for the fate of the world, and while in Ireland I was something of a celebrity among the faeries, in Denver, I was just Maggie O'Neill, recent high school graduate.

"Do you want to watch another movie?" Simon asked, bringing my attention back to him as we sat in his house in Denver. Finn and Erin had gone back to Ireland right after my graduation, so we were alone for the first time in a very long time.

"If you do," I told him.

"Not really," he said awkwardly. He turned to look at me and took my hands in his. "I was actually wondering if you wanted to spend the night."

The blush on his cheeks told me what I needed to know—what he was suggesting—and I nodded, unable to keep the smile from forming on my face.

I called my parents to let them know that I wouldn't be home. Since our time in Ireland, my relationship with my dad had changed significantly. He'd seen me murder the most powerful faery in the world, so I guess he figured I could handle myself in any situation. I also think that he trusted Simon in a way he never had before.

We walked to Simon's room hand-in-hand. We hadn't made love since the day Danu had given him his powers back at the Caretaker's Cottage. I was nervous, and I was certain Simon was, too.

After closing his door, he walked to me and put his hand on my cheek and I could feel the slight tremble in his fingers. He moved his other hand to my face and looked into my eyes as if he were seeing me for the first time.

"I love you," he whispered.

"I love you, too," I whispered back.

He stroked his fingers softly against my skin and coaxed my face to turn toward him, moving down to kiss me, slow and soft. We didn't tear at each other's clothes. We didn't rush to devour each other. We didn't need to. We had all the time in the world, and we made love the way we had the first time—a lifetime ago on my eighteenth birthday. It was tender and sweet, and it gave me hope that we were going to be okay.

෨෬

"Dinner's ready," I told Brandon and Simon. They were playing a video game in the living room and my mom and dad were in the back yard at the grill.

Simon put down his remote and stood up, but Brandon didn't look like he'd even heard me.

"Brandon, dinner's ready. Turn the game off."

Chill out, Maggie.

It was unmistakably Brandon's voice in my head. I was looking right at him when he said it, and his lips hadn't moved, so that meant only one thing.

Aw crap!

Epilogue
Five Years Later

"Where's my dress?" I asked as I frantically looked around the room.

"It's right here," Lexie told me. "You need to calm down, Maggie. It's just a wedding. It's not like you're going to have to go and slay an evil faery or anything."

I gave her a tolerant look as she handed me the bag that contained my dress.

"Keelin's meeting us at the church?"

Lexie nodded. "I just got a text from her and she's on her way—and we need to be, too."

I made a last check of the room to be certain we had everything, then the two of us walked to the limo waiting to take us to the church.

"I forgot the rings," I said before I got into the limo. I turned around to go back for them, but Lexie grabbed my arm.

"Simon has them," she said calmly. "I gave them to him this morning.

"You're sure?"

"Yes, I'm sure. Now get in the car."

I sat down next to her and closed the door, my foot tapping wildly with nervous tension.

"You seriously need to take some deep breaths, Maggie."

"How can you be so calm?" I asked, incredulous.

"It's just a wedding."

"*Just* a wedding? How can you say that?"

"It's not hard. Maybe you should give it a try. Repeat after me. 'It's just a wedding.'"

"It's just a wedding."

"Keep saying it."

"It's just a wedding. It's just a wedding."

I kept repeating the mantra to myself while we got dressed in the room reserved for the bridal party at the church. I continued to repeat it while Lexie and Keelin and the other bridesmaids and I posed for pictures, and was still repeating it when I saw the guests taking their seats.

"Are you feeling a little calmer?" Lexie asked as we stood in the vestibule of the church.

I nodded. I knew it was going to be okay. This wedding was inevitable. I could see that now.

Lexie hugged me and took my hand in hers, squeezing it while we waited for the wedding coordinator to give us the signal that the ceremony was ready to begin. When she told us it was time, I gave Lexie's hand one last squeeze before letting her go.

I stood at the doors to the sanctuary, waiting to walk down the aisle, and looked out at all of the people I cared about most in the world—faeries and humans and family and friends. Simon was there—of course—standing at the alter with Ian, smiling as I made my way slowly toward him. Brandon stood with him, as well, so tall and handsome. He'd brought a date to the wedding, and the thought of him dating still freaked me out, but he'd become more of a friend than a pesky little brother in the past five years. We still teased each other, but we also confided in each other and leaned on each other when life got a little annoying. He gave me a thumbs-up as I walked toward him and I smiled at his goofiness.

I walked to my spot next to Keelin, and winked at Simon before turning to watch Lexie walk down the aisle on her father's arm. She was so beautiful that it took my breath away and I knew Ian must have been thinking he was the luckiest man in the world at that moment. The two of them were so happy and this wedding was so right.

༄

"Who would have thought five years ago that those two would end up married?" Simon asked as we danced together at the reception.

"Not me, that's for sure. They were constantly at each other's throats."

"But they're so happy now."

"Yes."

"And I'm happy they're happy."

"Me too."

"Shall we be next?" he asked.

"Are you proposing?"

"I'm proposing that we think about proposing," he said with mischief in his eyes.

"Well, you let me know when you're ready for the real thing."

"Will do."

He reached in to kiss me deeply before resting his forehead on mine.

"I love you, *cushla macree.* Always."

"Always?"

"Always."

"You don't think you'll get bored with me eventually?"

"Never. I'd be happy living alone on a deserted island with you for the rest of my life. I'd be happy living in poverty as long as you were with me. I'd be happy walking through hell if it meant I'd see you when I returned. I'd be happy doing anything—being anything—with you. *With you.* Always with you."

Acknowledgements

I am so lucky to be surrounded by a group of people who believe in my books as much—and sometimes more—than I do. Each one of them is there to knock sense into me when I'm convinced my books are crap. They promote my books as much as I do, and share in every up and down. They get excited about every edit, and read and listen to my stories over, and over and over. I could not have gone through the difficult process of writing and publishing if it were not for each one of them: My mom, Bonnie Grable; my sisters, Maggie Grable and Breya Grable; my brother, Bradon Grable; and my dear friend, Robbi Makely. Thank you!!

My faithful group of beta testers: Michelle Findley Barnacz, Debbie Tu-Tygrs and Vicki Gonzales. Your suggestions are such a huge help!! Thank you! Thank you! Thank you!

I will be the first to admit that adopting a puppy while trying to finish a book was a very clear indication of my own insanity. Bailey, I love you a bunch, but between your naughtiness and cuteness, it's really hard to get any work done. This book would still be unfinished if it weren't for the staff at Bark Doggie Daycare. They love her and play with her and wear her butt out enough that she passes out and lets me get some work done. Melissa, Jessica, Cynthia, Rachel, Laura, Michael, Katie, Steve, Matt, Matt, Megan, Stacey, Rochelle, Jon, Jeff, Brandy, Kristen and Elizabeth: Thank you, each and every one of you!

Also by this author...

For more information about the author and her books, go to:
www.jilldaugherty.com

Made in the USA
Charleston, SC
13 May 2014